PROSECUTOR OF METALHAVEN

METAL AND BLOOD
BOOK 2

G J OGDEN

Copyright © 2023 by G J Ogden
All rights reserved.

No part of this book may be reproduced in any form or by any electronic or mechanical means, including information storage and retrieval systems, without written permission from the author, except for the use of brief quotations in a book review.

These novels are entirely works of fiction. The names, characters and incidents portrayed in it are the work of the author's imagination. Any resemblance to actual persons, living or dead, events or localities is entirely coincidental.

Illustration © Phil Dannels
www.phildannelsdesign.com

Editing by S L Ogden
Published by Ogden Media Ltd
www.ogdenmedia.net

1
LET'S GET TO IT

Finn Brasa lay on the queen-sized bed in his luxurious apartment in the prosecutor barracks and stared at the ceiling. It was spotless. In many ways this was good because it meant that his room was clean and fresh, not to mention warm, but it had also spoiled his ritual process of getting to sleep. His old apartment in the Reclamation sector was damp, cold and littered with mold spots, which Finn had counted as a way to relax and unwind. It was the Metalhaven version of counting sheep. Without mold to count, Finn had spent a restless night in his new home, though he doubted he would have slept much even if he had been lying on his old, rock-hard sofa bed. Too much had happened in the twenty-four hours since his trial had ended, with Finn Brasa the sole survivor. Too much had been lost.

"Owen..."

Finn spoke the name out loud, hoping that his friend would reply, which he knew was impossible. Owen Thomas was dead and his body was already ash. It was his fault. He should have felt angrier about that fact, and he should have felt upset, but the truth was that he felt almost nothing. Sliding his feet off the bed, Finn sat up and ruffled his hair with his bandaged hands. The Authority sector medics had treated the many wounds he'd sustained in the crucible, not least of which were his broken knuckles; a result of beating Corbin Radcliffe to death with his bare hands. Yet because of the medical technology that the golds possessed, he was even denied the penance of pain.

"What the hell I am doing here?" Finn said, directing the question to his robot, Scraps, who remained inactive on his desk, while he waited for the parts he needed to fix him. "A couple of days ago, I was slicing up tanks in reclamation yard seven and minding my own business, and now I'm a gold."

Finn huffed a laugh and shook his head. He couldn't lie to Scraps, even when then bot was unable to hear him.

"Minding my own business..." he repeated, sighing. "If only I had, then Owen would still be alive, and we'd been drinking shit-tasting algae beer and complaining about all the slackers in yard seven."

Scraps was unable to reply but even if the robot could answer, he wouldn't have simply hit Finn with the hard truths he deserved. That had been Owen's job. As his best and only friend – his brother in all but blood – Owen was the only person who had stood up to him. Time and again, Owen had warned him about the dangers of pissing off the Authority, but Finn hadn't listened. He was too angry and too arrogant, and far too certain that his double-five rating would spare him from the harsher punishments that others with lesser ratings would be subjected to. And for years, it had done. As a top-rated worker and one of the few genetically undamaged men in Zavetgrad, Finn could walk on a razor's edge, antagonizing the authority and pushing his luck far beyond the limit that any lower-rated worker could do without being sentenced to trial. Then one day he had pushed too far and everything had changed.

As punishment for injuring and humiliating him, Captain Viktor Roth, the sadistic Head Prefect of Metalhaven, had tortured Finn and sent him to the crucible. While being sentenced to die in a macabre blood-sport designed to tighten the Authority's iron grip on the workers of Zavetgrad was a harsh ruling, if he was honest, Finn had gotten what was coming to him. Owen, however, hadn't deserved to be dragged down with him, and as much as he hated Soren Driscoll – the bully who had driven him to lash out – and his oafish sidekick, Corbin, they hadn't deserve it either. Nevertheless, within twenty-four hours of striking and disfiguring Captain Roth, Finn was on trial and fighting for his life. Two hours after that, Owen was dead. He didn't have a chance to say goodbye. He didn't have a chance to say sorry. There wasn't even a funeral. Owen was just bagged, tossed into the back of a ground car and driven to the crematorium without ceremony. His body was likely burning at the same time Finn was being lauded as the Authority's latest gold and introduced to his lush new apartment and his privileged new life.

"Feel something, damn you!" Finn barked, slapping the side of his face hard enough to make his ears ring, but the analgesics he'd been given denied him the pain he so desperately wanted to experience.

Sighing again, Finn moved from his bed to his desk and began toying with the inanimate body of Scraps. He tried to clear his mind of dark thoughts and focus on what he'd need to do to fix the machine, but his head was still too full of the trial, as it had been throughout his restless night.

If I had just held my nerve and ignored Soren, as Owen had told me to do, none of this would have happened... Finn thought, spinning the oil-can body of Scraps in his hands. *If I had been stronger and smarter, he'd still be alive...* These facts were indisputable and confronting them should have made Finn hate himself but it didn't, and his continued absence of feeling sickened him. *Maybe I do deserve to be a gold...* Finn thought. *Maybe I'm just as fucked up as they are...*

Then there was The Shadow, Elara Cage. Considering the grotesque sequence of events that had led Finn to this moment, the revelation that the infamous Iron Bitch of Metalhaven was a rebel – a Metal – was easily the most shocking after Owen's death. Metals were infiltrators from Haven, a free city across the Davis Strait from Zavetgrad that had been founded by workers from the Reclamation sector after a revolt one-hundred and twenty-seven years ago. In the brief moments they had shared before Elara had left Finn alone in his room to recover, The Shadow had told him about Haven, and how it had been founded by one-hundred and forty-three chromes like him from Metalhaven, who had managed to steal skycars and escape beyond Zavetgrad's tall, electrified walls. In the years since its founding, Haven operatives called Metals, in honor of the blood sacrifice their brothers and sisters had made, had freed hundreds more. Those refugees, plus the people born free in Haven, now numbered in the thousands. How many thousands, even Elara didn't know for sure, but it was enough to form a new society. Maybe, even an army.

The Authority had done everything in their considerable

power to ensure the people of Zavetgrad never learned of Haven's existence, or that of the rebellion that led to its establishment. The least insidious of these acts was to wipe all records pertaining to the revolt from the archives, but this had only been the start. Everyone involved in the rebellion, or who'd had significant knowledge of it, had been executed. This hadn't been limited to the Metalhaven workers who had participated in the uprising, but over one-hundred Prefects and golds had also been murdered in order to ensure the Authority's secret. Yet rumors of Haven persisted like a virus that kept evolving to evade extinction. Finn had known people to disappear simply for mentioning the name of the rumored refuge in public, yet even he had doubted its existence. And despite what he had learned, he doubted he would ever truly believe until – if – he saw the place with his own eyes.

Elara Cage had told him all this freely, despite the grave risk to herself in doing so. She had trusted him implicitly, though as with much of what had happened in the last two days, he had no idea why. And now he was her apprentice. *But an apprentice of what? What's her plan? And why me, of all people?* All these were questions that Finn had no answers to. All he knew was that Elara Cage had saved his life in the belief that somehow he might be able to help the Metals of Haven free Zavetgrad, and perhaps even tear down the Authority itself. Nothing would satisfy Finn's broken soul more than seeing Nimbus burning in space, and the mental image of the orbital citadel in ruin was the only thing that made him feel anything at all, but it was fanciful. What could he, a lowly chrome from Metalhaven elevated to a position he didn't deserve – a false gold – do against the might of the Authority?

Finn laughed and gently set Scraps down on the top of his hardwood desk. In the end, it did him no good to dwell on the past, or even to contemplate the future. At that moment he was as powerless as when he'd been a worker in yard seven, except instead of being at the mercy of foremen and prefects, his fate was now entirely in the hands of Elara Cage.

Suddenly, the door chime sounded, and the noise jolted Finn so sharply that he almost fell out of his chair. It was a bass-rich, two-tone note, and despite it sounding nothing like the prosecutor's voice, all Finn heard was Bloodletter shouting his name - "Bra-sa!... Bra-sa!..." His pulse was racing and he felt sick with nervous energy but his body was frozen in place, as if the door chime had been a bell tolling a countdown to his execution. The buzzer was pressed again – *Bra-sa!... Bra-sa!...* – and Finn squeezed his hands against the arms of his chair and forced his body to stand but his legs were shaking. Then instead of the chime he heard a voice.

"Mr. Brasa, are you in there?" It was Trial Assistant Pritchard, his valet. "I can come back later if it's inconvenient?"

The sound of the mild-mannered man's voice set Finn at ease, and he felt ashamed and embarrassed at how easily he had been stricken impotent with fear.

"No, it's fine, come in," Finn said, shaking the tingling numbness from his arms.

The door opened and Pritchard walked in, carrying a bundle of items. The man was smiling, which was his default expression. "Good morning, sir, I trust you slept well?" he asked, setting down the bundle onto Finn's dining table.

"Sure, in fact I don't think I've ever slept so well," Finn replied. It went against his nature to be dishonest but telling Pritchard the truth would only worry his valet and subject him to a raft of questions that he didn't want to answer. "Whether it was the drugs the medics gave me, or that cloud-like mattress, I don't know, but I was out like a light."

"That's good to hear, sir!" Pritchard replied, cheerfully. He bustled over and checked Finn's bandages on his hands and neck without being invited to do so. Finn flinched but reined in his urge to grab the man's wrist and snap it like a twig. "These are healing nicely," the valet said, blissfully unaware of how close he'd come to being beaten bloody.

"I feel fine," Finn said, stepping back. It was another lie, or at least a half-truth. He wasn't in pain, but he was also hardly himself, whoever that person was now.

Pritchard nodded and smiled, then pressed his hands to his hips and remained in front of Finn, grinning like a buffoon. His yellow hair was lustrous like strands of golden silk, while his young face, at only seventeen years old, was unburdened by the stresses and pressures that made Metalhaven workers of the same age look like they were already in their late thirties.

"Was there a reason for the visit?" Finn asked. His valet was starting to make him feel uncomfortable.

"Oh, yes, my apologies, sir," Pritchard replied, darting over to the dining table and unpacking the bundle of items he'd brought in. "I fetched the items you requested."

Finn moved over to the table and sifted through the tools that Pritchard was methodically setting out on the surface. Everything seemed to be there, including the all-important power cell for Scraps. Furthermore, it was all grade-A, brand new equipment.

"I'm used to working with junk," Finn said, examining a precision multi-tool, which was probably worth more than the contents of his old apartment in Metalhaven. "This stuff is perfect, thanks."

"It's my very great pleasure, sir!' Pritchard replied, beaming with pride.

Despite being a gold, and despite his over-enthusiastic nature, Finn couldn't not like the man. He then noticed a mug beside the tools and he scowled at the container, which appeared to be leaking steam into the room.

"What's going on with that mug?" Finn asked, pointing to the container. "It looks like it's about to explode."

"Oh, that's just your coffee, sir," Pritchard replied, hastily transferring the mug from one side of the table to the other, so it was in front of him. "I didn't know how you liked it, so I just went with a medium-roast arabica, black." His valet then sifted through the remaining items he'd brought and set out a small silver tray next to the mug, with various packets and tiny sealed containers. "I brought some creamers and some cane sugar. If you'd let me know how you prefer to take it then next time I'll bring exactly what you want."

"I didn't know there was more than one way to take coffee…"

Finn picked up the mug and removed the lid to find a steaming hot brew that was blacker than Elara Cage's roundel dagger. He gave it a sniff, but it didn't smell anything like coffee to him. Even so, he sampled it and it felt like the taste blew the top of his skull clean off.

"I don't know what this is, but it's not coffee," Finn said, dumping two packets of sugar into the brew then tasting it again. The second time was even more blissful than the first.

"Of course," his valet replied, snapping his fingers in realization of his error. "I forgot that you don't have this kind of coffee in Metalhaven. Not to worry, I'll bring a broader selection next time, including latte, cappuccino, macchiato..."

Finn held up his hand to stop Pritchard mid-flow. "This will do, just fine, thank you. Black with two sugars." He tasted the coffee again and reconsidered. "Actually, make it three sugars."

"As you wish, sir, it would be my genuine pleasure," Pritchard said, still smiling.

Finn tried to detect any hint of insincerity in the man's response but there was none. Pritchard was genuinely happy to serve. More surprisingly, he didn't look down on Finn for being a 'fake gold' – the moniker that was applied to people like him who were not born into the privileged color of the Authority. Even so, the constant deference Pritchard showed him was jarring, not only because he wasn't used to it, but because he didn't agree with it either.

"Thank you, Pritchard, but you don't have to call me sir," Finn replied. "I've spent all my life subservient to prefects and foremen, bowing my head in obedience to the Authority. It wasn't right then, so it's not right now."

Pritchard looked suddenly uncomfortable and for the first time since he'd seen the man, he wasn't smiling.

"Actually, sir, I do have to pay you the proper respect," Pritchard replied, uneasily. "But, truly, it's no bother. It is, as I keep saying, a genuine pleasure to serve you."

Finn sighed under his breath and rubbed his face. The coffee had cut through his tiredness and he was feeling much more alert. "Would you get into trouble if I ordered you *not* to call me sir?"

"Yes, sir," Pritchard replied, now smiling nervously. "If I were caught not paying the proper deference it would go on my record and hurt my chances at promotion."

Finn laughed and Pritchard squirmed uncomfortably, perhaps worrying that Finn was going to use this power against him, but his valet had misunderstood. All he found amusing was that repercussions for a gold amounted to reduced job prospects, whereas for the worker class, repercussions meant a savage beating, or death via trial.

"In that case, carry on calling me, 'sir', in public" Finn replied, setting his valet's mind at ease. "But when we're alone, call me Finn. Can you do that?"

"Yes, sir," Pritchard replied, his familiar smile returned in full force.

Finn laughed again but his valet was clearly unaware at his unintentional witticism, and he didn't want to cause the man any more anxiety by pointing it out. Instead, he collected Scraps off his desk and brought the little robot over to the table, before preparing the tools he needed to start work on the repairs. Pritchard watched with interest.

"Is it correct that you built this robot yourself, while still a Metalhaven worker?" his valet asked. The man's cheeks then flushed with color and he looked worried. "I'm sorry, sir, I didn't mean to pry. It's not my place..."

"It's fine, really," Finn said, again holding up his hand to cut Pritchard off mid-flow. "If you're going to be my valet, you need to loosen up a bit."

"Yes, sir, sorry sir," Pritchard replied, clearly mortified at his failure to adapt to Finn's way of working.

"It's Finn, remember?" he replied. "You're not in performance review right now."

Pritchard smiled nervously and nodded and Finn sensed the man was suddenly desperate to leave. However, he didn't want his valet to scurry off with his tail between his legs, especially not after bringing him the parts, and the incredible coffee.

"This is a replacement power cell," Finn said, holding up the device and offering it to Pritchard to take it. The man understood his subtle invitation to remain and took the cell gladly. "It's much better than the one I originally salvaged and includes photovoltaic cells, so Scraps won't need recharging manually. Even the pitiful amount of sun we get in Zavetgrad will be enough to keep him going indefinitely."

"How marvelous!" Pritchard said, again without any hint of artificiality.

Finn sifted through the other components, which included metal panels to patch up the hole in Scraps' side, then found a can of paint. This was another item he'd requested but the color was not to his liking.

"This is gold," Finn said, holding up the can and giving it a little shake. It rattled like something inside it was broken.

"Yes sir, naturally," Pritchard replied.

Finn figured that it was an understandable response, considering everything around him was either gold or trimmed in gold, but there wasn't a chance in hell he would besmirch Scraps by painting him in the color of the Authority.

"Get me a can of chrome paint, will you?" Finn asked, rolling the can across the table. Pritchard caught it, frowned, then shrugged. "As you wish, sir." He set the can of gold paint down on the table, rather than keeping it in his hand. "But, if you'll allow me to give you a spot of advice, your robot will need to have some gold, otherwise it may be considered a labor force bot, rather than a personal robot."

Finn nodded. "Good advice, thank you."

The door chime sounded again, and the voice of Bloodletter rang out in Finn's mind. *Bra-sa!... Bra-sa!...* He flinched but managed to keep his composure, and Pritchard didn't notice his discomfort. Or, if the man had noticed, then he did not let on, which Finn considered just as likely. The door opened without invitation and Elara Cage strode inside, her boots clacking against the gold-edged hardwood floor with metronomical precision. The prosecutor turned her emerald eyes to Pritchard and the valet almost pissed himself.

"Good morning, Miss Shadow..." Pritchard said, his voice barely more than a timid squeak.

Elara merely stared at Pritchard until the silence became too awkward and his valet excused himself and vanished through the door faster than a bolt from The Shadow's crossbow.

"You certainly have a way with people," Finn said, feeling guilty that Pritchard's squirming had amused him.

Elara pressed a finger to her lips then closed the door and walked over to the dining table, brushing the components to one side.

"What are you..." Finn began, but Elara pressed her hand over his mouth to quieten him. Her touch was like ice and Finn was frozen. His mentor then attached an opaque strip to the inside of the lampshade in the center of the table and clicked a button on the tracker device that encircled her left wrist like a bracelet.

"Your room is bugged," Elara said, coolly. "As a former worker, they don't trust you."

Finn's mouth fell open but while his mentor's statement had shocked him, he quickly realized that he had no cause to be surprised. Of course the Authority didn't trust him. The Regent of Spacehaven and Captain Viktor Roth had both said as much, though not in such direct terms.

"Officially, it's against the law to covertly monitor any gold, but the Authority is above the law," Elara went on, while hiding additional devices in other places around his apartment. "These bug-killers will algorithmically alter anything you say in this room to something more innocuous, and also mix in false images to hide anything suspicious that you might do."

"Like covertly installing anti-surveillance devices?" Finn said.

Elara smiled, which was still an alien expression on her face and one that he was struggling to get used to.

"Exactly..." The Shadow answered. "Though it's still safer if we refrain from speaking about anything that might throw your loyalty into question while we are in this room."

Finn sighed and nodded. "What about outside of this room?"

Elara considered the question for a moment. "I would advise against it, but in the main, you should be safe. Bugging your room is one thing, but bugging a public place where the conversations of other golds could be intercepted is another matter entirely. Golds like their privacy, some golds more than others, and no-one wants to get on the wrong side of a head prefect or supervisor."

"Or a prosecutor?" Finn suggested.

Elara smiled again, though this was darker. "Especially a prosecutor."

Finn looked into the lamp where Elara had affixed one of the bug-killer devices, but he couldn't see the thing no matter how hard he looked.

"I suppose these bugs employ the same tech the golds use to fake elements of the trials, so that the public don't see everything that goes on?" Finn asked.

"Yes," the prosecutor replied, in her trademark plain-speaking manner. "You may be surprised to learn that the gold sector isn't as shiny and perfect as you've been led to believe."

Finn huffed a laugh. "Honestly, at this stage, nothing much would surprise me. Hell, I'm not even sure you're real. You could be a figment of my imagination for all I know."

His stomach then rumbled aggressively and Elara scowled at him, like he'd just broken wind.

"How long is it since you last ate or drank something?" Elara asked.

Finn thought about the question but time had become fluid since the moment of his arrest, and he wasn't even sure if that was two or three days ago, or longer.

"I snagged a protein bar during the trial," Finn said, shrugging. Then he pointed to the coffee that Pritchard had brought him. "Other than that, I'm running on coffee."

Elara nodded. "Then let's eat. We have a big day ahead of us."

His mentor walked to the door and waited for Finn to join her. He reached for the button to open it but Elara covered the switch with her hand, and he ended up pressing his fingers to her skin instead. *Ice cold... Is she even alive?*

"Pritchard, your new valet, is one of the good ones," Elara said. "I chose him myself."

Finn frowned. "Is he a Metal too?"

Elara scowled at him for breaking her golden rule only seconds after establishing it, and Finn looked suitably penitent.

"No," his mentor answered. "But one day, maybe." She activated the button and the door opened. She pressed a finger to her lips again and Finn nodded his understanding.

"Are you ready to begin your training, Prosecutor Apprentice Brasa?" Elara asked.

Finn wanted to say 'no' but he imagined that wasn't the answer his mentor was looking for.

"Yes, ma'am," Finn replied. "Let's get to it."

2

FIRST STEPS INTO A NEW WORLD

Following Elara out of his apartment and sanctuary was a bigger deal than Finn had expected it be, and he immediately felt exposed. The sound of the door thudding shut to his rear made him jump and this didn't go unnoticed by his mentor.

"You'll get used to it," Elara said, apparently sensing the cause of his discomfort. "Remember that you're a gold now. You belong here and you should act as though you belong here, even if others try to make you feel differently."

Finn nodded and blew out a shaking breath. The stimulant effect of the coffee was a double-edged sword and it felt like a million tiny ants were crawling over his skin.

"I feel like a foreman or prefect is going to jump out at any moment and club me with a nightstick," Finn said, following behind his mentor, who was advancing along the corridor at a mercifully slow rate. "A few days ago and I'd have been shot on sight for merely being here."

"That feeling is natural," Elara replied, without looking back at him. "It'll pass…"

Finn wasn't so certain but he chose to trust his mentor, as she had asked him to do. After all, he had little other choice. She was the only person in the Authority sector who understood him and who was truly on his side. Pritchard, for all his enthusiasm and good graces, was still a true-born gold, and that made him different, whether he thought of himself that way or not. Then Finn realized why Elara was so in tune with his thoughts, which was because she too had been required to make the transition from worker to gold. He wondered if she had done so without the benefit of a sympathetic mentor like he had.

"Did you feel like this when you first arrived?" Finn asked. "Like a fish out of water, I mean?" He knew it was a personal question considering they barely knew each other, but if he was to truly trust Elara with his life, he needed to know who she really was.

"Yes, I felt out of place," she replied, still looking ahead, rather than into his eyes, which he preferred since The Shadow's stare still unsettled him. "The difference is that while others didn't want me here, I was determined to stake my claim to gold status."

"Did your mentor help you to adjust and fit in?" Finn asked.

Elara stopped walking and this time she did look at him. Despite knowing that she wasn't a threat, he still felt afraid, worried that the prosecutor might stab him through the neck with her roundel dagger at any moment.

"My mentor hated me and the feeling was mutual," Elara said, and every word dripped with resentment. "He was bitter that I had killed his co-prosecutors, his friends, in order to secure my position, but he hated more that I was a worker from Metalhaven. Despite the rules of the trial granting me my right as a gold, he didn't treat me as one. He made every single day a battle but it was a battle that I was determined not to lose."

Finn found that his mouth had gone dry and wished that he'd brought the portable cup of coffee that Pritchard had served up with him.

"Who was your mentor?" Finn asked, as fearful as he was intrigued to learn who had sculpted Elara Cage into the formidable Iron Bitch of Metalhaven.

"His name was Magnus Drexler, though you probably knew him as Ironclaw," Elara replied. She turned and resumed her progression along the corridor, boot-heels clacking against the stone floor with military precision.

"I remember him," Finn said. Though he hated watching the trials, like all workers, he had been forced to do so and was unable to forget any of them. They were inscribed on his mind like tattoos on skin and once the ink had dried the memory was indelible. "He used a blade-tipped gauntlet to cut people to shreds like a wolverine. The bastard was even more of a sadist than Bloodletter."

"Yes he was, and I'm sure you won't be surprised to learn that Ironclaw and Bloodletter were friends," Elara replied. "He was an obnoxious, cruel tyrant that made my life a living hell, but he at least taught me well. He's dead now, of course."

Finn and Elara continued in silence for a while but there was something about Ironclaw's death that was significant, and it was bothering him that he couldn't remember. He knew that at the time of his passing, Elara's mentor had been the top-ranked prosecutor of all time, with a horrific one-hundred and seventy total kills, but that wasn't the fact he was trying to remember. Then it came to him and he confronted Elara.

"Didn't Ironclaw die from the wounds he suffered in the last trial he prosecuted?" Finn asked. It was a leading question and the sideways glance that his mentor gave him suggested she suspected he was hinting at something.

"Yes, that's correct," Elara replied. She narrowed her eyes at him. "Do you consider that surprising?"

Finn looked at his bandaged knuckles then flexed his fingers. Considering how damaged they had been less than twenty-four hours ago, he shouldn't have been able to unfurl his hand, let alone articulate each digit without the slightest hint of pain.

"I was half-dead coming out of the crucible. So were you," Finn replied. "But the medical tech in the Authority sector is borderline magic. I just find it hard to believe that a tough sonofabitch like Magnus Drexler would have succumbed from his injuries. As I recall, he wasn't that badly hurt."

Elara raised her eyebrows and looked ahead, though there was a curious Mona Lisa smile curling her lips. Finn's suspicions crystallized into a full-blown theory and he smiled.

"He didn't die of his injuries, did he?"

Elara stopped dead again and her emerald eyes drilled into him. "Some poisons are very difficult to detect," the woman replied. "And some have no known cure."

With that, The Shadow turned again and this time her pace quickened, preventing Finn from asking a follow-up question. However, while he would have preferred a straight answer, he didn't need one to know that Elara Cage had assassinated her own mentor. He wasn't certain whether that made him more afraid of her or more convinced that she was the right person to oversee his training. Perhaps it was both, he decided.

By the time Finn had caught up with her they were already at the entrance to another room. There was no door, only a wide archway that opened into a dining hall. The sound of clattering crockery and boisterous conversation was flowing through the opening, not unlike the atmosphere of a recovery center, but without the odor of stale sweat and strong beer.

"The other apprentices and their mentors will already be inside," Elara said, eyes focused into the room. "Walk in like you belong and don't stare. Once we're seated, I'll give you a rundown of who you will be spending the next few weeks with."

Finn recoiled from his mentor. "Weeks? Is that how long I'll be here?"

Elara raised an eyebrow at him. "Did you think that training to become a prosecutor was something that could be achieved in mere days?"

Finn shook his head. "No, it's just that I thought I'd be out of here sooner and an on a skycar to..." He caught himself just before saying 'Haven', and the relief on his mentor's face was palpable. "... a skycar to my first trial," Finn added, swiftly digging himself out of a hole.

"All in good time," Elara replied, which Finn noted was becoming something of a catchphrase for her. "For now, you train. But before that, you must eat."

Elara walked into the dining hall and it was apparent that

every eye in the room was on her. Some were open about it while others, mainly Finn's fellow apprentices, who were obvious by virtue of their youth, did so more furtively. Then Finn strode in, head held high and chest puffed out, and suddenly no-one was watching The Shadow, because all eyes were on him. His fame had clearly preceded him but it was also abundantly clear that the attention he had garnered was not of the positive kind. The other apprentices and their mentors were looking at Finn as if he were a shit-stinking vagrant that had just wandered in off the streets.

"If looks could kill, you'd already be dead," Elara said, as Finn joined her at the buffet table. "But well done for not buckling under the pressure. They might not want you here but there's not a damned thing they can do about it. Remember that."

Finn sighed and nodded then cast his eyes over the buffet table. He was suddenly ravenous but the sight of the food was making him feel nauseous rather than hungry.

"The last time I ate from a buffet table like this, I was face down in my own drool a few minutes later," Finn said, recalling how Captain Withers had drugged his 'last meal' before he and his fellow offenders had begun their trial in Spacehaven. "I assume I'm not going to take a bite of bread then find myself hanging from a noose in the parade square outside?"

"Everything here is fine to eat," Elara said. As if to offer him comfort, she was already loading up two plates, one for her and one for him. "Focus on proteins and carbohydrates. You're going to need as much energy as possible."

The instruction was unnecessary since his mentor was already taking care of his breakfast plate for him. As she did so, Finn continued to scour the contents of the table, which was even more impressive and exotic – by worker-class standards – than the buffet he'd eaten before his trial. There was eggs, scrambled, fried and poached, a dozen different kinds of real bread, bacon and other meats, a juice drink, coffee, and many more items that he didn't recognize. Finn had used his illegal data device in his old apartment to study what humanity had eaten before the Last War, so it surprised him that some of the produce was unknown to him. He wondered if there were perhaps modern delicacies that had been invented by the Authority since the foundation of Zavetgrad, and he picked up a spongy-looking round bun as an example.

"What the hell is this?" Finn asked, giving the foodstuff a sniff. It smelled sweet, but there were earthy tones too that he didn't recognize.

"It's a local delicacy, though I don't care for it," Elara replied, taking the bun from Finn's hand and placing it onto one of the plates, which he assumed was destined to be his. "They're called Spiced Brioche and are made with a mix of sausage and apple, flavored with cinnamon and a mixture of other herbs and seasonings that are apparently a secret recipe. If you ask me, they taste like shit."

Finn laughed. It was good to hear Elara Cage speaking like a regular person. Unusual, but good, and he liked it.

"For a moment there, you sounded like any other Metalhaven worker complaining about the food in the recovery centers," Finn said, smiling at his mentor. He meant it as a compliment, but the icy glare he got in return told him that he had erred.

"Don't ever let anyone hear you talking like that, not even

me, at least not in public," Elara said, speaking in little more than a whisper. "Everyone in this room will claw and scratch at you, looking for a hint of chrome underneath that glossy gold training uniform. Don't let them see it. Don't let them see who you were."

Not for the first time, Finn's mouth was dry and he felt foolish and afraid, but he kept his back straight and his body strong, hoping that no-one would see it, especially not his mentor.

"I'm sorry," Finn replied. "It won't happen again."

Elara continued to stare into his eyes for several seconds and it took all his nerve not to look away, until she finally broke off and returned her attention to the breakfast trays.

"I'm not asking you to forget, Finn," Elara said, while pouring two glasses of the juice drink. "I'm just asking you to lock that side of you away, at least until you need it again."

Finn nodded though Elara didn't see it since she had already turned her back and begun heading to a vacant table by the far wall. Finn saw that he'd left his tray on the table and he picked it up and followed her. Again, all eyes were on him, and he felt terrified, like a kid on his first day at a new school, desperate not to trip and fall in full view of everyone.

"I'm surprised one of the other apprentices didn't stick out a foot to trip me up," Finn said, making it to the table with his breakfast intact. "I suppose that bodes well."

"Don't be so sure," Elara replied, speaking from behind her glass of juice. "This may not be a school, but you should expect playground tactics, and not only from the apprentices."

"Great..." Finn said, picking up his drink and swilling it

around the glass. "And here's me thinking that being a gold might actually be fun."

He took a sip of the juice, which was almost as cloying as the probiotic algae goop he was forced to drink every morning in Metalhaven, though it did at least have the advantage of tasting good.

"That contains a cocktail of nutrients that will help to keep you strong," Elara explained, again as if reading his mind. "I know what you're thinking and it's broadly the same thing, apart from that its base is fruit juice, rather than algae."

"Not exactly a taste of home but it's nice that at least something is vaguely familiar about this place," Finn said, setting down the glass half-finished.

"This is your home," Elara said, detectably annoyed that Finn had again broken one of her edicts only moments after it had been established.

Finn cursed and held up his hands. "Sorry. I'll get used to it."

"Get used to it faster," Elara said, placing her empty juice glass on the table and starting work on her eggs and bacon.

The sight of his mentor forking bacon into her mouth was enough to kick his own hunger into gear, and he suddenly couldn't care less whether the food was drugged or not. He demolished his eggs before Elara had gotten half-way through hers, then began work in earnest on the salmon and grilled chicken which, while mundane foods to a gold, were like caviar and foie gras to him.

"Slow down," Elara said, eating in the same way that she moved, with methodical precision. "Golds have decorum, remember."

Finn stopped eating and looked up to discover that

curious glances had become appalled stares. He wiped a flake of salmon from his chin then picked up a napkin and dabbed his mouth in what he hoped was a 'proper' manner. Elara snorted a laugh and the hint of chrome showed itself again, before it was gone just as quickly.

"Better..." Elara said, while pouring two cups of coffee from a carafe that was already on the table.

"Can I assume that it's not just my bad table manners that are causing us to be talk of the town?" Finn said, Spiced Brioche in hand.

"You're the first worker to be elevated to gold since I was," Elara said, lowering the tone of her voice while also hiding her mouth behind her coffee cup. "That we're both from Metalhaven makes them nervous and suspicious, especially in light of that sector's infamous history."

"I'm surprised they paired us together," Finn replied, adapting his mentor's tactic by shielding the movement of his lips with the brioche.

"They didn't but I insisted," Elara replied, and suddenly she was The Shadow again, ominous and unknowable. "I can be very persuasive."

Finn raised an eyebrow but on that occasion he thought it best not to probe any further. Instead, he cast his eyes across the sea of people in the room, some of whom were still looking at him, while others had returned to their own conversations, or their breakfasts.

"Okay, so let me know who I'm up against," Finn asked. The food had filled a hole in his stomach, but not the gap in his knowledge. "I want all the gory details."

He took a bite from the spiced brioche but it was revolting and he spat it out onto his plate. Suddenly, the attention of the entire room was upon him again and he patted his mouth with the napkin, trying to look nonchalant, before side-eyeing his mentor, expecting her to look furious. However, she was still hiding behind her coffee cup, hand trembling as she gently shook with laughter.

3

MASTER AND APPRENTICE

Finn discarded the offending brioche onto a side plate then pushed it as far away from him as he could reach. He hadn't imagined it possible that something the golds revered as a delicacy could be so disgusting, but then he was quickly learning a lot about the Authority sector. Much of it was as expected, especially the latent hatred that was being directed at him as a former worker, but some had been surprising too, such as the fact that not all golds were utter assholes. His valet, Pritchard, immediately sprang to mind.

He took a sip of coffee to wash away the taste of the bun, then began to furtively survey the room. His mentor had stopped laughing at him and the cold, clinical prosecutor was back in control. Elara was also surveying the room, waiting until interest in them had subsided to a sufficient degree that she could begin her analysis of Finn's fellow apprentices without this being obvious to everyone in the dining hall.

"I count only five other apprentices," Finn said, turning his body toward his mentor so as to appear disinterested in what was going on around him. "I'd thought there would be more."

"Becoming a prosecutor's apprentice is a great honor, and places are hotly contested," Elara replied. For the first time since they'd sat down, no-one was watching them, at least not openly. "Hundreds apply every year, but only those most likely to succeed are selected. Aside from your background, that's another reason why the others resent you. In their minds, you didn't earn this honor, you were given it on a technicality."

The idea that surviving a brutal contest to the death was somehow considered 'a technicality' made Finn angry and he snorted his contempt. This caused several of the prosecutor mentors to shoot angry glances in his direction, but Finn was careful not to meet any of their eyes. As a worker, simply looking at a prefect the wrong way would land you a beatdown, so Finn was very well-practiced in the art of minding his own business, at least when it suited him.

"Do the others already have prosecutor aliases?" Finn asked, nonchalantly sipping his coffee. The prosecutors he'd aggravated had returned to their own conversations.

"No, you all receive your prosecutor names and customized gear at the end of the training cycle," Elara explained. "Your style and persona is part of what will be developed while you are here."

Finn almost snorted again but managed to hold it in this time. He'd forgotten how this was all a game to the golds. The prosecutors were more than just trained killers, they were celebrities, each with their own unique character, like comic book vigilantes.

"At least we're all starting on a level playing field," Finn commented. "That's something, I guess."

He was trying to find anything positive in what his mentor had told him but Elara was shaking her head, suggesting that even that assumption had been incorrect. She leaned in toward him to ensure that her voice didn't carry beyond their table, and Finn had to fight his instinct to shrink away. From across the other side of their table, The Shadow was out of striking range, but the closer she came, the more intimidating she was. It was like the difference between looking at a viper that was behind a glass barrier in a zoo, compared to one that was tasting the air at his feet.

"Some of these people were born to become prosecutors and have been trained to fight and hunt since they were children," Elara said, either unaware of Finn's discomfort or ignoring it. "Take him for example..."

Elara flashed her emerald eyes in the direction of a man who sat eating in the far corner of the room. He was muscular and even seated behind a table Finn could tell that he was tall, perhaps six-three or six-four. He had black hair and dark eyes that were periodically appraising the competition in the dining hall, looking at everyone like they were his blood-sworn enemies. Then their eyes met briefly and Finn looked away first, heart suddenly thumping in his chest. It was pure instinct, like turning away from a prefect, but he cursed under his breath, knowing that the man would now see him as weak and vulnerable.

"Who is he?" Finn asked, fighting the urge to look back at the table in case the muscular apprentice was still watching.

"His name is Walter Foster and he was developed right here in the Authority's birthing center, using seed from a

Genetic Rating Five worker," Elara explained. "His biological mother was a pure-born gold, and a former prosecutor. She was unable to have children, but her eggs were harvested and genetically-edited before being fertilized and given to a gestational surrogate to carry to term."

Finn snorted again though in a more restrained manner that didn't attract any attention. This time it was the notion that the fertilized egg was 'given' to a surrogate that had prompted his disgust. This was simply language designed to make the process sound perfectly normal and consensual, when in fact neither the sperm donor nor the surrogate had consented to the procedures. They had both been forced to comply on penalty of death.

"Walter has been trained since he was a boy for this very role," Elara went on, snapping Finn back to the moment. "That means he already has ten years of conditioning under his belt."

Finn scowled then chanced a second look at the man, who was thankfully now focused on one of the other apprentices in the room.

"Ten years in training? The guy looks like he's barely twenty years old," Finn said, doubting that he'd ever looked as healthy and as youthful as Walter in his entire life.

"He began at age seven, which is younger than most," Elara replied. Finn realized that this actually put Walter's age at seventeen or eighteen, and he let out a low whistle. "He's dangerous, but not only because of his size and abilities. The fact he was born to do this means he resents your presence more than anyone." She paused then corrected herself. "Well, more than *almost* anyone, but we'll come to him later."

Finn didn't want to wait and was intrigued to learn who

hated him more than the genetically-modified brute who sat in the corner, when he noticed another man at Walter's table. This was someone who needed no introduction.

"That's Walter's mentor," Elara said, also having spotted the new arrival. "His name is..."

"Frost..." Finn said, finishing her sentence. "I know him alright."

André Regan, known better by his prosecutor alias, 'Frost', was the third-highest ranking prosecutor by number of kills made during trials, and was rapidly climbing the ranks. The man was as big as his apprentice and wielded a comically-sized warhammer in the crucible, which he employed to brutal effect. He was named 'Frost' because the man showed no emotion, even when prosecuting his kills in the arena.

"If Walter Foster has the ego of a mountain then André has an ego the size of a planet," Elara said. She was scratching her nails on the table and looking at 'Frost' with dagger eyes. "But Walter will listen to him, because Walter respects strength." Elara turned to Finn and leaned in closer still, so that he could smell the thick fruit scent from the juice drink on her breath. "That means the next time Walter looks you in the eye, you don't look away."

Finn nodded. He'd wondered if Elara had seen his slip and now he knew. In hindsight, he should have never doubted it.

"I understand," Finn replied. He could have said more but his mentor appeared to appreciate that her message had struck home. "So, who's next?"

Elara drew back, and the air surrounding Finn felt less suffocating. She reclined in her chair and looked around the room, before fixing her gaze on a young woman at the center table.

"Do you see the apprentice in the middle of the room?" his mentor asked. "Short, blond hair and a lithe, wiry physique."

Finn had already spotted her. Elara's description of the woman was accurate, in terms of her physical appearance. From the way she was sitting, relaxed but alert, and the diamond-hard look in her eyes, Finn also gauged that she wasn't intimidated by her location in the slightest. Perhaps, she had even chosen to sit in the dead center of the room so as to make that very point. She was clearly confident, but there was more to it than that. She was hungry, and not for the food on her plate, which was largely untouched. Rather, her hunger was to prove herself, perhaps even more so than the others.

"I see her," Finn said, toying with the knife beside his plate. "What's her story?"

"Sabrina Brook is nineteen and the daughter of a prefect supervisor from Volthaven," Elara explained. "She was a prefect initiate, destined to follow in the jackboot steps of her thug father, until she graduated top of her class. That's when the prosecutors took notice."

Finn nodded, understanding why Sabrina was putting herself front and center. Prefects were a dime a dozen and while being an honor graduate set Sabrina a rung above the regular officers, she was amongst an entirely different category of people at the Prosecutor Academy. If she was going to make a name for herself, she'd have to prove her worth. In that respect, she was not unlike himself, though Finn was under no illusion that the mountain he'd have to climb was taller and steeper than for any of the others.

"Sabrina's mentor is Ayla Price, or 'Death Echo', and they're a good match," Elara continued. "Death Echo specializes in setting traps that ensnare offenders, allowing her to get in close and kill with a stiletto dagger. She'll ensure that Sabrina uses her head and plays to her strengths. We must do the same."

Finn nodded his agreement again, and while he was deeply curious to learn what Elara considered to be his strengths, he didn't interrupt his mentor to ask.

"Next is Zach Spencer, twenty-two years old," Elara said, with barely a pause for breath. "He's a wild card, and even I'm not sure what to make of him yet."

Finn followed the line of Elara's gaze and saw a man sitting alone, isolated from the rest of the group, even more so than himself and Elara. At a first glance, Finn considered Zach to be entirely unremarkable. He was ordinary to look at, with tufty brown hair and a slim build that made him look puny next to the titan, Walter Foster.

"He looks nervous," Finn said, though even as he spoke the words he was uncertain of his own assessment. "Or maybe he's just anxious to get started, I can't tell."

"That's the problem," Elara replied, seeming to agree with him. "Zach may not look like much, but until he was seconded here, he was a prefect supervisor in Stonehaven."

"He can't be much more than one-sixty or one-seventy pounds tops," Finn said, scowling at the man, who was habitually scratching the back of his neck as if he couldn't stop himself. "Metalhaven workers love a good drink and a fight, but Stonehaven is the roughest work sector by far. They'd eat him alive out there."

"Don't be so certain," Elara said, sounding a word of caution. "Zach was notorious at instigating savage beatdowns, and his record lists four fatalities against his name in just the month leading up to his transfer."

Finn's scowl reversed and his eyebrows shot up instead. It wasn't uncommon for workers to die during a beatdown, but he'd never heard of a prefect tallying four kills in a month, all by himself. The fact that instead of being punished, Zach had been rewarded for his murderous antics summed up the Authority perfectly, Finn thought.

"What's with the scratching?" Finn asked. Zach was still rubbing his neck and the sight was making Finn itch all over. "I've seen workers will all kinds of stress-related ticks but never a gold."

"I don't think it's stress in his case, but it's fair to say that Zach Spencer isn't entirely stable," Elara replied.

This got Finn's attention and he stopped toying with the knife on his plate. "Are you saying that he might have some kind of genetic anomaly?" he asked, and Elara nodded, shocking Finn again. "I didn't think that was possible."

"The authority would never admit that a gold is anything less than a four on the genetic rating scale, but that isn't the case," his mentor said. She had turned her head away so that no-one could see her lips moving besides Finn. "That's why they continue to harvest rating four and five seed from the worker class, because there isn't enough within their own community to go around."

"And they call *me* a fake gold," Finn said, masking his mouth with his hand while pretending to itch his nose.

"It's why entry to Nimbus is so heavily regulated," Elara continued. "The Authority knows that the golds in this sector are tarnished. Only those that it considers perfect make it to the citadel."

Finn doubted that it had been Elara's intention, but he suddenly felt far less out of place in the dining hall than he had done upon first entering. The worker class had been conditioned to believe they were lesser humans when in fact the only significant difference between them and the golds was the food they ate and the clothes on their backs. With a natural genetic rating of five, Finn suspected he was more 'gold' than anyone else in the room.

"Zach's mentor is Cleo McKay, or Garrote," Elara said. Finn looked around the dining hall and saw the prosecutor in question speaking with Sabrina's mentor, Death Echo. It seemed that even Cleo didn't want to be near his twitchy student. "She's a blunt instrument who will only force Zach to double-down on his natural aggression. Everyone in this room is dangerous, Finn, but Zach is dangerous *and* unpredictable. Don't take your eyes off him."

Finn sighed then took another sip of coffee. It was going cold but he was drinking it to wet his lips and lubricate his dry mouth, rather than to quench his thirst.

"The fourth apprentice is Tonya Duke, who up until a couple of weeks ago was an administrative worker for the Bureau of Labor Statistics," Elara said, moving on from Zach. "She's the tall red-head at the table by the door."

Finn had already noticed Tonya, because she was impossible to miss. Tall, athletic and with flowing red hair that didn't have a strand out of place, she was stunning to look at. She knew it too, and was basking in the attention she was receiving, from apprentice and prosecutor alike. One apprentice, in particular, was enthralled by her, and from the way she twirled her hair and shot him furtive glances, it was obvious that Tonya was encouraging his affections. The man in question was the final apprentice, the one Elara had suggested would begrudge his presence more than anyone else, even Walter Foster. There was something about this final apprentice that was disturbingly familiar but he couldn't put his finger on what.

"Most men can't keep their eyes off Tonya, but you've barely looked at her," Elara said. While he had been watching the mystery final apprentice, she had been watching him. "Are red heads not your type?"

Finn raised an eyebrow at his mentor's curiously catty comment, but his 'type' wasn't a subject up for discussion, especially not with someone he barely knew, and who had recently held a knife to his throat.

"An administrative worker doesn't seem like a smart choice for a trained killer," Finn said, ignoring Elara's probing question. "How did she end up getting selected?"

Finn detected a brief flash of annoyance from his mentor, who like all golds – born or made – was used to being obeyed, but it didn't linger for more than a heartbeat before she resumed her evaluation.

"Tonya is a blood descendent of one of Zavetgrad's founders," Elara said, her tone a little sharper. "She has little talent but a lot of ambition, and the connections to get what she wants."

Finn laughed under his breath. "It seems that nepotism wasn't a casualty of the Last War."

"No, and she's not even the worst example," Elara replied.

Her eyes flicked across to the final apprentice as she said this, but his mentor wasn't yet done with Tonya Duke. "Kurt McCullough will oversee her training, providing he can take time out from patronizing all of the Authority sector's brothels."

Finn had to think hard, but then managed to connect the Prosecutor's real name to his alias.

"McCullough is Blitz, right?" Finn said. "I thought he'd retired?"

"He did, but he's a friend of the Chief Prosecutor, so he hangs around like a bad smell," Elara said, no longer caring to moderate the volume of her voice. "The good news is that he'll only be here as often as required, since his retirement plan of screwing every sex worker in Zavetgrad clearly takes precedence."

Finn checked the room but true enough 'Blitz' wasn't there, not that Tonya Duke appeared to mind. Considering all the attention she was receiving, he wondered if the woman was even aware of the fact her mentor was absent. Nether Duke nor McCullough interested him, though. The apprentice he really want to hear about was the only one yet to be introduced. Elara was also now focused on the man and had resumed scratching lines into the table with her fingernails.

"The man you're looking at is Ivan Volkov," Elara said, eyes narrowed and attentive.

Finn didn't have to think to recognize the name. Every worker knew the name Volkov, no matter which sector they came from.

"Volkov, as is in Maxim Volkov, the Regent of

Spacehaven?" Finn asked, hoping he was wrong, but knowing he wasn't.

"Yes..." Elara replied. She'd scored a furrow in the table several millimeters deep. "Every Regent offers a son to the prosecutors. Sometimes it's their least favorite son, and sometimes it's their most troublesome. In Ivan's case, it's both. Even so, he is the Regent Successor of Spacehaven, and effectively royalty. People will be deferential toward him. He'll get special treatment. You need to be wary of him most of all."

Finn nodded, and was no longer concerned with Zach or Walter, or the other apprentices. Elara was right. A Regent's son was a problem, but the offspring of the Regent of Spacehaven even more so. This wasn't only because Maxim Volkov had presided over Finn's trail and personally warned him to keep his nose clean, but because the Regent of Spacehaven was the highest-ranking aristocrat, besides the President himself, the Voice of Authority, Gideon Alexander Reznikov. Maxim Volkov was not only a Regent but the current Mayor of the Authority sector too.

"Who is Ivan's mentor?" Finn asked. He counted only three Prosecutors he recognized in the room, besides Elara, and he already knew that Kurt 'Blitz' McCullough was otherwise engaged.

"She's in the corner, watching everything and everyone," Elara said, though she didn't take her eyes off Ivan Volkov. "Her name is Sloane Stewart, and she's not a prosecutor, but a bodyguard and assassin, and also Ivan's personal courtesan."

It took Finn a moment then he spotted the woman, and as soon as he did, he noticed she was looking straight at him. He almost looked away, as he had done with Walter Foster, but this time he held his nerve, and it was a full three seconds before Sabrina Brook happened to walk between them and force them to break eye contact. Despite only losing sight of her for a second, by the time Finn looked again, Sloane was gone.

"What do you mean, she's also Ivan's personal courtesan?" Finn asked. He was looking for the woman, but it was as if she'd vanished like smoke from the tip of a cigarette.

"Every prosecutor and apprentice has an assigned paramour," Elara replied. "You will too."

Finn's stomach knotted and he stopped looking for Sloane Stewart and turned to his mentor, blocking out everything else around him.

"Whoa, what do you mean I'll be assigned a paramour?" Finn said, heart racing. "I didn't use the wellness centers as a worker and I sure as hell won't be forced to screw someone as a gold."

Elara stopped scratching the table and folded her arms. "You won't be forced to do anything. Play tiddlywinks with her if you like, I don't give a shit, but you *will* have a courtesan."

"What the hell is Tiddywinks?" Finn asked. In his mind it sounded like some depraved sex game but the rolling of Elara's green eyes suggested he'd made a fool of himself again.

"Like I said, you can do whatever you like, but you will meet up, and you will spend time together," Elara said, becoming more forceful. "Remember what I told you. This is no place to buck authority. You have to fit in, whether you like it or not."

Elara's assertions that he wouldn't be forced into a sexual

relationship with a stranger gave him comfort, but it also raised some questions.

"Do you have a paramour?" Finn asked, tentatively.

He realized he had no right to ask, considering how he'd brushed off his mentor's question about his 'type' earlier, but he thought he'd chance his arm. For reasons he couldn't understand, he wanted to know and was nervous to learn the answer, but the arrival of someone new into the dining hall spared his mentor the need to respond. Suddenly, chairs were shoved back and everyone stood to attention, including Elara. Finn remained seated, mainly because he was caught by surprise, but his mentor's hissed demands of "stand up!" jolted him into action, and he was on his feet before anyone had noticed his error.

"My name is Chief Prosecutor Dante Voss," the new arrival announced in a thunderous voice that sounded amplified though it wasn't. "I am the Judge General, and the arbiter of who lives and dies inside our great crucibles where justice is done. You will call me Apex."

There was a coordinated cry of "Apex!" so loud it shook the floor and tables. Elara joined in, chanting the word loud enough to mask the fact that Finn remained dumbstruck.

"Prosecutors and apprentices," Apex continued, opening his hands to the room like a king addressing his court. "Let the training begin!"

4

THE OCTAGON

Finn filed in beside his mentor and followed the other prosecutors and apprentices out of the dining hall. At the same time, a small army of robots entered from a different door and began to tidy up the used plates and crockery and take the uneaten food away. At first, he didn't recognize the machines, but as one walked past he noticed that it was a modified foreman with a different head. Instead of the scowling eyebrows and stern mechanical expressions of the robotic middle managers, these machines wore affable smiles, like they were dancers on a stage in one of the Las Vegas casino bars that had been razed to the ground during the Last War. They were even wearing clothes, which only served to make them look more ridiculous in Finn's eyes.

"Oh, I do beg your pardon, sir," one of the robotic service staff said, pausing to allow Finn to move ahead of it. "My mistake, I'm terribly sorry."

"That's okay..." Finn said, waving the machine on, and it dutifully scurried past him.

"How was your breakfast, sir? I hope it was to your

satisfaction?" the machine added, bowing slightly while balancing a stack of thirty plates in one hand like a circus performer.

"Um… great, thanks," Finn said. He was so used to telling the machines to fuck off that he was bamboozled by the fact one was being nice to him. "Erm, compliments to the chef…"

The machine bowed lower then floated away, picking up a dozen more plates enroute with implausible dexterity.

"Compliments to the chef?" Elara said, side-eyeing him. "Where the hell did you learn a phrase like that?"

Finn felt his face burn hot. He hadn't thought his mentor had been paying attention and needed to get used to the fact that Elara Cage didn't miss a beat.

"A few years back, I found a data device with a natural language interface in a wrecked vehicle," Finn explained. "I smuggled it into my apartment and studied it most nights. You could say that I'm something of a historian."

Elara seemed impressed. "So that's how you managed to build your little robot friend. I had wondered. I don't suppose you studied martial arts or combat skills of any kind?"

Finn shook his head. "No, I learned about weapons and a little about how they work, but it didn't really interest me."

"That's a shame, it would have helped for what comes next," Elara said, picking up the pace so that they didn't drop too far behind the rest of the group.

"What comes next?" Finn said, afraid to hear the answer.

Elara side-eyed him again. "Fighting, and a lot of it."

"I'm no stranger to fighting," Finn said. Rather than worry him further, his mentor's answer had buoyed his confidence. "I've been doing it all my life."

"This is different."

They turned a corner and the corridor widened into a hangar-sized hall, filled with more equipment than Finn had ever seen in one place. Some he recognized from his data device, such as training weights and punching bags, and there were even several octagon-shaped fighting rings, while much of it was new to him. He was about to step inside when Elara grabbed his arm and held him back. She waited until the rest of the party had moved ahead before speaking again.

"Up to now you've been resisting, not fighting, and they're not the same. In here, you need to be smart, and you need to listen to me."

Finn nodded. "I understand the rules," he said, but Elara was not done with him.

"You don't understand, not yet," his mentor said. Since stepping into the training room, she had switched persona and The Shadow was now firmly in control. "We have twelve weeks of this, and if we're to make it to the end, you need to do as I say. No arguments. No push backs. No resistance."

"I understand," Finn said, angrily shaking himself free of his mentor's grasp. "I know what's at stake."

Elara glowered at him for a moment, considering saying more, but the other prosecutors and apprentices had already assembled in front of Chief Prosecutor Voss, and Apex was looking in their direction.

"I hope so, Finn, for both of our sakes," Elara said.

The Shadow extended a hand into the room, and Finn gladly accepted the invitation to move ahead, since the atmosphere between them had become suffocating. He filed in behind Sabrina Brook, who winked and smiled at him. It was such an unexpected gesture of kinship then he smiled back, until he caught Sabrina's mentor, Ayla 'Death Echo' Price scowling at him, and the smile was quickly wiped from his face.

"Apprentices, this is the training hall," Chief Prosecutor Voss began, speaking from inside one of the octagon rings. "You will train in here every day for the next twelve weeks, honing your existing skills and learning new ones that will enable you to become effective prosecutors of the law."

There was a chant of "Apex!", and everyone pumped their fists into the air, except Finn, who still had no idea how the ritual was supposed to work. Thankfully, no-one seemed to notice.

"As you all know, those born gold train from the age of thirteen to learn the combat skills necessary to defend our city against those who may rebel against the Authority," Voss continued, and though the Chief Prosecutor didn't look at Finn as he said this, Ivan Volkov and several others did. "Some of you, including myself, have trained since an even younger age, and are already proficient in many forms of combat. These skills will serve you well inside the crucible, but none of you are yet prosecutors. This twelve-week training regimen will not only hone you into a weapon of justice, but it will also identify your unique abilities and style. At the end of the program, you will have earned your prosecutor alias and that will be how you are known from that day until the day you die."

There was another chant of, "Apex!" with an accompanying fist pump. Finn partly anticipated it this time, recognizing that the chants occurred whenever Voss ended a sentence with a rising intonation. He managed to half-heartedly join in but felt foolish doing so, and even a little ashamed. It felt as if every chant of the Chief Prosecutor's name was an affront against those who had died in the crucible, many at the hands of men and women who were in the room with him. Voss then held out his hands and the assembled group quietened down.

"You will undergo intense physical training to condition your bodies, masterclasses in hand-to-hand combat, instruction in everything from bows and arrows to laser weapons, and become proficient assassins, able to move and kill without being seen."

Finn almost chanted "Apex" but recognized that Voss had concluded this part of his speech without a flourish and held his tongue. Elara was watching him out of the corner of her eye, as she always was, and appeared to appreciate the fact he was learning, and learning quickly.

"But before we begin your individual and group training in earnest, I want to find out what each of you is capable of now," Voss continued. "You and you! Show me what you can do."

Voss had pointed to Ivan Volkov and Walter Foster and both men did not hesitate to climb into the octagon ring and take up positions in opposite corners. Their mentors moved into position just outside the ring, while Voss remained in the center as observer and perhaps referee.

"This should be interesting," Finn said, whispering to his mentor, just as other apprentices were whispering to theirs. The anticipation in the room had become feverish. "Based on what you told me about Walter being bred for this role, I'd expect him to wipe the floor with Ivan."

Elara raised an eyebrow at him. "Are you prepared to wager on that?"

"Wager with what?" Finn asked. The only 'currency' he'd ever owned was chits for beers and cigarettes.

"How about ten Gideons?" Elara suggested, nonchalantly. "You're paid at the end of each week, so you can owe me."

"Only if I lose," Finn replied, showing his defiant side. He had no idea how much a Gideon was worth, and for all he knew he could be wagering an entire week's worth of pay, but he was never one to pass up a challenge. "You're on."

Elara nodded and smiled, and Finn worried that he'd just made a terrible mistake, but the deed was done, and the outcome of the fight – and their bet – would soon be known. Ivan and Walter had been prepared for the contest, and each was now wearing gumshields and open-fingered gloves that Finn figured weighed no more than four ounces apiece.

"Fight!" Voss announced, before dancing back to a neutral corner.

Finn was used to watching people fight, since brawls were a common occurrence in the recovery centers of the worker districts, but in his wildest dreams, he'd never imaged he'd witness two golds square off against each other. At first, Ivan and Walter were tentative, testing each other with snappy jabs while moving around the ring with light-footed precision. Given his size, Walter was no less agile than Ivan, who gave up at least thirty-pounds in mass to the bigger man.

"I said fight, not dance!" Voss yelled, and the Chief Prosecutor's intervention jolted the action into a higher gear.

Ivan took the initiative and attacked with restrained aggression, but Walter blocked the punches before soaking up a kidney shot that made his perfect face wince. There was a flash of anger, and Walter pushed Ivan back then harried the smaller man into the corner before unleashing a torrent of head and body shots. Ivan ducked and weaved but he was trapped and despite his obvious skill in the ring, Walter snuck an overhand right through his guard that rocked the Regent's son and sent the man down to one knee.

"Good, continue!" Voss yelled, pushing Walter back to allow Ivan to regain his footing.

"Looks like I'm going to be up ten Gideons," Finn said.

He grinned at his mentor, though Elara remained stony faced and focused on the fight, and Finn realized that she was studying the combatants' every moves. He cursed under his breath and returned to the contest with a fresh pair of eyes, remembering that he wasn't supposed to be a spectator, but a student.

The two men returned to their corners and spoke to their mentors, before moving into the center of the ring for another round. Despite his fall, Ivan was again the aggressor, but this time the man had switched techniques, and was no longer boxing, but employing a form of martial arts, testing Walter with kicks at range. Suddenly, the Regent's son snapped a kick at Walter's leg that unbalanced the bigger man, and Ivan tried to capitalize on his advantage by closing in with a combination of elbow and knee strikes, but Walter was unfeasibly quick. Walter blocked the attack then rocked Ivan with a left hook before grappling the man to the mat and placing him in a choke hold. Within seconds, Ivan tapped out and Walter released him, leaving the Regent's son red-faced and gasping for air.

Finn glanced at Elara again, though this time he reined in his natural urge to gloat, though even if he had, his mentor would have been unaffected. Despite Walter's clear dominance she still didn't look concerned, and suddenly Finn's doubts were amplified tenfold.

What the hell does she know that I don't?

Ivan slapped the mat angrily then picked himself up and returned to his corner. Finn noticed that Sloane Stewart, Ivan's mentor and paramour, was not in his corner. Instead, the mysterious woman had been speaking to Walter's mentor, Frost. The conversation was already over and Sloane was heading back to Ivan's corner, but it was clear that the mood in Walter's camp had changed. Frost was speaking to his apprentice and Walter looked pissed, though was nodding his head in agreement with whatever his mentor had told him.

"What the hell is going on?" Finn said, speaking the words out loud.

"You're about to lose your bet."

Finn might have expected Elara to have said this, but instead it was Sabrina Brook. Like his mentor, it seemed that the apprentice and former Prefect Honor Graduate had ears like a fox.

"Fight!" Voss said, and again the two men advanced toward each other inside the octagon ring.

Walter's body language had changed and the man's guard was lower and lazier. Ivan was again the aggressor, but this time his attacks were successful, and Walter soaked up three headshots before being forced into a neutral corner. In the previous two rounds, the bigger man would have easily blocked the shots, and Finn finally worked out what was going on. Ivan Volkov, son of the most influential Regent in Zavetgrad, could not be allowed to lose. Walter was throwing the fight.

Walter bounced out of the corner and threw hands at

his opponent, but the shots were sluggish and wayward, and Ivan evaded them with ease. Still employing a martial arts style, Ivan thumped a roundhouse kick into Walter's side that sent the man reeling against the ropes, then a spinning elbow strike cleaned his clock and Walter was down on the mat, blood and drool leaking from his swollen lips.

"Excellent!" Voss announced. He took Ivan's wrist and raised the victor's hand. "Ivan Volkov is the winner by knockout!"

There was generous applause, especially from Tonya Duke, the stunning red-head who had captured everyone's eye, including Ivan's. Tonya then wolf-whistled like she was a siren trying to lure the Regent's son into her watery lair. Frost entered the ring and helped Walter up, then out of nowhere two robots entered the hall and began tending to the apprentice's injuries. Like the machines in the dining hall, they were foremen adapted into medics, and though they appeared to be well-equipped and proficient, Walter was not interested in their ministrations.

"Get off me!" the man yelled, shoving one of the machines through the ropes and out of the ring. It clattered onto the hard floor, sounding like a stack of pots and pans falling off a kitchen worktop. "I'm fine, get lost!"

The other medical bot retreated then Finn watched as Ivan Volkov walked over to Walter. The two men looked at each other, then Ivan offered his defeated opponent his hand. Walter took it and Ivan help the man to stand. They shook hands and exchanged looks of appreciation and respect, and Finn felt foolish for not foreseeing the conclusion, as his mentor had done.

"Better luck next time," Sabrina said, slapping Finn on the butt and winking at him again.

"You win some, you lose some," Finn shrugged.

Death Echo then called to her apprentice and Sabrina moved away, but it wasn't long before he felt his own mentor breathing down his neck.

"I'll expect payment promptly at the end of the week," Elara said, with a touch more smugness than Finn appreciated.

"You knew that Walter would let him win?" Finn asked, turning to his mentor.

"Of course."

Finn sighed and shook his head. "Why? Just because he's the Regent's son? That's stupid."

"No, it's smart," Elara said, sternly. "You need to learn to be smart, Finn. Not every fight is won with fists and knives."

"We will have another contest!" Chief Prosecutor Voss called out.

The chant of "Apex!" filled the room and this time Finn was in tune.

"You and you!"

Finn's mouth went dry and his stomach knotted. Voss had pointed to himself and to Sabrina Brook.

5

LESSONS LEARNED

Finn looked over at his fellow apprentice and soon-to-be opponent, but Sabrina's reaction was the exact opposite to his. She'd pumped her fist and hurried to the octagon, eager to prove herself to her fellow trainees and to the Chief Prosecutor, who held her future prospects in his calloused hands.

"Voss paired you with Sabrina for a reason," Elara said. Her emerald eyes were boring into him like lasers and he could barely stand to look at her. "He knows you can fight, because he's seen you in the crucible, but he wants to see how fighting a woman changes you. As a prosecutor, you'll be tasked with killing anyone who is put in the arena with you, no matter their age or gender."

"But I'm not going to be a prosecutor," Finn whispered. "We're just biding our time until whatever the hell you have planned."

"You need to put that out of your mind, right now." She was angry and barely holding back. "For the next twelve weeks you are an apprentice prosecutor, and you have to act like one."

"But I'm almost twice her size!" Finn complained.

"Then end the fight quickly," Elara replied, unmoved by anything he'd said. "But make sure you end the fight as the winner."

"Brasa, get your ass in here!" Voss roared, waving him over from inside the octagon ring. The man wasn't angry, just impatient.

"Yeah, get in here, chromeboy!" Sabrina added.

Everyone in the hall laughed at her reference to his lowly origins, and Chief Prosecutor Voss didn't call her out for using the unkind nickname. It was clear that Finn was a gold in name only and that the color of his birth would never be forgotten.

"Fight to win," Elara said, shoving him toward the arena. "No mercy."

Reluctantly, Finn climbed into the ring and Elara fitted his gloves and gumshield. He wanted to talk more but Voss was too close and the man could easily overhear anything they said. Across the other side of the ring, Sabrina was already kitted out and ready, dancing from one foot to the other, and shaking out her arms. She had the same hunger in her eyes that Finn had noticed when he'd first seen her in the dining hall.

"This contest is for three falls, assuming either of you last that long," Voss cut in, looking at Finn as he spoke. "Fight hard and show me what you can do."

Voss motioned for the two fighters to engage then danced into the corner to observe. Unlike with the fight between Ivan and Walter, shouts and taunts rang out all around the ring, and none of them were in his favor.

"Kick his ass, Sabrina!" Tonya called out.

"Show him how a real gold fights!" Ivan added to a chorus of cheers from Walter and the others.

Finn blew out a sigh and raised a guard. Unlike his fellow trainees, he'd not been trained to fight. Everything he knew he'd learned on the snowy streets of Metalhaven or the sticky, beer-stained floors of the recovery centers, but brawling with drunken louts was a million miles away from a formal one-on-one contest, and he was out of his depth. Sabrina circled around him, practically floating across the canvas, smiling and taunting him with feints that lured him forward, only for her to dance away and leave him looking clumsy and amateurish.

"Come on, chromeboy, I know you've got some moves," Sabrina said, mumbling through her bright red gumshield. "Let's see what you've got!"

Sabrina's taunts were at least good-humored, rather than malicious, and Finn figured that she was a better opponent than anyone else Voss might have chosen. Had Walter stepped into the ring with him, for example, he imagined that he'd already be flat on his back and missing a few teeth.

Sabrina feinted again then attacked for real, kicking and punching with lightning speed. Finn managed to block some of the blows on instinct, but many more landed. Then he was winded and knocked down by a straight front kick that had beaten his guard with embarrassing ease.

"That's one fall to Apprentice Brook," Voss announced, to cheers of appreciation from the spectators. "On your feet, Apprentice Brasa. Let's go again."

Finn recovered quickly and got up. He looked at Elara, hoping that she might impart some words of wisdom, or give him a strategy to employ, but she'd barely moved since the fight had begun. She wasn't wearing her chameleonic armor but she was as good as invisible to him.

"Fight!" Voss called out.

Sabrina danced forward again, buoyed by her early success, and this time Finn didn't have time to think. A kick was snapped at his head and he blocked it on instinct before launching a counterattack, throwing hands like he was in a street brawl in Metalhaven. One punch landed flush on the side of Sabrina' face, and the woman went down like a sack of wet hay. Finn winced and rushed to his fellow apprentice's side.

"Shit, sorry, Sabrina," Finn said, looking into her glazed eyes as she lay, flat on her back. "Are you okay?"

Before he knew it, Sabrina's legs were wrapped around his body, clamping his lungs and squeezing the breath from his chest. She pivoted from underneath him then his arm was yanked free and pulled between Sabrina's thighs, elbow joint hyperextended to the point of excruciating pain. Finn yelled and slapped the mat hard to submit, but Sabrina held on for a second or two longer, before releasing her hold then climbing to her feet. Cheers rang out and her arm was being raised in victory before Finn had even realized he'd lost.

"Sabrina Brook is the winner!" Voss announced to yet more cheers.

Finn spat out his gumshield and rolled out of the ring, tearing off his gloves and tossing them to floor. His arm was throbbing and he saw the medical robots tiptoeing toward him, but the look of pure thunder he shot the machines convinced them to keep their distance.

"Better luck next time, chromeboy," Sabrina said.

She was leaning on the ropes, smiling at him. The woman winked then pushed away and returned to her corner, where Death Echo was waiting to congratulate her.

"What the fuck was that?"

Finn spun around and Elara Cage was there, looking ready to hit him. He opened his mouth to answer, but Elara grabbed his aching arm and maneuvered him away from the octagon and out of earshot of the others.

"I told you no mercy, and you fucking apologize for hitting her?" Elara hissed. "You had her beaten and you threw it away."

"Look, I'm sorry," Finn said, throwing his arms out. "I've only ever fought in self-defense and I've never hit a woman before. I don't think that makes me an asshole!"

"You're not here to be a knight in shining armor, you're here to train," Elara hit back. "They all think you don't belong and you're just proving them right. If you're weak you won't last two weeks let alone twelve."

Finn glanced over Elara's shoulder and saw Ivan, Walter and some of the others looking at him like he was their next meal. He cursed under his breath, knowing that his mentor, as usual, was right.

"You made yourself look weak and vulnerable," Elara continued, struggling to keep her voice down. "You need to listen to me."

"I am listening to you," Finn hissed. "But you didn't tell me I'd be beating the shit out of a nineteen-year-old girl!"

Now everyone was watching them and Elara kicked open a door and yanked Finn through it. The door slammed, then before Finn could say anything more, Elara stunned him with a straight right that sent him staggering against the wall. By the time his eyes had cleared, he felt the sharp edge of a black roundel dagger at his throat. He hadn't even noticed that his mentor was carrying it.

"I risked everything to get you here, but compromise me and I'll kill you myself!" The Shadow was speaking now. "We have twelve weeks, no more, no less. You have to show them that you belong. You have to fight every instinct in your body and be a gold, even if it makes you want to throw up. That's how you survive and get out of here."

Elara removed the knife from his throat and sheathed it, though Finn still couldn't see where or how she'd concealed the weapon. She backed away and The Shadow begin to give way to Elara Cage, his mentor.

"It's not just your life on the line, Finn, it's mine too," Elara said, whispering the words, despite them being alone. "And if you fail then all those who were lost so that you could be here will have died for nothing."

The reference to Owen and the others who were killed in the trial was clear and Finn hated her for it. For a blissful hour or two, he'd forgotten that his friend was dead, and the cold, stark reminder of that fact had been intentionally cruel and calculating. Yet, at the same time, Elara was right, and he hated her for that too because he hated being wrong. Suddenly, the handle of the door was turned and Finn and Elara separated, like two teenagers that had been caught smoking in a restricted area of school. Chief Prosecutor Voss entered, looking at them both with deep suspicion.

"Everything okay in here?" Voss asked.

There was little real concern in the man's voice and Voss was merely doing what was expected of him. Given a choice, Finn doubted he would lower himself to speak to them at all.

"Yes, I was just instructing my apprentice on the importance of showing no mercy," Elara replied.

Voss grunted. "Well, there's no one better than you to teach that lesson," the man replied, though rather than a genuine compliment, it sounded more like a forced admission. "Return to the hall, while I have a word with Mr. Brasa."

"With respect, Apex, I should be present for any discussion you have with my apprentice," Elara replied.

"You two chromes can reminisce later," Voss said, and Finn was shocked by the casual disregard of Elara's status, which had been hard-earned. "Now do as I say."

Elara hesitated a moment and Finn wondered if she was considering employing her roundel dagger again, before she glanced at Finn, eyes imploring him to behave, then left.

"What can I do for you, Apex?" Finn asked, falling in line as his mentor had asked.

"Let's cut the shit, Brasa, I don't want you here," Voss said, and Finn felt threatened. "I know what the rules of the crucible say, but the prestige of this academy is sullied by your presence, just as it was by the presence of your mentor, who stubbornly refuses to die in the arena and spare me from having to see her face."

Finn's instinct was to defend his mentor and poke the Authority in the eye but he held his tongue. He was learning.

"Anyway, if you continue in the same vein as today, you won't last long, and I'll be spared the dishonor of two chromes walking my halls," Voss continued, already bored of the conversation. "But while you're here, you have an additional obligation. As a former worker, you must undergo a regular loyalty evaluation."

Voss removed a card from his pocket and pressed it Finn's chest. The man had released the card before Finn had taken it, but he managed to catch it on reflex before it fell to the ground, much to Voss's obvious disappointment. The man had probably hoped to see Finn bowed down at his feet, in his proper place.

"Don't miss the appointment," the Chief Prosecutor added, jabbing a finger at Finn. He felt like biting it off. "And do better tomorrow. If you can…"

6

ROOM 616

Finn waited until Chief Prosecutor Voss had returned to the training hall to conduct the final rounds of sparring then read the card he'd been given. *Prosecutor Apprentice Finn Brasa, Loyalty Evaluation. Room 616. By order of the Special Prefecture.* He scowled and tapped the card against the back of his hand.

"But where is room 616, and what time is my appointment?" Finn asked out loud. It was in moments like these that he wished Scraps was already repaired, because he felt sure that the little robot would know the answer.

"I'll take you to the interview room."

Finn jumped then spun around to see Elara behind him. That she'd managed to open the door and sneak up on him without a sound was a special and disturbing talent. His mentor then took the card out of his hand and tapped it to his wrist. A band of light lit up on his cuff then then the date and time of his appointment was displayed. It was in five minutes.

"I thought Voss ordered you back into the training hall?" Finn said.

He was still pissed at his mentor for holding a knife to his throat, but he was angrier at himself for letting her down, and the combination of so much pent-up frustration meant he was radiating negativity like a toxic cloud.

"He did," Elara replied, offering no further explanation for her absence. She returned the appointment card to Finn then removed a capsule from her pocket that was the size of a small button. "Swallow this."

Finn took the capsule and examined it but it was entirely nondescript. "If you wanted to kill me then you could have just slit my throat earlier, instead of feeding me poison."

"If I wanted you dead, Finn, then you'd already be dead," Elara replied, drawing on her Shadow persona to deliver to the statement with a convincing degree of authority. "That capsule contains an inhibitor that will attach to your nervous system and mask the physiological indicators of when you're lying."

Finn continued to scowl at the capsule then swallowed it. It felt larger than it looked sliding down his gullet without the benefit of a drink to wash it into his stomach.

"Why do I need something that hides when I'm lying?" Finn asked.

He could have asked this question prior to swallowing the device but he understood that his mentor needed to see a gesture of trust and compliance from him. He didn't know for sure that it had worked but after swallowing the capsule he found himself more in the presence of Elara Cage than The Shadow, and he realized that this was by far his preference.

"The loyalty evaluation is really an interrogation," Elara said, setting off along the corridor and forcing Finn to jog a couple of steps to catch up. "The questions will start easy then quickly become more challenging and much more personal. You need to be prepared."

Finn nodded. Elara's earlier message, delivered at the point of a knife, was still buzzing around his head like a detuned radio.

"I can't come in with you, but it's important that you find a way to answer the questions truthfully as much as possible," Elara said. "This will help to train the device you just swallowed to understand when you're being honest and how to mask the signals that indicate when you're not."

Finn held out a hand and stopped his mentor in her tracks. He knew he didn't have long before the appointment, but something she'd just told him had rung alarm bells.

"How can I be honest without incriminating myself?" Finn asked. "I mean, what if they ask me what I know about Haven?"

"Then you tell the truth up to a point, and lie about the rest," Elara said. "The Authority knows that rumors of Haven's existence circulate in the recovery centers of every work sector, so it's reasonable to expect you might have heard the name before. That's truth. But when they probe deeper, you have to lie, and lie convincingly. The device will help to conceal that lie from them."

"And if this device doesn't work?" Finn asked. He had a damned good idea what the answer was going to be, but he wanted to hear it from his mentor straight.

"You've lied to foremen and prefects all your life, Finn, this is no different," Elara replied, dodging his question, which was perhaps for the best. "Just be as brief as possible, and whatever else you do, rein in your natural urge to be a dick."

Finn was offended and he made sure that his pouty expression articulated that fact, though he had no right to be annoyed with his mentor, because Elara – once again – was right about him. The screen in Finn's cuff then flashed up a warning that they were going to be late, and Elara hustled him through the maze of corridors inside the Prosecutor Barracks until they were outside room 616. A single prefect stood guard but it was a style of officer that Finn hadn't seen before. The man's armor was like a carapace, colored black with gold trim, and an opaque visor hid the officer's face above the nose so that only his clean-shaven, square jaw was visible.

"Prosecutor Apprentice Finn Brasa, here for his evaluation," Elara said to the guard.

Finn waved the appointment card at the officer who snatched it out of his hands then scanned it using his C.O.N.F.I.R.M.E device. He was surprised to see that officers in the Authority sector still used the wrist-mounted computers, the acronym of which stood for Centralized Observation Network for Forensic Identification, Registration, and Monitoring of Entities. Finn had thought that they were only used for monitoring workers, then he remembered Elara's comment about how the Authority sector wasn't as perfect as he imagined. Whoever the jackbooted officer was, he clearly represented a higher tier of the Authority and Finn made a note to be extra vigilant.

"I'll see you once this is done," Elara said, suddenly gripping his wrist, adding enough pressure to cause him pain. "Remember what I told you."

Finn nodded – his mouth was too dry to speak – then the door was opened and the special prefect stepped aside. He wasn't explicitly invited to enter, but he saw no reason to dally and walked into the dimly-lit room without delay. Inside was a simple metal desk and two metal chairs, one of which was occupied by a foreman robot, though like the prefect, it was a class he'd not seen before. Taller and stockier than a regular foreman and with heavy armor, it looked like it had been designed for fighting instead of conducting interviews. The desk was empty apart from a single block-shaped device that sat on the far side. Wires snaking out from the device were connected to the back of the foreman's head.

"Welcome Apprentice Prosecutor Brasa," the robot said, without standing up. "I am a class-five evaluator attached to the Special Prefecture and will be conducting today's interview."

"You look like a foreman to me," Finn said. Try as he might, the sight of the robot servants of the Authority filled him with a deep-rooted hatred, and he spoke without thinking.

"As I already explained, I am a class-five evaluator," the machine replied. Its tone was polite but impatient. "Please sit down."

Finn blew out a sigh then dropped into the chair opposite the robot. It was hard and unforgiving, and he expected that his robot interviewer would be the same. The special prefect then closed the door and stood in front of it, blocking the exit. The man was armed with an electrified nightstick and a sidearm, both of which remained stowed, but within easy reach. The evaluator robot then pressed a sequence of buttons on the slab-shaped device and a compartment popped open, facing Finn. Inside was a black fabric glove.

"Please insert your left hand into the glove," the evaluator said.

"What will it do?" Finn asked, while complying with the directive and wiggling his fingers inside the tight-fitting glove. He figured that the robot might be more conversant if his questions were paired with acts of compliance.

"The glove allows me to monitor certain aspects of your physiology," the evaluator replied. "This includes your pulse, perspiration, involuntary movements and more. Coupled with the scanners in this room, and my own personal suite of assessment tools, I will be able to determine the authenticity of your every response."

"So, you're a glorified lie detector?" Finn asked.

The robot raised a mechanical eyebrow and Finn again kicked himself for allowing his emotions to control him, rather than the other way around. The device on the table bleeped then the evaluator opened a drawer and removed a logbook. To Finn's surprise, the machine also picked up a pen, then opened the book to a blank page and began writing. The movements were swift and fluid and the script was graceful, like an old hymn book, but because of the lights in the room, one of which was shining in his face, Finn couldn't see what the evaluator was writing.

"Very interesting," the evaluator said, while continuing to write notes into his book.

Finn wanted to fire back a petulant retort, such as 'I'm glad one of us is having fun...' but he managed to rein in his urges. Even so, the machine bleeped again and Finn was fearful that it could even detect his unspoken thoughts. If so, he would betray himself without speaking a word.

"How do you know all this equipment is accurate?" Finn asked. He felt that this was a reasonable question to ask and was focused on remaining reasonable.

"I have been programmed solely to assess the loyalty of my interviewees, and my accuracy rating is 99.3%," the evaluator said, smiling smugly.

"I feel sorry for the 0.7%," Finn replied, before kicking himself again.

The evaluator maintained its smug smile. "I am detecting irritation. Based on your worker file, this is normal behavior for Finn Brasa. On every occasion where you have been required to comply with a directive, such as to attend a wellness center or donate a seed sample, you have resisted." The robot set down its pen and leaned in closer. "Why is that, Mr. Brasa?"

Finn was no stranger to interrogations and had noticed a consistent pattern in all of them, which was that interrogators always asked questions that they believed they already knew the answers to. It was standard practice for the authority to presume guilt and despite his newly-minted gold status, Finn realized he was in a fight for his life. He straightened up – he hadn't even realized he'd been slouching until that point – and every neuron in his brain switched on.

"I can't deny that as a worker I was less than compliant, and that I resented being forced into certain actions," Finn said, taking Elara's advice and mixing truth into his answers where he could. "But my arrest and trial taught me the error of my ways. Now, I have a second chance, and I don't intend to waste it."

The second part of his answer was truth mixed with lies and he hoped that the device Elara had given him was able to separate them out and feed the evaluator's machine only the data that would keep him alive. For several seconds the evaluator merely stared at Finn, and he stared back, forcing his breathing into a regular rhythm and compelling his body to remain calm.

"Very interesting," the evaluator eventually replied, before picking up his pen and scribing some more notes into the logbook.

"Please describe your feelings when you received the news of your elevation to gold status as an apprentice prosecutor?" the robot asked, eyes down while still writing.

Finn shifted in his chair. This seemed like an easy question, which made him oddly more nervous. "I was shocked, of course," he replied. *Where you can, tell the truth...* "I didn't really know how to process it."

"Are you excited at the prospect of dispensing justice inside the crucible?"

"I want to play my part," Finn answered. *Keep your answers brief...*

"As a prosecutor you will be required to kill offenders," the evaluator continued. "These will be workers, such as you once were. Does that... bother you?"

Shit! Already with this? They're not holding back...

"I don't want to kill anyone," Finn replied. *Tell the truth...* "But I understand what my role is and what it will require of me."

The robot stroked its chin, as if it were covered in metal filaments to mimic a beard, where in reality it was polished smooth, like the rest of its body.

"Very interesting," the evaluator replied. Finn was already growing to hate that phrase.

"I wish to understand your opinion about the division of society into the Authority and Worker tiers," the robot went on. "Do you believe it is a fair system, and if so, why?"

"I don't think it's fair, but fairness isn't what matters," Finn replied. *Truth mixed with lies...* "The survival of the human race is what matters. I understand that now."

The robot wrote in his logbook while Finn continued to force his breath into a rhythm. He could feel that his heart rate was above normal and he felt hot, but his body refused to sweat. *Is that the device at work?*

"Do you agree that a worker tier is necessary to the survival of Zavetgrad and that the authority is correct to use force to ensure societal stability?" the evaluator asked.

Finn was getting used to the questions now and he knew how to answer them with a blend of truth and lies.

"Without the work sectors and what they produce, Zavetgrad couldn't survive," Finn replied. He was pleased at how he answered that part of the question without really answering it. "And maintaining order through the use of force is essential. I see that now."

"Very interesting..." The evaluator replied.

The scribble of pen against paper felt like the robot was writing directly onto his brain. The evaluator then stopped suddenly and looked into his eyes, which seemed to glow like the residual heat of a lightbulb filament.

"How did you feel when Owen, your friend and worker buddy, was killed?"

Finn's heart began to race and the machine on the desk bleeped more urgently, but there was simply no device or technology in existence that could mask the guilt and pain he felt over Owen's death.

"How do you think I felt?" Finn snapped. *Get a grip, for fuck's sake!* ... "He was my friend. I was... upset."

"Do you blame the Authority?"

Deep breaths... keep in control...

"I blame Corbin Driscoll, the low-life piece of shit who killed him."

"Do you seek revenge?"

The evaluator was trying to rush him, to force Finn to make a mistake without thinking. He wasn't going to fall for it.

"Justice was already served," Finn replied, waiting a few seconds before answering to slow the pace of the interview. "In that respect, he was my first kill as a prosecutor."

The robot narrowed its mechanical eyes at him, which were even more expressive and probing than those of a head foreman, a class of machine he'd dealt with on hundreds of occasions.

"Very interesting..." the evaluator said, before jotting more notes into its book.

Finn desperately wanted to see what the machine was writing, and he suspected that this was the entire point of the physical logbook. Digital screens could be turned off, but paper and ink was permanent and its mere existence, just out of reach, was part of his torment.

"As a worker in Metalhaven, were you ever involved in subversive or rebellious activities against the existing social order?"

"What?" Finn said. The new line of questioning had come out of the blue and caught him off guard.

"As a worker in Metalhaven, were you ever involved in subversive or rebellious activities against the existing social order?" the evaluator repeated, this time louder and more forcefully.

Out of the corner of his eye, Finn could see that the special prefect had gripped the handle of his nightstick and he forced down a dry, hard swallow before compelling himself to stare down the evaluator.

"No," he answered, just as forcefully.

"Are you aware of a rebel stronghold called Haven?" the evaluator barked.

"I've heard rumors," Finn replied. *Truth...* "People talked but I paid it no mind." *Lie...*

"Tell me everything you know about Haven."

"I don't know anything more than what you've just told me," Finn replied. *Lie... A big one. Shit, I hope this device in my body works...*

"Have you ever heard the phrase 'Metal and Blood'?"

The evaluator was firing off questions at the rate of a machine gun and Finn felt that he should have been sweating buckets, but his skin was dry, like his mouth.

"I heard a worker shout that phrase at the beginning of a trial in Metalhaven's yard seven." Finn replied.

"Do you know what it means?"

Deep breath... "No."

"Are you a Metal?"

Boom! The question was shot at him like a cannon but Finn was ready for it.

"No..." His answer was definitive, back straight and eyes level.

"Is your mentor, Elara Cage, otherwise known as The Shadow, a Metal?"

Finn hadn't anticipated this but he held his nerve, and suddenly Elara's warning that it wasn't only his life on the line hit home. They already suspected her.

"The Shadow almost killed me in my trial, and I barely escaped with my life," Finn answered. *Find a way to mix in truth with the lies...* "She's one of your top prosecutors and a one-hundred percent solid-gold bitch."

That part came from the heart and Finn was confident that no method of sensory interrogation could determine otherwise. Even so, the evaluator continued to stare into his eyes for several more seconds, and he stared back, not even blinking once. Then the robot smiled.

"Thank you for your time, Apprentice Prosecutor Brasa," the evaluator said, brightly.

The lights in the room came up and the door opened. The special prefect who had been guarding it had stepped aside. The man's hand was no longer wrapped around the handle of his nightstick.

"I can go?" Finn asked. He wanted to be sure it wasn't part of the interrogation. A cruel bait and switch.

"Yes, we will update you shortly with the date and time of your appointment next week," the robot said.

"We're doing this again?" Finn said, pulling his hand out of the glove in the machine. He'd expected it to be dripping wet with sweat, but like his skin it was bone dry.

"Yes, we will continue with the evaluations until the Authority is entirely satisfied that you are gold, Finn Brasa, and that no trace of chrome remains."

Finn nodded and stood up. His legs were like jelly and he

hoped that this wasn't obvious as he walked out of the door, which thudded shut behind him. Elara was there waiting for him.

"I think I passed," Finn said.

"You did," Elara replied, with the hint of smile. "I know because you're not dead."

7

SCRAPS OF GOLD

Finn pressed his thumb to the ID panel and the door to his apartment slid open with a satisfying whoosh and thump. There were no squeaks from age-worn gears or grinding sounds as the bottom of the door dragged against the floor, it just worked. Everything in the Authority sector was like that, Finn had discovered. While the infrastructure in the work sectors was left to rot, maintained only when absolutely necessary, no expense was spared to ensure the golds lived in luxury. It disgusted him, but he was learning to hide his disgust and his experience in room 616 only reinforced how necessary this was, not only for his survival, for his mentor's too.

Stepping inside, the door whooshed and thumped shut behind him and Finn found himself at a total loss for what to do next. The concept of downtime was unfamiliar to him. Normally, by the time he'd returned to his apartment after a shift in the reclamation yard, he barely had time to eat a basic meal before being required to attend the wellness center or donate at the gene bank, before heading out for his mandated drinking session in the recovery center. Most of the worker class staggered home late and collapsed onto their sofa beds, only to be rudely awoken at five o'clock the next morning to drink their hangover-relieving probiotic goop and begin their next twelve-hour shift. Quite often these hours were extended for a multitude of reasons, which in Finn's case was usually because he'd insulted a foreman or thumbed his nose at the Authority in some other way. As such, if he'd managed to get one hour in twenty-four that was completely to himself, it was a luxury. As a gold, he had several hours every day set aside purely for his own recreation and he didn't have the slightest clue where to start. Then he saw Scraps sat on his desk, still inert due to his broken power core, and suddenly his afternoon plans were set.

"Okay, let's see if we can't fix you up, pal," Finn said, sliding into the desk chair and setting out the tools he needed. He was about to begin when the doorbell chime sounded, *bra-sa!... bra-sa!* ... invoking more unpleasant memories of Bloodletter, and Finn almost jumped out of his skin. "Come in!" he called out, louder than was probably necessary.

The door whooshed and thumped and his valet, Pritchard, entered, carrying a square box that was roughly the size of a medium-sized toolchest.

"Good afternoon, sir!" Pritchard said, setting down the box on his dining table.

"Finn, remember? We're alone at the moment," he replied, reminding his valet that he needn't speak to him like an aristocrat while they were in private.

"Of course, sir, I'm sorry, sir," Pritchard waffled apologetically. The man then smiled. "I'll get it right one day!"

Finn laughed then got up to greet the man with a handshake, which Pritchard was at first hesitant to accept, then reciprocated gladly and with gusto.

"How was your introductory training session, sir?" Pritchard asked, while removing the packaging from the box. Finn still had no idea what it was.

"Let's just say it could have gone better," Finn replied, hesitantly. His elbow and shoulder still ached from where Sabrina had grappled him into an arm lock.

"And your interview with the evaluator?" Pritchard added. There was a palpable degree of tension in the man's voice as he asked this.

"That was unpleasant, but I'm still here, so I'm assuming it went well enough," Finn answered.

"Quite so, sir!" Pritchard said, visibly relieved to hear it.

The packaging was finally removed and neatly folded away, then Pritchard opened the box and removed a steaming cup of coffee that had been stowed inside.

"I took the liberty of bringing you a coffee," his valet said. "Pure arabica, three sugars, black."

"Just how I like it, thanks," Finn said, accepting the drink. His throat was hoarse after the interrogation and he welcomed the soothing sweetness of the coffee. He then frowned at the object that his valet had miraculously produced the coffee from, like a rabbit from a magician's hat. "What have you brought me this time?" he asked.

Pritchard breamed a smile at him. "This, sir, is a portable spray booth." Finn looked at him, clueless, and the man dutifully elaborated. "It's for your robot, sir. Just place the little machine inside and program the booth with the color scheme you desire, and voila!"

"Voi-what-now?" Finn said.

Pritchard politely dismissed his confusion with a waft of his hand. "What I mean to say is that it's instant and simple." He smiled again. "So, shall we give it a try?"

"I haven't actually replaced his power core yet," Finn said, returning his attention to his desk. Then he had a thought and shrugged. "But it's a simple task to replace the body panel, so maybe we can paint him now, and I can fix him after."

Pritchard clapped his hands together gleefully, bizarrely far more excited at the prospect of painting a robot made from junk than even Finn was.

Finn went to collect Scraps and picked up the body panel that he'd already prepared to replace the damaged one that had been punctured by Elara's crossbow bolt. The installation was simple and the door hinges screwed into place securely. He tested the fit and the new panel opened and closed with gold-standard precision, just like his own front door.

"Here you go," Finn said, passing the robot to Pritchard, who handled the machine with reverence, as if it were an ancient relic.

"What color-scheme would you like?" Pritchard asked, while placing Scraps inside the booth with supreme care and attention.

"I want him to be chrome, remember," Finn said, stepping beside his valet to watch him work. "So chrome plus whatever gold accents are needed to ensure he's not seen as a labor bot."

Pritchard nodded and set to work. A screen popped out from a compartment at the rear of the device, showing a rotating 3D representation of Scraps, as he currently looked, in a hodge-podge of different rusted metal colors. Then the image changed and the bot was a lustrous metallic chrome.

"This is standard Metallic Shimmer Chrome from the official color palette," Pritchard explained. "It's the color that you wore in Metalhaven."

Finn shook his head. "Not quite, that's the color of prefect body armor. Workers didn't get to wear anything so glossy and expensive looking."

Pritchard shrugged then tapped the keypad on the device and the color-scheme switched to a darker shade of silver.

"This is called Liquid Luster," Pritchard said. "It is the color that the Prefect of Metalhaven wears on his robes."

Finn snorted a laugh. "Perfect..." he said, smiling. "Scraps is Metalhaven royalty, as far as I'm concerned, so let's paint him in that shade."

Pritchard nodded then tapped the control panel again and seconds later the image was updated with gold accents on Scraps' upper arms, like he was wearing shoulder pauldrons made from solid gold.

"This will ensure that your little machine is clearly identifiable as a personal robot," Pritchard said, finger hovering over the button to activate the booth. "Shall I proceed?"

"Do your worst," Finn said, brightly. Pritchard frowned at him and he clarified his instruction in terms that someone who hadn't frequented a Metalhaven dive bar would understand. "I mean yes, please go ahead."

Relieved, Pritchard activated the painting booth then stepped back as it began to trundle and whir, sending high-frequency vibrations rattling through the table. Finn was about to ask how long the process would take when the machine stopped suddenly and pinged, like his food-heating station in his old apartment.

"Is that it?" Finn asked, as Pritchard switched off the machine then lifted the lid.

"Yes, it's a quick process." His valet reached inside then lifted Scraps out of the box. The robot was gleaming like an authority sector skycar flying overhead in the midday sun. "It's quite dry," the man added, holding Scraps out for Finn to take.

"He looks incredible," Finn said, taking the robot into his hands. He expected to get paint all over him, but whatever process the spray booth had used was instant. "Thank you, Pritchard."

"It is my genuine pleasure, sir," his valet replied, with a subtle bow. A computer wrapped around the man's left cuff then bleeped and he read the message without delay. "My apologies, sir, I have some clerical work to attend to." Pritchard pointed to the spray booth. "Shall I leave this here?"

"No, you've done an incredible job," Finn said, examining Scraps in more detail. In every way, the robot looked factory fresh, apart from the fact he was still broken. "Now, I just need to get him working."

"There are technical people in the sector that could do that for you?" Pritchard suggested.

"No, I'll fix him myself."

His answer was delivered snappily and Pritchard knew not to press the matter further. Instead, the man merely bowed again then made his apologies and left, taking the spray booth and its packaging with him. Finn picked up his coffee, returned to his desk and set Scraps down in front of him. He'd already prepared the components he needed and so got straight to work, popping open his freshly-painted chest panel and inspecting the damage. It wasn't as bad as he'd thought and in less than hour, fueled by his sweet coffee, the new power cell was fitted and connected. He stood Scraps up on his desk then shuffled his chair back and drew in a deep breath of purified air.

"Here goes nothing..."

Finn activated Scraps and power surged through the machine's circuits. His eyes began flashing as the robot's boot-up cycle began then his arms and legs articulated and the process culminated in a cheerful bleep. Finn let out the breath he'd been holding and leaned in closer.

"Scraps? Are you in there, pal?"

"WA-WA!" the robot yelled and Finn jolted back so sharply that he toppled over the back of his chair and ended up flat on his back. "Lady-bad-man! Lady-bad-man! Shot-shot!"

"No, Scraps, you're okay!" Finn said, hauling himself off the floor. "Lady-bad-man is gone. You're okay. I fixed you."

Scraps stopped screaming and the little robot narrowed his eyes at Finn, before looking around the room with a mix of intense curiosity and deep suspicion.

"Not Metalhaven?"

"No, pal, this isn't Metalhaven," Finn replied, smiling to comfort the machine.

"Trial over-over?"

"Yes, I won the trial, pal," Finn explained. "I'm a gold now. We're in the prosecutor barracks in the Authority sector."

Scraps nodded but his mechanical eyes remained narrowed. Then the machine noticed his new paint job and jumped back with surprise, knocking over the lamp Finn had positioned to help him work.

"Scraps good as new!" the robot said. Then he saw the gold patches on his arms and shoulders. "Scraps also gold?"

"Yes, you're a gold now too!" Finn said, laughing. "And that means I don't have to hide you anymore."

"Yay-yay!" Scraps said, and the robot sprouted its rotors from the top of its head and began hovering around the room. "Apartment nice-nice!"

"Yes, it is!" Finn said, laughing some more as his robot buddy buzzed around the space, whipping through his kitchen then bouncing on his bed, before returning to the lounge and circling his dining table. After a whistlestop tour, Scraps finally returned to the desk and landed in front of him, eyes narrowed again. "Where Owen?"

Finn felt his blood run cold and his stomach knotted so tightly that he winced from the pain. From the heights of happiness he was now scraping the depths of despair. *Owen...* he thought. The loyalty evaluation followed by Pritchard's arrival had districted him enough to forget that his friend was dead, but now the memory came gushing back, like blood pouring from a severed jugular. He felt sick with sadness and guilt and his little robot could sense every ounce of his sorrow.

"Owen gone-gone?" Scraps asked, but in his circuits the robot already knew the truth.

"Yes..." Finn said, the word catching in his throat. "He was... killed."

Confirming the news to his robot seemed to suck all the air out of the room and Finn was unable to say anything more, but he didn't have to. Scraps leapt at him and grabbed the fabric of his training uniform, hugging him tightly.

"Scraps sorry..." the robot said.

"I know, pal..." There was musical plink... plink... and Finn realized that he was crying, and that the sound he could hear was his tears drumming on the robot's oil-can body. "I'm sorry too."

Finn wrapped his arms around Scraps and for a time they consoled each other in silence. Then, once he was able to function again, he told his robot friend everything that had happened, from the moment Elara had incapacitated him with a crossbow. He explained how he'd fought Bloodletter and lost, only for Owen to save his life at the last second. He remembered the elation he'd felt in that moment, knowing that they'd defeated both prosecutors, and he remembered even more keenly the abject despair that had engulfed him when Corbin had shot Owen through the heart in a selfish act of callousness and wanton cowardice. Scraps listened attentively and passed no judgement, even after Finn admitted to bludgeoning Corbin to death with his bare hands. The robot's only concern was for Finn, and his loss.

"And Soren?" Scraps then asked before growling like an angry shih-tzu. "He bad man!"

"Soren got out," Finn said. He didn't thank the robot for reminding him about that. "Cora did too, so that's something, at least."

Scraps nodded his agreement at this then scratched his head. It was an amusingly human gesture for an oil-can-shaped robot to perform, but it oddly suited him.

"And lady-bad-man?" Scraps asked. "She also dead-dead?"

Finn blew out a sigh and rocked back in his chair. "Now,

that part is going to take some explaining." Scraps moved the edge of the desk and sat with his little legs dangling over the side, as if waiting for Finn to tell him a bedtime story. Finn was about to begin when he had a thought. "Are your security protocols active, pal? Whatever we say to each other has to be encoded."

Scraps nodded. "Data safe-safe."

Finn pointed around the room to the various locations where he recalled Elara installing bug-killer devices.

"And can you scan the room?" Finn added. "There should be devices installed in various locations that intercept any listening devices and modify the signals that are transmitted to the Authority."

"Bug-killers?" Scraps asked, and Finn nodded. A sensor dish sprang from Scraps' back and the robot scanned the room for several seconds, turning its mechanical gaze precisely toward the location of each bug-killer device. "Room safe-safe. We speak. No problem!"

Finn nodded, the blew out another sigh. "Here's the thing, pal. Lady-bad-man, The Shadow, Elara Cage, is actually a Metal."

"No-no!" Scraps said, clasping his little hands to his mouth, as if Finn had just revealed the major plot twist of a murder-mystery novel. "Lady-bad-man is lady-good-man?"

Finn had to think about that for a moment before nodding. "She's still a pain in my ass, but she's one of the good guys, yes." He laughed and shook his head. "I can still barely believe it myself."

Finn went on to detail everything that had happened since he was proclaimed a gold and delivered by skycar to the prosecutor barracks, where his new mentor had been waiting for him. Scraps was blown away by it all and Finn worried that any more revelations might overload the robot's Foreman Logic Processor. The door chime rang before he could say anything more, not that there was much more to say. The truth was, he'd barely spent any time in the Authority sector and it was all still a blur to him.

Bra-sa! ... Bra-sa! ... the door chime sounded, and Finn growled through his teeth.

"I don't suppose you can re-program that damned thing so it just goes 'ding-dong' or any other sound?"

"Yes-yes!" Scraps nodded then zoomed over to the door and interfaced with it. Seconds later the chime sounded again, but the tone was a musical chirrup instead, and Finn felt his blood pressure fall.

"Finn? Are you in there?" The voice from beyond the door was that of his mentor.

"Yes, come in," Finn called out.

The door opened and Elara Cage walked in before she sensed something and her fingers tightened around the handle of her concealed roundel dagger.

"Hi-hi!" Scraps said, waving at her.

"Er, hi..." Elara replied, sliding her hand out from inside her jacket. The two stared at each other for a moment, before she added, "Sorry about the crossbow bolt."

"No bother!" Scraps chirruped, before patting his body. "Scraps all new!"

His mentor smiled and suddenly it was Elara Cage from Metalhaven in the room with them and not The Shadow. "I like the paint job," she said. "The gold is a nice touch."

"We have Mr. Pritchard to thank for that," Finn said, pushing out of his chair and walking over to greet his mentor.

"He's thoughtful and kind, everything I'd thought golds were taught not to be."

"They're not all bad," Elara replied. The fact she'd used 'they' rather than 'we' while in the safe-space of Finn's apartment was telling, he thought. His mentor then shrugged. "Though most of them are."

"Do I have more training?" Finn asked, suddenly wondering why Elara was there. He was still getting used to his training schedule but he felt sure there was nothing planned until early the next morning.

"No, I just wanted to let you know the results of your evaluation," Elara said. She moved to the dining table and sat down, and Finn joined her. Scraps then buzzed over their heads and flew into the kitchen.

"Scraps make coffee!" the robot said, happy for something to do. "Or tea-tea?"

"Tea is good, thanks," Elara said, again smiling at the robot. She'd smiled at Scraps more in last couple of minutes than he'd ever seen the woman smile in the whole time he'd known her. "There's always a selection of herbal teas in the cupboard above the water faucet. There's a lavender blend, including rose petal, vanilla and saffron that I quite like."

Finn raised an eyebrow at his mentor's choice. He thought he'd been subtle about it, but of course nothing escaped her attention.

"Don't look so surprised," Elara said. "The Shadow might turn up her nose at anything so extravagant, but Elara Cage isn't immune to the finer things that being a gold can offer."

"I didn't say anything," Finn replied, holding up his hands.

His mentor continued to scowl at him. "You didn't have to."

There were an awkward few moments while Scraps prepared the tea then Finn remembered why Elara had visited in the first place.

"You said you had news about my loyalty evaluation?" Finn asked, suddenly nervous.

"Yes, they rated you an eighteen," Elara said, again smiling at Scraps as the robot deftly lowered a tea tray on the table. Finn had no idea the machine even knew how to make tea. "The ratings are based on the old system of caratage, which is how people measured the purity of gold before the war."

"Is eighteen good then?" Finn asked. The scent of the tea was distractingly intoxicating.

"It's borderline," his mentor replied, frankly. "Twenty-four is pure, though for nonsense political reasons, only the Zavetgrad aristocracy are given that rating." She sipped her tea and Finn could see the muscles in her shoulders relax. "Twenty-two is the rating expected for all natural-born golds. This equates to a loyalty evaluation score of ninety-two percent or higher."

Finn nodded. While the system was quaint in the way it gelled with the Authority's notion of purity, it at least made sense.

"I guess eighteen isn't so bad then, considering I'm not a natural born gold?" he asked, hopefully.

"It's the minimum threshold for a gold," Elara replied. "It means that you are under suspicion and at a higher risk of sedition. Below that is fourteen, the typical threshold for workers, then 'P' or pyrite, which is fool's gold. That's reserved for traitors."

Finn laughed, which his mentor didn't seem to appreciate, but he couldn't help himself.

"How the hell did I manage to rank eighteen?" Finn asked. "Surely, I'd rank the lowest of the low?"

"Thank the device you swallowed, because without that you'd already be dead," Elara explained. "But this doesn't mean you can relax. You must have lied well in order to score eighteen, but you need to lie better. If we can increase your score to twenty-two then, whether Voss or the other prosecutors and apprentices like it or not, you're as loyal as they are. It will take the pressure off and make what comes next easier."

"And what comes next?" Finn asked, trying his luck. He didn't like that Elara was being so secretive, but he could at least appreciate why.

"All in good time," Elara said, and in hindsight, Finn realized he should have expected this exact response.

Finn nodded then tried the tea, which he actually enjoyed. This must have been self-evident from the look on his face because Elara was smiling again.

"Not bad, right?" she said.

"I hate to admit it, but yes," he replied. "Though do you know what I really fancy right now?"

Elara raised an eyebrow, and Finn realized that his question could have been misconstrued, so he quickly explained himself.

"I really fancy a pint," he said, and Elara laughed, shocking him with how 'normal' she could appear. "I never had much of a taste for the stuff, but whether it's the drugs they put in it, or just the ice-cold alcoholic kick, I could sink a pint in one and still hanker for another."

"I'd like to say the urge goes away, but I'd be lying," Elara replied.

"Really?" Finn asked. He wondered how many more times his mentor could shock him in the space of a few minutes. "I never had you down as a beer drinker."

"Once a chrome, always a chrome," Elara said, saluting him with her tea.

Finn returned the salute then drank, but as soon as the cup touched his lips the door chime sounded. He looked at Elara but she seemed as surprised as he was, which meant the guest was not expected.

"Come in," Finn said, a little hesitantly.

The door opened and behind it was a young woman in a close-fitting white satin suit edged in lustrous gold, like the color of her hair. She stepped forward and Finn sprang to his feet, though he wasn't sure why. The woman was striking and had an aura that seemed to penetrate every inch of his room, as if royalty had just walked in.

"Hello, Finn," the woman said, smiling and pressing her hands together in front of her stomach. "My name is Juniper Jones. I'm your paramour."

8

FIRST DATES

Juniper Jones took another carefully-measured step inside the room but not far enough for the door to close behind her. She smiled at Finn then at Elara before spotting the two half-drunk teacups on the table and adopting a more apologetic expression.

"I'm sorry, I'm interrupting," Juniper said, a slight flush of rouge tinting her cheeks. "I can come back later."

She turned to leave but Finn called out for her to stop. It was absurd, but he felt guilty for having been caught entertaining another woman, even though he and Juniper were complete strangers and he'd had no foreknowledge of her arrival.

"It's okay, you weren't interrupting," Finn said, smiling at the woman as she paused in the threshold and half-turned back.

"Actually, you did interrupt us," Elara said, rising from her seat. Finn didn't detect any irritation in her voice, but since he was never entirely certain about his mentor's current mood, he had a feeling she was annoyed. "But it's not a problem," Elara added. "I was just leaving."

Finn frowned at Elara and the white lie she had just told. He couldn't figure out if she was simply trying to spare Juniper's blushes or whether the awkwardness of the situation had compelled her to make a speedy exit.

"You don't have to leave," Finn said. He realized then that he didn't want her to go. "You haven't finished your tea."

"I have some of it at home," Elara replied. She smiled but it was forced and Finn realized that his mentor had become suddenly self-conscious. "I'll catch up with you later, Apprentice Brasa, so we can discuss tomorrow's training schedule."

"Sure, but..." Finn replied, still frowning at her, though Elara was already headed toward the door at speed. *Apprentice Brasa? Why the hell did she just call me that?* he thought, baffled by her sudden formality.

Juniper stepped aside to allow Elara to leave, bowing her head slightly as the prosecutor slipped past without giving either him or his new paramour a second glance. The door then thudded shut with its usual precision and suddenly they were alone. If his apartment had a window, Finn would have thrown himself through it on order to avoid the situation that was now forced upon him, but there was no escape.

"I'm sorry, I wasn't expecting you," Finn said. He could feel the skin on his face radiating heat like a sun.

"That's okay, Finn, there's not need to apologize," Juniper replied. She approached him, gliding across the floor like a cloud, and before he knew it, she had taken hold of his wrist. "All of your regular appointments are stored in your personal diary, but perhaps no-one has shown you how to access them?" Juniper tapped the center of his wrist twice and the material morphed into a screen. "You can cycle through your entries like this..."

Juniper stroked her finger across the screen and the display reacted by cycling through his training schedule and personal schedule, which were on different pages. She then drew her finger gently from left to right along his forearm to scroll through the entries, and the thrill of her touch sent a chill rushing through his body. The burning sensation intensified and he felt ashamed.

"Thank you," Finn said, easing his arm free, though Juniper's touch lingered for a heartbeat longer than necessary, prolonging and intensifying the tingling sensation in his body. "You're right that no-one has shown me how to work this, even my valet, Pritchard."

"He probably assumed you already knew how," Juniper replied, still with the same sweet smile, which made Finn feel immediately comfortable in her presence. "I can still come back later if you're busy?"

"No, I'm not busy," Finn said. He then laughed. "To be honest, I'm not used to having free time, so I'm glad of the company."

Juniper nodded then took two paces back, perhaps concerned that her sudden proximity was unnerving him, which was the truth, though likely not for the reasons she had assumed. She was unlike anyone he'd ever seen before and Finn found himself gawking at the woman like a creep. Men and women in Metalhaven all wore the same heavy-duty overalls and no-one had time or inclination to attend to their appearance. The work was dirty and if you weren't covered in grime by the end of the day then you'd certainly be covered in beer.

Juniper Jones, on the other hand, looked like she'd been crafted out of marble by a renaissance master. She was wearing a satin-white pants suit with gold trim and a golden-yellow crop-top that revealed a toned mid-riff. She was probably about the same age as the apprentice prosecutors, Finn guessed, but her clothes and immaculately-styled hair made her look older, and closer to his own age. And because of the three-inch lift in her golden open-toed shoes, she stood an inch taller than him too.

"It is standard practice for paramours to wear a suit on a first meeting, after which we can discuss what you'd like me to wear," Juniper said. Finn just returned a confused frown and the woman elaborated on her statement. "The way you were looking at me, I thought you were displeased with my appearance," she said, looking down at her toes. "I just wanted you to know that I can dress differently and appear…"

"No, that's not what I was thinking at all," Finn said, cutting her off. He hated that everything he did seemed to make the woman feel uncomfortable and unwanted. "I've just never seen anyone like you, that's all."

Juniper blushed and looked away and Finn cursed his clumsiness. He didn't know why he was acting like a teenager but if his face got any hotter, he was afraid it would melt right off his skull.

"Then you like how I look?" Juniper asked. Her head was still tilted slightly down, but she was looking into his eyes, desperate for his approval, and he was powerless not to give it.

"You look… beautiful," Finn said, cringing as he spoke the word, which was perhaps the first time in his life he'd ever uttered it. "And for the record, you can wear whatever the hell you like. I don't see why I should choose."

"Because that is your right," Juniper replied, a little surprised by his answer. "I am your paramour, Finn. I am yours to do with as you please."

Finn felt a spark of anger ignite a familiar flame inside him. Everything about this encounter was foreign to him, from the quality of the apartment they were in, to the exquisite clothes and splendor of the woman in front of him, but Juniper's answer bore the hallmarks of the Authority, and this was something he knew well.

"I don't care what the Authority told you, but no-one owns you, and you're certainly not mine to do with as I please," Finn said, with feeling.

Juniper tilted her head slightly to one side. "They warned me that you might be resistant to the idea of a paramour."

Finn laughed and the woman again looked at her feet, clearly worried that she'd offended him. He drew in a long breath and tried to keep in mind that he had to act like a gold, even if doing so went against his every instinct.

"I'm not laughing at you," Finn said, moving nearer and taking Juniper's hand in an effort to comfort her. She looked up slightly but now seemed afraid to meet his eyes. "It's just that I'm not used to all this gold stuff yet, and I still have some hang-ups from before."

Juniper squeezed his hand gently then lifted her chin and finally met his eyes. Another thrill tingled through his body but he didn't pull his hand away, conscious of not humiliating her any more than he already had done.

"You were from Metalhaven, right?" Juniper asked.

"Yes," Finn said. He wanted to let go of her hand but it was like they were magnetically drawn to one another.

"They gave me a dossier about you, which said that you refused to use the wellness centers in the sector, so I can understand how this is difficult for you." Juniper added.

Finn doubted that she understood but he didn't want to say so and ruin the progress they'd made. Instead, he finally managed to pull his hand free from hers, then use it to gesture to the dining table.

"Would you like to sit down?" Finn said. "Or we could sit on the couch, whichever you prefer."

Juniper returned her hands to the front of her stomach, one held gently inside the other.

"Where would you like us to sit?" she asked. "It is your choice, not mine."

Finn felt his hatred of the Authority stirring inside him again but he kept a lid on his emotions and shook his head gently. "Look, Juniper, if we're going to spend time together, it will be as equals," he said. "I can't have it any other way."

Juniper nodded. "Well, since I have to do as you say, I accept your terms."

Finn had to think about that sentence for a moment, but while it still amounted to the woman obeying his command, he consoled himself with the knowledge that his order had reset the balance between them. Or, at least he hoped it had.

"And the table is fine," Juniper said, sliding over to the chair that Elara had vacated earlier and gently lowering herself into it.

"I guess we'll need some more tea," Finn said, testing the pot with the back of his hand and finding that it was no better than lukewarm.

"Scraps make!"

The robot suddenly darted out from the kitchen area and moved into a hover in front of the table. Finn recoiled in shock but to his added surprise, Juniper wasn't alarmed in the slightest.

"Hello, what's your name?" Juniper said, beaming a smile at the robot. He had that effect on people.

"Scraps!" Scraps replied. "Finn built Scraps! Finn clever."

"Yes, he must be to have built such a wonderfully perfect robot!" Juniper said.

Scraps spun around in mid-air like a whirligig, making a sort of "weeeeee!" sound like a child whizzing down a helter-skelter. The machine then stopped and landed beside the teapot.

"Juniper want tea?"

Juniper nodded then she clicked her fingers and leaned in closer to Scraps. Finn felt oddly jealous that the machine had struck up such an easy rapport with the woman, while he'd fumbled and floundered like a stranded fish.

"I do, but how about I show you both this wonderful little tearoom in the cultural quarter of the Authority sector?" Juniper said. "I just know you'll both love it."

"Like a date-date?" Scraps said, before turning to Finn. "Scraps come too?"

Finn shrugged. He'd never been on a date and wasn't even sure what one entailed. Then he realized that having Scraps tag along would make the experience a whole lot easier to stomach. The robot was like an emotional support animal but with the added benefit of also being able to speak and containing an encyclopedic knowledge of everything in the known world.

"I mean, sure?" Finn said, shrugging again. He saw no reason to refuse. "Metalhaven workers don't go on dates, though, so I'll have to follow your lead."

"Then this will be your first date!" Juniper sprang out of the chair and practically danced to his side, before hooking her arm through his. She then glanced back at Scraps and winked. "Are you coming?"

Scraps looked to Finn and he nodded, then the robot burst into flight before dropping onto Finn's shoulder and clamping on tightly with his little metal feet. Juniper steered them both out of the door, and Finn felt exposed again, like he'd done when Elara had taken him to the dining hall. The feeling soon passed, however, because with Juniper Jones as his guide, he felt safe and even as though he belonged. The paramour guided them out of the prosecutor barracks, reassuring Finn when he looked nervous that one or more of the prosecutors might chase after him for deserting his post. Soon they were moving through busy streets, populated by other people in fine clothes, though none of them could hold a candle to Juniper Jones, who stood out like a jewel in the center of a crown. Many of the other golds also had personal robots, and Scraps waved and shouted to them as they passed. Even though most of the machines thumbed their mechanical noses at him, Scraps remained undeterred and unbreakably cheerful.

Before long, they had turned off the main sidewalk that ran alongside the barracks and entered a monorail platform. A train arrived almost immediately and Finn recognized it as similar to the freight trains that ran through Metalhaven, bringing fresh scrap from the salvage teams and taking away the reclaimed metal that he'd spent backbreaking hours producing.

"Where are we going?" Finn asked, as they entered the train car. It still felt like he was on the run, and were it not for Juniper's unconcerned expression and hold on his arm, he might have resisted boarding.

"The Central Authority sector is only a couple of minutes ride away," Juniper explained. "You can think of it as the entertainment district." She flashed her eyes at him and he noticed the subtle sparkle of golden eyeshadow for the first time. "It's the place to see and be seen."

"I don't think anyone wants to see me," Finn said, feeling the eyes of other passengers on him.

"You're with me, so you'll be fine," Juniper said, hugging his arm more tightly.

Finn smiled then looked out of the window. This was the first time he'd seen the wider Authority sector from ground level and what struck him most of all was how clean everything was, as if it had just been built. Snow managed to cling to parts of the buildings but the sidewalks and roads were clear, like they were heated from beneath which, Finn wondered, perhaps they were.

"Fancy-fancy!" said Scraps and Juniper laughed.

"Yes, that's the gold sector all over," she replied. "No expense spared..."

The train slowed and Juniper stood, pulling Finn up with her. Other passengers had begun to gather by the doors and Finn noticed how they made a hole for him as he approached, as if he stank like a vagabond. He wondered whether they could smell the chrome on him, or whether it was the prosecutor training uniform that had intimidated them to stay away. Perhaps both, he wondered.

"Welcome to the cultural quarter," Juniper said, extending her free hand to the buildings surrounding the monorail platform.

Finn recognized some of the architectural styles from studying pre-war history on his old data device, noting Stalinist, Byzantine and other Muscovite-inspired looks, all juxtaposed with Zavetgrad's uniquely ostentatious gilt-edge showiness. Juniper set them on a course directly down the center of what he assumed to be a road until he realized there were no cars. The area was entirely pedestrianized and appeared to be dedicated to showcasing oneself and one's finery.

"I feel underdressed," Finn said, as they slipped by another couple dressed like they were about to attend the opera, which, Finn figured, might have been the case. "I'd suggest I go back and change but I don't have any other clothes."

"I can help you there," Juniper said, nodding and smiling to others as they passed. Each of the other promenaders greeted her in return, though none looked at Finn, which he was glad of, since he was unfamiliar with Authority sector social etiquette. "But not today. Today, we keep it simple and just have tea."

"Fine with me," Finn replied, grateful that Juniper was already leading them off the promenade and toward an English Victorian-era tearoom.

Juniper slid her arm free in order to speak to the hostess of the tearoom, and Finn felt like he'd been cast adrift in the ocean, but it wasn't long before they were being led to a table.

The tearoom was lavishly decorated with tall ceilings, chandeliers and paintings of people that looked older than time itself. Finn was completely lost in the place, as was Scraps, and neither noticed Juniper place an order on their behalf. Soon, a pot of tea had been brought to the table along with two delicate China cups and a serving stand with three tiers, some containing sandwiches with the crusts removed and others dainty cakes and scones.

"Yum-yum!" Scraps said.

The robot jumped down onto the table and began examining the cakes with scholarly curiosity. A number of 'tuts' and disproving stares were directed at their table but Juniper ignored them, focusing her attention entirely on Finn. This impressed him more than anything else she'd said or done, because it meant that Juniper didn't care what others thought of them. It was a kind of free-spirited individualism that he could get behind.

"The tea is Earl Grey, which is sometimes served with milk, but often taken black with a slice of lemon," Juniper said, pouring the steaming liquid into Finn's cup first. "The sandwiches are cucumber and cream cheese, smoked salmon, and chicken and mayonnaise."

Juniper then pointed to the next tier, but Finn started detailing the contents before she could start.

"The baked scones are typically accompanied by clotted cream and strawberry or raspberry preserve, then we have a variety of sweet pastries, cakes and petit fours." Finn pointed to a circular confection that had a delicate pastel pink color. "And that, I believe is a macaron. I've always wanted to try one."

Juniper reeled back and looked at Finn like he'd just torn

off a mask and revealed himself to be none other than the sector's Regent. However, while she was shocked she wasn't annoyed. If anything, Finn thought she looked amused.

"I didn't realize that afternoon tea was a popular pastime in Metalhaven..."

Finn laughed. "It's not, but some years ago I salvaged an old pre-war data device, so I've been studying history for some time." He then worried that he might have spoken out of turn. "You're not compelled to report on me, are you? I wouldn't want to get either of us into trouble."

"No, what happens between us stay between us, and us alone," Juniper said. Her statement was resolute which Finn appreciated. "And no-one cares about what you did as a chrome. All your past transgressions are forgiven."

Finn snorted. "Tell that to my loyalty evaluator," he said, feeling a sudden surge of aggression as he pictured the robotic interrogator's smug mechanical face. He took a deep breath then smiled and pushed the feeling deep down. "But as a pure-born, twenty-four carat gold, that's not something you have to worry about, right?"

"I'm not actually a gold..."

Finn almost spat out his tea, but just managed to swallow the mouthful without choking on it or forcing it to spill out over his chin.

"Well, not yet, anyway," Juniper clarified. "I'm what they call a bronze. I was born twenty-one years ago as a product of the Authority's Nimbus population initiative, using seed from rating-five workers combined with a surrogate mother, but I didn't quite pass 'inspection'."

"What?" Finn blurted, setting down his teacup so hard

that he almost smashed the fine bone-China saucer. "But you're perfect!"

Juniper smiled and blushed and all Finn wanted was for a black hole to open up and swallow him.

"I just meant that you don't look defective," Finn said, and this time Juniper laughed. In trying to dig himself out of the hole, he'd only made things worse. He huffed and shook his head. "Damn, I'm sorry. I really don't have the first clue what I'm doing."

"Don't worry, just give it time," Juniper said, squeezing his arm and pressing some of the tension from it.

"But how are you not a gold?" Finn asked. He wondered if he was prying, but at the same time, Juniper had raised the topic. "You're dressed in gold and you look more like a gold than any gold I've seen."

"A routine examination when I was thirteen detected certain genetic anomalies that were missed when I was being gestated," Juniper explained, serving Finn and herself a selection of delicacies from the tiered plates. "They're minor, but even minor defects disqualify me from entry to Nimbus. I could have accepted twenty-two carat status, but I was born for Nimbus and Nimbus is where I want to be, so I forfeit that grade. Now, if I work for five years as a paramour, I will earn enough credit to have these genetic anomalies corrected. Then, I will be permitted to travel to the citadel."

Finn was trying to take it all in, but of the dozens of questions that were floating around in his mind, one stood out. "So it was your choice to become a paramour?" he asked, and Juniper nodded.

"I could have remained in the Authority sector, working

any number of roles, but I grew up dreaming of Nimbus and my heart is there," Juniper explained.

"How many years do you have left until you can ship out?" Finn asked. He tried the pink macaron and it was heaven.

"You're actually my first assignment," Juniper said. "But I'm hopeful this will work out and we can remain partners for the full five years."

"What happens if it doesn't work out?" Finn asked. Juniper looked down and he felt the need to explain his question. "I'm not saying it won't, I'm just curious, is all. This is all new to me."

"If I fail in my duties, I'll be reassigned," Juniper explained, still looking down.

"Reassigned where?"

"That's not important," the woman replied, forcing herself to smile at him. "I'm sure it won't come to that. Besides, there is a rigorous process that matches paramours to their intended partners, and our match rate was very high. I'm sure you'll like me, if you give me a chance."

Finn was flattered by the suggestion that Juniper apparently liked him enough to want to be shackled to him for five years, but he still had deep issues with the idea of a 'paramour'. Juniper had admitted to knowing about his refusal to use Metalhaven's indentured sex workers, and he'd already explained that she was not 'his' to own. Yet, he liked the woman and if proving that he was gold meant complying with the directive to have a paramour, he couldn't imagine anyone better. Even so, it had to be on his terms.

"You've read my file so you already know everything about me, or at least what the Authority thinks they know,"

Finn said, become more earnest. "And while I struggle with the idea of a paramour, I like you Juniper." She beamed a smile and squeezed his arm tighter. "But..." Finn added, and concern tainted her joy, "... if we're going to do this then it has to be real. I don't want you to do or say anything that's not genuine, or your choice. Does that make sense?"

Juniper thought for a moment then nodded. "Yes, I understand."

"Good, then it's agreed," Finn said. He blew out a sigh of relief then was about to reach for another macaron when he had a thought. "Hey, what's your real name? I'll bet this macaron that it's not Juniper Jones."

Juniper flashed her eyes again. "No, it's not my real name," she admitted, before snatching the macaron out his finger with cat-like reflexes. "But if we're being real then that's a level of connection that we have to earn, right?"

"Right," Finn said.

Juniper took a bite of the macaron, whereas Finn would have eaten the thing whole, then set it down on her plate, before laughing and covering her mouth with her hand.

"What have I done wrong now?" Finn said.

He quickly checked himself to make sure he hadn't spilled tea on his uniform or left his flies undone, but Juniper wasn't looking at him. Instead, she was looking across to a nearby table, where Scraps was sitting beside another personal robot. The two machines were holding hands and looking into each other's eyes, adoringly.

"It looks like someone is a fast mover," Juniper said, breaking off another chunk of macaron.

"You're right," Finn said, feeling suddenly paternal. "Scraps and I need to have words..."

9

CHARMING MAN

THE ALARM on Finn's bedside table sounded a polite alert, like birds chirruping softly outside a window, and Finn reached over to silence it. The clock read 06:00 but he'd been awake for the last hour already and was dressed and waiting for his mentor to arrive.

"Scraps stay here?" his robot asked. The machine was sitting on the bed next to him.

"Yes, pal, you stay here," Finn said, patting Scraps on the head. Then he reconsidered, wondering whether there were technically any restrictions on his personal robot wandering the building alone. "Though I guess you could stretch your legs if you get bored. Don't leave the barracks, though." He wagged a finger at the robot like a schoolteacher telling off a wayward pupil. "I saw you and the other personal robot yesterday..." he added, playfully.

Scraps giggled and smiled. "Nice to have friend."

Owen was suddenly front-and-center in his mind and his gut churned. Scraps seemed to notice this and shuffled closer.

"Sorry-sorry..." the robot said.

"You don't have anything to be sorry about, pal," Finn said, hugging the machine. "It's just that sometimes I forget."

"Finn lucky," Scraps replied, dolefully. "Scraps never forget."

The door chime sounded, and Finn was pleased to discover that the modified ring-tone had persisted. The one that reminded him of Bloodletter's war-cry from when the prosecutor had hunted him in the crucible was long gone, but the nightmares remained. That had been the main reason he was up so early. The comfortable bed didn't spare him from disquieting dreams.

"Come in," Finn said, pushing himself up and walking toward the door, which swished open as he did so.

Elara was standing outside but his mentor didn't enter straight away, instead inching her head across the threshold as if she were concerned someone or something might leap out at her.

"Are you alone?" Elara asked.

"Of course I'm alone, why wouldn't I be?" Finn said, frowning at her. "Well, apart from Scraps, anyway."

Scraps hovered into the middle of the room and landed on the dining table. "Hello, Elara-good!" the robot exclaimed, waving at her.

"I just wanted to be certain, that's all," Elara replied, waving at Scraps then finally stepping inside.

Suddenly it dawned on Finn that his mentor thought Juniper Jones might still be with him. He didn't know whether to be insulted that she believed he'd bedded his paramour on the first night, abandoning a lifetime of abstinence in protest against the Authority's policy of compulsory sex workers, or impressed that she considered him such a stud.

"I told you that I don't agree with having a paramour," Finn replied, allowing his disappointment to color his words. "I went out with her, like you told me I should, and I was the perfect gentleman." He shrugged. "And quite charming too, I think."

Elara snorted a laugh at this, which only soured Finn's mood further, then took another step forward to allow the door to thud shut behind her.

"Like I said, I just wanted to make sure," Elara said. Her arms were folded and she looked annoyed at him, though for what reason Finn had no clue. "It's none of my business what you did or didn't do, anyway."

On the one hand Finn agreed with this, but there was also the inescapable fact that their relationship was more complicated than simple master and apprentice. They were, in essence, co-conspirators and traitors, which meant their bond – or at least their obligations to one another – ran deeper.

"I don't know about that," Finn replied. "It feels like we shouldn't have secrets from one another. Our fates are too intertwined for that."

"Intertwining is what your paramour is for," Elara replied, still inexplicably cross with him.

"You know what I mean," Finn said, unamused.

"Yes, I know what you mean," Elara replied.

Is she annoyed that I went on a date with Juniper or annoyed that I actually got on with her? he wondered, though even if either were true, he didn't know why that would bother his mentor. An awkward silence persisted for several seconds, during which time Elara's expression of annoyance become more one of concern.

"You should still be careful," Elara said. This was now his mentor speaking, he realized, logical and without emotion. "Juniper Jones is trained to make you feel comfortable and safe, even loved, but she's still a part of the system, and she has her own motives. Remember that."

Finn nodded, recalling what Juniper had told him about her goal of reaching Nimbus, though the time he'd spent with her had, admittedly, eased his concerns.

"I will, but she seems harmless enough," Finn replied. "She's not even a full gold, not yet anyway."

"I know that she's a so-called bronze, but she's still more gold than you or I will ever be," Elara said. "And no-one who wears gold is harmless."

Finn frowned. "You've been digging into her background, haven't you?"

"Of course, it's my job," Elara replied, returning his scowl with more vigor.

The tension between them was palpable and Scraps had picked up on it, the same way a dog can sense fear and stress. The little robot was looking from him to Elara and back again, perhaps concerned that they were about to come to blows.

"Elara sleep good?" Scraps said, offering a timely intervention.

Elara smiled at the robot, whose natural charm could win over the devil himself, then nodded. "Yes, thank you, Scraps," she replied. "Did you get a full charge in overnight?"

"Scraps fully charged!" Scraps said, before leaping into the air and doing a rotor-assisted summersault, which made both Elara and Finn laugh.

"What about you?" Elara said, turning her attention back to Finn.

Finn could sense that she'd been hesitant to ask the question. More than anyone alive, Elara Cage understood what it was like to go to bed one night on a rock-hard mattress in a frozen room and wake up the next in gold-infused luxury. And she also knew what Finn had lost. Elara had remained tight-lipped about her own past, but it was safe to say that she'd sacrificed and suffered and could empathize with his situation.

"I slept fine," Finn said, choosing not to tell Elara that he'd been woken early by a nightmare. He didn't see how revealing that would help either of them. "Metalhaven got me used to functioning on four or five hours a night, so I don't need much sleep."

Elara's emerald eyes probed Finn for a second or two. He could sense that she doubted him but was relieved when his mentor didn't question his answer.

"Then let's get to breakfast," Elara said, stepping back and hitting the panel to open the door. "Perhaps today, we can make a better impression on your fellow apprentices, and on Chief Prosecutor Voss."

Finn was surprised to discover that the disappointment implied in his mentor's reply actually smarted and made him want to perform better. Spurned on, he smiled at Scraps who waved goodbye then followed Elara as they made the short walk along the corridor to the dining hall. He could hear the chink of cutlery against crockery that suggested the other apprentices were already inside, as eager to please as he was.

Reaching the entrance archway, Finn strode into the hall with his head held high. The other trainees and their mentors didn't give him a second look at first, until they realized that the false-gold had arrived with his Metalhaven mentor in tow, and the chatter of discontent began in earnest. Some were subtle about it, while others, mainly Ivan Volkov and Walter Foster, were vocal in their condemnation. Finn suddenly noticed that the hall had been laid out differently to the day before and that the apprentices were all now gathered together on a large circular table. Their mentors, on the other hand, were sat on a long table at the head of the room, watching over their trainees with a ready eye.

"Shit, I don't have to sit with them, do I?" Finn asked, as Elara set to work loading her breakfast tray.

"Yes, from now until the end of your training, apprentices sit and eat together," Elara confirmed. "The idea is that you build a rapport, so try to rein in your natural tendency to be an asshole and fit in."

Finn froze, croissant in mid-flight toward his plate. "Hey, that hurts..."

"I'm serious, Finn," Elara said, unmoved by his fake display of outrage. "It does you no favors to make enemies of these people. You need to be one of them, or at least seen to be one of them."

"It's okay, I get it," Finn said, depositing the croissant onto his plate along with some bacon. "I can be quite charming when I want to be."

"I'm sure Juniper will be thrilled to hear it," Elara said. It was a needlessly catty comment but Finn let it slide, not wanting to cause a scene in front of the others. His mentor then turned to face him, tray in hand. "I'll be watching from the mentor's table. Let's see you put this supposed charm to good use."

With that said, Elara turned and walked away. Finn scowled at the back of her head then noticed that the other apprentices were watching him, perhaps trying to figure out if he was planning to join their soiree. He picked up a glass of the juice drink that Elara said was good for him then set off in the direction of the circular table. The elaborate eye rolls and heavy sighs suggested that some of his co-apprentices were hoping he would sit alone. Then, to his surprise, Sabrina Brook smiled and pulled out the chair next to her.

"Hey, chromeboy, sit here," Sabrina said, patting the seat.

Ivan and Walter scowled at her but Finn had parked himself on the chair before any of them had chance to object.

"Thanks Sabrina," Finn said, tucking in the chair. He offered her and the group a smile but only Sabrina smiled back.

"No problem, chromeboy," Sabrina said. "You don't mind me calling you chromeboy, do you?"

Finn shrugged. "Would it make any difference if I said yes?"

Sabrina's smile became wicked. "No, but I thought I'd ask." Then she snapped her fingers. "Oh, but if you manage to beat me in a sparring session, I promise to stop."

"Sure, though that means I'll have to stop going easy on you," he said, returning the wicked smile. "In other words, no more mister nice chromeboy..."

Sabrina laughed and slapped him on the back hard enough to make his chest cavity resonate like a drum.

"I like you chromeboy," Sabrina laughed. She then pulled her hands back and looked shocked, as if she'd just broken a priceless vase. "Sorry, was that too rough? I know your arm must still be sore."

"No, it's fine," Finn said. He raised his arm, waggled it, then gave Sabrina the middle finger. "See, it works just fine."

Sabrina laughed again then Zach joined in and even Tonya Duke cracked a smile, though she wiped it off her face as soon as she saw Ivan Volkov's thunderous expression.

"This sort of food must be unusual for you," Ivan said. It was not a polite inquiry but a reminder of Finn's lowly origins. "And it must be nice to sleep in a room that isn't infested with rats and freezing cold."

Finn knew his mission was to charm his fellow apprentices but he also knew that Ivan Volkov, as the son of Zavetgrad's most prestigious Regent, was predisposed to hate him. He couldn't imagine any circumstance where he might win him over, but he was still willing to try.

"Things are certainly different here," Finn said, choosing a diplomatic answer. He picked up a croissant and took a bite. "But I intend to make the most of it," he added, mumbling though a mouthful of food.

Sabrina laughed again as did Zack and Tonya, and it seemed that the novelty of having a worker-class apprentice at their table was amusement enough to overcome their earlier prejudices. Ivan remained staunchly disapproving, however, and Walter sat by his side like a bodyguard, ready to leap into action should Finn challenge the prominent aristocrat in any way.

"You weren't at training yesterday afternoon," Ivan said.

The man was speaking to him in the same accusatory and condescending manner that Metalhaven prefects and foremen used to do, and Finn's gut reaction was to tell Ivan to fuck off and mind his own business. He despised the golds and their privilege, Ivan most of all, because of his hereditary title. Then he caught sight of Elara in his peripheral vision. She was watching him with the keenness of a vulture waiting for a deer to expire from exhaustion, and he repeated her instructions in his head.

I need to be charming... Finn said, using his inner monologue to drum home what he needed to do. *I need to make them like me or at the very least tolerate me...*

"As you know, I was made a gold after winning my trial in the Spacehaven crucible," Finn said, hiding the shame and guilt he felt over his victory and what it had cost. "So as a former worker, the Authority pulled me out of training to run a loyalty evaluation, which is why I wasn't there."

"Well, it looks like you passed," Sabrina said, chomping on a piece of sausage. "Otherwise, you'd already be swinging from the rafters in the training hall."

The others smiled and laughed politely at the joke, despite its darkly truthful undertones. All except Ivan.

"There's still time," the Regent Successor said. "The stench of Metalhaven doesn't wash off in one day. You still have a lot to prove."

Finn scowled then sniffed his armpit. "Do I smell?" he asked, playing up to his audience. "I did shower this morning."

He got the laugh he was hoping for though this only seemed to further irritate Ivan, whose plan had clearly been to poison the others against him.

"Come on, Ivan, lighten up a little," Sabrina said, throwing a piece of fried mushroom at him. It missed, though Ivan didn't even flinch. "He might have come from the gutter but he's one of us now. If he fails in training then fine but let's at least give chromeboy a chance."

Finn felt that the weight of opinion around the table was with him so he decided to seize on the opportunity. He took a sip of his juice drink to wet his lips and sweeten the taste of the sour and deceitful words that were about to come out of his mouth.

"Look, I know I'm an outsider here, but I want you to know that I appreciate the chance I've been given," Finn said. "The Authority has given me the opportunity of a new life, and I don't intend to screw it up. I know I wasn't born gold like all of you, but maybe one day I'll earn your acceptance."

"Bravo!" Sabrina put down her fork and began to clap, though as with everything the honor graduate did, it was extravagant and showy and more than a little cringeworthy. This meant that no-one joined in with the applause, but no-one voiced their dissent either, even Ivan. That was a start, Finn thought.

"I heard you had a friend that got killed in your trial," Walter said. The man's voice was rich and powerful and commanded the attention of everyone at the table.

"Yes, his name was Owen," Finn replied. In his thoughts he added, *thanks for reminding me, asshole...* "He was killed by another offender."

"As a gold, you must be glad that justice was served?" Walter added. "If he died then he was guilty as charged."

Finn smiled. It was a test, one of many that he expected his fellow apprentices to hurl in his direction, to check if he really was gold.

"Do you have any friends, Walter?" Finn asked.

"Of course I do," Walter replied, the muscles in his

enormous neck tensing up. "What does that have to do with my question?"

"If you have friends then think how you'd feel if one of them was killed," Finn answered. He had to tread carefully.

"So you don't think he deserved to die?" It was Ivan again.

Finn felt like he was back in room 616 being interrogated all over again.

"He was killed during the trial so the law says he's guilty, and I accept that," Finn replied. *Truth mixed with a lie...* "But that doesn't mean I can't feel sad that he's dead, just as you would mourn the loss of your friends."

"You broke the law too," Ivan added, bitterly. "You struck a head prefect. If anyone should have died in that crucible it was you."

"But I didn't die," Finn said, quick to counter. "Like it or not, I'm here."

His response was sharp and the mood around the table shifted like quicksand. Now, everyone was watching Ivan for his next move. He glanced at Elara and it was clear she'd been listening in. Her eyes were full of fear. *Careful, Finn...* he urged himself. *Tread carefully...*

"You're right though," Finn added, before Ivan responded, and this admission was enough to give him a stay of execution. "It was my fault that Owen, Soren and Corbin were sent to trial. I was jealous of the golds and wanted what they had, so I lashed out." He looked directly into Ivan's eyes and the man didn't even blink. "The truth is it was me who deserved death, but that's not how it went down, and now that I am here, I intend to make the most of it. The Finn Brasa from Metalhaven is dead. Good riddance. I am

Prosecutor Apprentice Brasa, and when I complete this training, and I *will* complete this training, I'll be worthy of the gold in my uniform."

The trainees all listened attentively, each of them focused on Ivan, waiting with bated breath for the aristocrat's reaction. And it wasn't just the apprentices. The table of prosecutors, and even the robotic serving staff, were frozen in place for fear of interrupting the contest of wills.

"Nice speech," Ivan said. He still hadn't blinked. "But you'll need more than words to impress me."

Sabrina slammed her hands onto the table, causing the crockery and every human being and robot in the dining hall to jump an inch off the ground.

"Ignore Ivan, he's just jealous that you're already more famous than any of us will likely ever be. The Hero of Metalhaven, that's what they call you, right?"

Finn raised an eyebrow at the woman. "Who are 'they'?"

"You really haven't heard?" Sabrina said. "It's all over the newswire. Yours was the most-watched trial in Zavetgrad's history, across all sectors, including this one. You're famous, chromeboy."

"Sure, but let's see how those chrome bastards react when you kill one of your own in the crucible," Walter said, and Ivan and Tonya laughed. "You won't be so popular then."

"You're wrong about that," Finn said. "I know the worker class, and if there's one thing they love most of all, it's a good trial. They'll love me not because I'm the Hero of Metalhaven, whatever that means, but because I'll be the best prosecutor this city has ever seen."

Walter snorted and hurled his napkin on the table while Ivan and Tonya muttered together about how impossible his boast was, but Finn had changed the narrative. Now, the conflict between them wasn't about who was gold and who was chrome, but about who was the best.

"Fuck you, chromeboy, I'm going to be top dog around here!", Sabrina said, lobbing a piece of scrambled egg onto his shoulder. He flicked it off and it smacked into her cheek, causing her to laugh hysterically.

"Bullshit, I'm better than all of you," Tonya chimed in. "Just wait and see. That Honor Graduate position is mine."

"You're already looking at an Honor Graduate, red hair," Sabrina cut in, playfully. "You guys don't stand a chance."

"You Prefect types aren't even worthy enough to shine my boots," Walter said. "I was born for this."

"Keep dreaming, muscles for brains!" Tonya said, jostling Walter with her shoulder, though she barely moved him. "I already beat your time on the assault course."

"I let you win," Walter said, jostling her back and knocking her off her chair. "I don't want to show you everything I can do in week one."

Finn allowed himself to take a breath and a quick glance in Elara's direction suggested he'd pulled off the impossible, which was to make at least some of the other apprentices accept him, and even like him. Ivan and Walter were exceptions, but despite the unlikely odds of winning them over, he would keep trying. Then he looked at Zach, who had barely said a word all breakfast.

"What about you, Zach?" Finn asked, and the others stopped laughing and joking to pay attention. "Do you think you have what it takes to be honor graduate?"

Zach thought for a moment then shrugged. "I'm just here because I like killing people."

An eerie silence descended over the table and the other apprentices exchanged awkward glances. Then Sabrina whacked the table again and burst out laughing.

"Fucking hell, Zach, that was dark!" Sabrina roared. "But I guess if killing is your bag then you're in the right occupation."

An alarm sounded to signify the end of breakfast, and Finn realized he'd barely touched his bacon and croissants. He shoved the food into his mouth and chewed quickly, then Chief Prosecutor Voss rose to address them.

Everyone stood up and the chant of "Apex!" rang out. Finn remembered to join in but spat out a piece of croissant in the process. It landed on the shoulder of a robot waiter and Sabrina stifled a laugh, while Elara rolled her eyes and shook her head.

"Training begins in ten minutes," Voss announced. "But before you leave, I have some exciting news. At the end of your training, should you reach the end, you will receive your prosecutor identities then immediately be examined in a live trial with real offenders."

Finn suddenly regretted wolfing down his food, because his stomach turned over and over like a washing machine. He looked at Elara but her green eyes were focused somewhere into the near distance and she had not reacted to the news.

"The trial will not be broadcast, but in all other regards, it is the same," Voss continued. "You will dispense justice by killing the offenders. Then, and only then, will you be a fully-fledged Prosecutor of the Authority."

The others began chattering amongst themselves, excited by the news, while Finn was frozen in place, staring at Elara, who continued to remain aloof, as if she wasn't even in the room.

"Dismissed!" Voss barked, and everyone quickly dispersed.

Finn headed out with his co-apprentices, conscious of not wanting to look out of place, but Elara was quickly by his side. Her pace was slower than usual and Finn matched it, so that before long a gap had opened up between them and the others.

"You said I wouldn't have to kill anyone..." Finn said, hissing the words under his breath.

"I know what I said," Elara answered, coolly. "I also told you to trust me." The group turned the corner and they were suddenly alone. Elara grabbed Finn's arm and pulled him aside. "*Do* you trust me?" she asked, so close he could smell the fruit scent on her breath.

"Yes, I trust you," Finn said. He didn't have to think about it. It was her life on the line as much as his.

"The test trial is how you get out," Elara said, whispering the words so quietly that Finn had to strain to hear. "Come with me after training, and I'll show you how."

10

METHODS AND TACTICS

Finn raced past the marker post and a buzzer sounded to signal that he was on the last stretch of the assault course. Ahead of him were Ivan and Walter, but it was the Regent's son that was firmly in his sights. Leaping over a stack of logs, he landed smoothly and put on a burst of speed, drawing level with Ivan and causing the aristocrat to grit his teeth and dig in harder, but Finn was faster and his competitor knew it.

Finn had never considered himself much of a runner. If you were caught running through the streets of Metalhaven, a prefect would likely assume you'd committed a crime and shoot first before asking questions. Even so, a decade's worth of arduous manual work had benefited him with a surprising level of stamina and strength, aided, he imagined, by his rare genetics. This had combined to make him an effective athlete and no-one appeared more surprised by this than Ivan Volkov, whom Finn was leaving in his dust.

"Stop!" Ivan yelled, his technique faltering as exhaustion kicked in. "Wait!"

Finn had no intention of stopping and he wasn't going to

wait for anyone, Regent's son or not. Walter may have been content to let Ivan beat him, and maybe Elara was right that he'd been smart to do so, but if Finn was to earn the respect of his fellow apprentices, then they'd have to earn his too. He smiled at Ivan and increased his lead, forcing the man to overextend in an effort to catch up. Ivan tripped and tumbled off the track like a loose wheel flying off a ground car and bouncing down the road.

Walter was next and Finn could see the man at the final obstacle, a fifty-meter vertical wall with only a rope to help the trainees climb it. Walter was already ten meters up by the time Finn reached the bottom, heart fit to burst, but he grabbed the coarse fibers and drew himself up, hand-over-hand. The climb was grueling but he fought through the pain, as he'd been required to do so many times in the reclamation yards of Metalhaven in order to hit a quota. Walter glanced down and saw that he was gaining, and Finn took a moment to revel in the look of disbelief in the man's eyes. Walter was stronger than him by far, but the extra muscle mass also needed more oxygen to fuel it than Finn's wirier physique did. Thirty meters up and Finn had drawn level, and now he saw the same panic in the man's eyes that he'd seen in Ivan's. It was the panic and dread fear that a lowly worker like him might actually beat the golds.

"Push, push, harder!" yelled André "Frost" Regan, Walter's mentor.

The Prosecutor was slapping the side of the wooden wall in an effort to gee-up his apprentice, but the harder Walter worked, the harder Finn worked to keep pace. Elara Cage was also on the sidelines, but like her prosecutor alias, she moved silently across the ground like a shadow. He didn't chance a look at her face, but while she may not have been yelling and pumping her fists like Frost was, Finn knew that her pulse would be racing, willing him to succeed.

Suddenly, Walter swung across then lashed out with his foot in an effort to kick him off the rope. Finn cursed and dodged the first attempt before Walter's size-eleven sneaker thudded into his ribs and his grip faltered.

"You fucking bastard!" Finn spat as Walter powered ahead, focused on the summit.

The rope to his other side then shook and Finn saw that Ivan had recovered and was already climbing. Running may not have been the man's forte, but climbing certainly was, and he was drawing himself up at twice the speed that Finn could manage. Biting down against the pain in his side, Finn resumed his climb and reached the summit a few seconds after Walter, but Ivan was already almost with him.

The final stage of the assault course was a straight sprint and Finn took off, knowing that he had the legs to outpace the less agile frontrunner. Wind streamed past his face and he could see the finish line, staffed by two modified foreman-class robots, one of which was acting as timekeeper and the other as a camera in case there was need of a photo finish. Soon, Finn was alongside Walter again, while Ivan was only a few seconds behind. With the finish line almost within reach, Walter flung out his massive arm and bashed Finn across the chest. He stumbled and went down, barreling across the rough track and coming to rest mere meters from the line. Walter had already crossed, the victor, then Ivan soared past, literally jumping over him to add insult to injury.

More shouts erupted from behind him and Finn spat blood onto the track then glanced back. Sabrina, Tonya and

Zack were also on the home stretch, but while he might have been cheated out of his victory, he wasn't about to come last. Hauling his aching body up, he dragged himself forward, ignoring the fact that his right foot was clearly broken. The timekeeper robot recorded his third place then seconds later Sabrina came in fourth, followed by Tonya and Zack almost neck-and-neck. Tonya went to congratulate Ivan, who was standing with Walter, both grinning at him like a pair of playground bullies, and before he knew what he was doing, Finn was up in Walter's face.

"You're a cheating fuck!" Finn growled, pushing the man hard in the chest and driving him against the wall of the finish-line shelter. "I had you beaten, and you knew it!"

Walter came at him and threw a punch but even with a broken foot, Finn was quick enough to evade it. His own hand closed into a fist and he was about to pop Walter on the nose when Frost dove between them and pulled them apart.

"That's enough!" the prosecutor bellowed, holding Finn by the collar of his training uniform. "We're all on the same team here!"

"Tell your cheating fuck of an apprentice that!" Finn yelled, pointing a finger at Walter like it was a gun.

Walter slipped loose from Frost's grip and was about to launch into another attack when Elara stepped up and the glint from her black roundel dagger was reflected in the man's eyes.

"Step back..." Elara snarled. She hadn't fully drawn the dagger, but the threat was real. "Right now..."

Walter considered testing Elara's resolve but in the end he backed down, snorting like a bull and spitting onto the ground close to his mentor's feet.

"This isn't over, Finn," Walter said, wiping his nose on his sleeve. "We'll settle this in combat training tomorrow."

Frost spoke into Walter's ear and the man finally stepped away, then the prosecutor squared up to Elara. He glanced at the still partly-unsheathed dagger and shook his head.

"I had this handled, Shadow," Frost grunted, as Elara concealed her weapon. "Next time, control your apprentice."

"Control me? ..." Finn blurted.

He was about to say more but the thunderous look on Elara's face convinced him to stay any further protests. Then Chief Prosecutor Voss appeared from inside the finish line shelter, and Finn understood the need to bite his tongue.

"That was an enjoyable contest," Voss said, addressing the apprentices like a proud father. "Spirited competition is healthy, and I saw no issue with the methods and tactics employed during this race." The man turned to Finn directly. "Wouldn't you agree, Apprentice Prosecutor Brasa?"

A week ago, Finn would have given Voss the middle finger and told him to shove his methods and tactics up his ass. Instead, he swallowed his bitterness and nodded.

"Yes, Apex," Finn replied, giving the answer expected of him. "I agree completely."

"Good, then gather your things and return to the barracks," Voss said, returning to addressing the group as a whole. "You have two hours until your next session."

There was a chant of "Apex!" and Finn dutifully joined in, though with less gusto than his compatriots. Walter and Ivan continued to grin and gloat for a few moments, before the group dispersed to collect their rucksacks and revive themselves with specially-formulated isotonic drinks. Finn hobbled to his pack and dropped heavily onto his backside, hissing with pain from his broken foot.

"You could have handled that better," Elara said. She was standing behind him and, as usual, he hadn't noticed her sneak up.

"I didn't tell Voss to eat shit and I didn't break my knuckles on Walter's face, so all things considered, I think I handled it fairly well." Elara raised an eyebrow and Finn sighed. "Okay, I could have maybe handled it a *little* better."

Elara waved one of the robots over and the machine duly obliged, carrying a crate of medical supplies along with it.

"Your foot is broken," Elara noted, and for once Finn knew something before she did. "Let the robot deal with it here. It'll heal quicker."

Finn nodded then stretched out his legs in front of him and allowed the machine to cut away his sneaker with a laser scalpel. His foot was swollen but there was surprisingly little pain and it didn't look like a bad break. Nevertheless, in Metalhaven, an injury like that could cost a man his life. This was not because the wound itself was fatal, but because it would make working impossible, and an incapacitated worker was a liability the golds would not tolerate.

In contrast, the task of fixing a broken foot in the Authority sector was no more troublesome than tending to a headache. Within the space of a few minutes, his bones had been set, fused and pinned, and healing accelerants were injected directly into the bone to speed recovery. A special therapeutic shoe was then slotted over his foot, which used advanced ultrasound technology and electrical stimulation amongst other remedies to induce rapid healing.

"Please do not remove this for at least eighteen hours," the robot medic said, while packing away his equipment.

"Then what?" Finn asked, but the robot was confused by his question. "I mean, after I remove it, then what do I do? Will you visit my apartment to finish the treatment?"

"In eighteen hours, your treatment will be finished and your injury will be healed," the robot replied. "Have a nice day."

Finn looked to Elara for confirmation but she didn't appear concerned by the machine's optimistic estimate of his recovery time.

"Don't worry, by the time you wake up tomorrow, you'll never know you broke it at all," his mentor said. She offered Finn her hand then helped him to stand. The shoe felt like he had a brick strapped to the bottom of his foot. "Now, come with me. I said I had something to show you, remember?"

"Now?" Finn asked.

Elara narrowed her eyes at him. "Yes, now." She pressed her hands to her hips. "Unless you have a hot date with Jupiter Jones," she added, getting his paramour's name wrong on purpose.

"It's Juniper, and you know that I don't," Finn said, narrowing his eyes right back.

"Good, then follow me." Elara turned on her heels and set off toward a waiting skycar.

"Can't I even shower first?" he called after her.

"No..."

Finn huffed and tutted then limped after his mentor. He heard laughter and he glanced back to see Ivan, Walter and Tonya huddled together, making fun of his invalided condition.

"Looking good, chromeboy!" Sabrina called out, causing another ripple of laughter. She was mimicking his hobble but overplaying it like a pantomime actor.

"I still beat you didn't I?" Finn called back, giving as good as he got, and Sabrina gave him the middle finger.

He didn't mind this, and even expected it from Sabrina, because jokey banter was a part of who she was. Walter and Ivan, on the other hand, were not playing games, and the muscular man's statement that they would settle their score in combat training was no idle threat.

"Can you hurry it up a little?"

Elara was already waiting by the skycar, looking bored, and Finn didn't know who was more cruel and heartless – Ivan Volkov and his cronies, or his own damned mentor.

"I'm literally going as fast as I can," Finn said, through in truth he had been dawdling.

Finally, he reached the skycar and pulled himself onto the front seat, passenger side, before slamming the door shut. The rotors spun up a moment later, drowning the cabin in white noise.

"Where are we going, anyway?" Finn shouted.

Elara didn't answer. She just checked her instruments then flipped a cascade of switches to disable internal and external comms, before turning to face him.

"I'm going to show you the location of the test trial at the end of your training," his mentor said. "I'm going to show you how you're getting out of Zavetgrad."

11

THE TEST CRUCIBLE

Elara piloted the skycar toward the edge of the Authority sector, in a direction that Finn had never been before, and soon the towering fence that encircled Zavetgrad was looming large in front of them. The difference between what was inside and outside the boundary was stark, as if the fence demarcated the point at which life began and ended. Yet Finn knew this was not true. Somewhere across the Davis Strait was another pocket of human existence and civilization, and he realized that the fence was not designed to protect those in Zavetgrad from the radiation-hardened creatures that lurked beyond it, but to keep the population contained. Zavetgrad was nothing more than a giant prison and the golds of the Authority sector were its jailers.

"Can't you just fly this thing over the top of the fence and make a run for Haven now?" Finn asked his mentor, suddenly curious as to why no-one had done that before.

"That's how the founders of Haven got out but ever since that failed revolution, all skycars are limited to a maximum altitude of one hundred and ninety meters," Elara explained.

"That barrier is two-hundred meters tall and electrified with enough power to vaporize the liquid in your body and turn you into a human torch."

"I guess that means trying to scale the fence is also out of the question?" Finn said, deciding that sarcasm was the only response to his mentor's gruesome explanation.

"People have tried, foolishly believing that insulated gloves and clothing would offer them protection," Elara said, surprising Finn again. "But anyone who has ever touched that fence has burned."

"Then how do the Metals get in and out?" Finn asked. "Surely, it can't only be done during a trial?"

"There are ways," Elara replied, mysteriously. She nodded toward a structure that was now coming into view out of his side window. "And I'm going to show you one of them."

Finn looked at the building, which resembled an ancient Roman coliseum but many times larger in terms of its internal volume. It was broken up into multiple sectors, like Zavetgrad itself, and Finn even noticed a rocket launch tower.

"That's the test crucible?" Finn asked and his mentor nodded.

"It's designed so that prosecutors can get direct experience of hunting in each of Zavetgrad's work sectors, before they take part in a televised trial," Elara explained. "Every sector is represented, apart from the Authority sector, of course."

"Of course," Finn snorted. "It wouldn't do to throw golds to the lions. That's an honor reserved for the worker class."

Elara dropped lower and circled around the test crucible to give Finn a better look. The Spacehaven mini-sector contained two rocket-launch towers, smaller than the ones that had been present in the crucible Finn had fought in, but similar in most respects. The Stonehaven sector was a construction site for a mid-rise habitat block, offering plenty of opportunities to hide amongst the part-completed buildings, in what would end-up being a tense close-quarters fight. Volthaven was centered around a power substation with a small field of solar panels offering some variety in terrain, and Seedhaven was largely an open field of towering vertical farming units. As Elara swooped closer, Finn could see tomatoes growing in the topmost bays. Makehaven was a series of small industrial units plus a factory building and Metalhaven was a miniaturized version of a reclamation yard. In some respects its familiar piles of junk were comforting, like seeing your hometown after an extended period away, but it gave him no pleasure to see it again, because it only served as a reminder of what he'd lost. The final work sector was Seahaven, represented by a small port, a couple of fishing boats and a body of water at the edge of the crucible, closest to the electrified fence. Autohaven, technically not a sector but a transport network, was embodied by a mono-rail terminal and system that circumvented the arena in a closed loop to nowhere.

Elara leveled off then aimed the skycar at a mid-rise building in Stonehaven. The structure was incomplete and didn't yet have a roof, but Elara managed to weave the craft between the scaffolds and set-down on the tenth story of the building. Elara powered down the rotors then opened the gull-wing doors, and the descending whine of the blades quickly gave way to the sound of wind whistling through the gaps in the electrified fence, which stretched another hundred and fifty meters above their elevated landing site. It was ghostly howl that sent a shiver racing down his spine, and not only because the air was freezing cold.

"Come on, we can climb to the top," Elara said, removing her harness and jumping out.

Finn followed but more cautiously on account of the fact they were fifty meters up on a half-constructed building with nothing to stop them falling to their deaths.

"Isn't this high enough?" Finn said, hugging one of the steel pillars close to where they had landed. He hadn't known he had a fear of heights until that moment.

"The view is much better from the top," Elara said. She was already on the way up, using beams and pillars to aid her ascent, like climbing a giant tree.

Cursing, Finn edged over to where Elara had begun her climb then made the mistake of looking down. *Shit... shit... shit! ... don't do that again...* Focusing on swirling sky didn't help and he found that his head was spinning. Then there was a tap on his shoulder and he peeked open an eye to see Elara dangling down from above. She was holding out her hand.

"Take my hand, I'll help you," his mentor said. "The trick is to just focus on the metal of the scaffolds and beams and forget everything else."

Finn took her hand then started to climb, tentatively at first but growing in confidence with each step, thanks to the comforting presence of his mentor. Before long, he'd scaled the eleventh storey and they were maneuvering to make the last part of the climb to the twelfth and final floor.

"Why are you teaching me to climb if that fence can't be scaled?" Finn asked, pulling himself up onto a crossbeam.

"Because I want to show you what we're aiming for," Elara said.

Elara lifted herself up then perched on the edge of a narrow section of completed roof, like climbing out of a swimming pool. For a brief, agonizing few seconds, she moved out of sight, then her face appeared over the edge, and she reached out her hand. He took it, eagerly, and she pulled him up, but was immediately struck with a dizzying sense of vertigo, like the world was spinning around him. He stumbled close to the edge but Elara caught him and pulled him close.

"Focus on me," Elara said, turning his head so that they were eye to eye. "The sensation will pass. Just look at me."

Finn did as his mentor asked but staring into her emerald eyes was almost as unsettling as gazing into the gaping depths beneath his feet. He could feel Elara's heart thumping against his chest, then wondered if it was actually his heart beating so hard and not hers. Soon, their breathing synchronized, his dizziness subsided, and his entire world became Elara Cage.

"Feeling better?"

"Yes," Finn said. He smiled and tried to look calm but his heart was still racing.

"Trust me," Elara said. She took his hand and slipped behind him, her other arm wrapped around his waist. "Do you see?"

Finn couldn't think of anything beyond the feel of Elara's hand on his stomach and the warmth of her breath on his neck. Given where he was, perched atop a building like sailor in a crow's nest at high seas, he should have been terrified but he felt completely safe.

"What am I looking at?" Finn asked.

"Haven," Elara said.

The word tickled Finn's ear and sent electricity racing down his spine. Elara had aimed them toward the Davis Strait, visible in the distance thanks to their lofty lookout. It was like they were already in a skycar, making their escape to Haven.

"I wish we could see it from here," Finn said, seeing only the ice-cold swells of sea water. "I wish we could be sure that it's really out there."

"It's there," Elara said. There was no doubt. "And you'll see it soon."

"How can you be sure?" Finn turned on the spot like a delicate pirouette, so that he and Elara were facing one another again. "You've never seen it, so how do you know?"

Elara smiled at him. "We all have to believe in something."

Their closeness should have been awkward but for once he didn't feel self-conscious, and it shocked him to realize that all he could think about was kissing her, and the feel of her lips on his. He inched closer and so did she, and for an agonizing, exhilarating moment, he thought it might happen. Then Elara looked away and the thrill of possibility was replaced by the mortifying weight of humiliation.

"We should climb down," Elara said, hurriedly attaching a rappel line to an upright. Finn hadn't even noticed she was wearing a harness. "There's something else I need to show you."

The descent to the eighth-storey happened without either of them saying another word, and Finn discovered that crushing embarrassment was a good foil for his fear of heights. *What the hell was I doing?* he asked himself. *I'm such a fool. What must she think of me now?*

"Look out there, toward the Seahaven mini-sector," Elara said. She had swiftly disconnected herself from the tether, her head turned away, so he couldn't see her face. "That's the way out."

"Can the boats fly too?" Finn asked.

"This isn't a time for jokes, Finn," his mentor said, though it was mostly The Shadow who was present now. "I need you to focus."

Finn nodded and forced the minute quantity of saliva that was still in his mouth down his throat, though it felt like swallowing barbed wire. He figured that humor would be a good way to reset the mood, but not for the first time, he'd misjudged his mentor's feelings.

"The Seahaven mini-sector borders the northern fence, and there's a tunnel that reaches below ground directly to a drainage outlet just beneath the water line."

Finn squinted his eyes and his mind worked to estimate the distances involved. From their vantage, it was clear that the stretch of water that formed part of the Seahaven mini-sector was no more than twenty meters from the fence, closer than any other part of the trial crucible.

"Thirty minutes into your test trial the hatch covering that drainage outlet will open," Elara continued. "Metals will be waiting outside the barrier fence. All you need to do is swim through that hatch then climb into the tunnel system, and you're out."

Finn ran over what Elara had said in his mind but it seemed suspiciously simple. Then he had a thought.

"Why can't we just head down there now and escape?" Finn asked. "We could force the hatch and make a run for it."

"We can't because the fence runs below ground too,"

Elara explained. "The crucible isn't connected to power until the day of the trial, at which point they have to siphon energy from the grid, effectively stealing it from the fence below ground. That's the only time this particular exit is accessible."

Finn nodded. He was beginning to piece together the different elements that had to align to allow any rescue attempt.

"I assume that's another reason why the Metals mostly use trial days to get people in and out?" Finn asked. "Protecting the Regents and policing the streets is a distraction, but the extra power usage means the fence is at its weakest too."

Elara nodded. She hadn't looked him directly in the eyes since they'd climbed down from the twelfth floor. Not that he minded; he needed to focus. What Elara had explained sounded simple, but in the heat of a trial, even a test trial, there were a hundred different ways that a plan could fall apart.

"Thirty minutes doesn't sound like much, but once the trial begins, those minutes could feel like hours," Finn said. "Won't the prosecutors suspect something if I don't hunt down the offenders, and just hang out at the Seahaven mini-sector?"

"You won't have to make a kill, but you'll have to make it look like you're trying," Elara said. "And those thirty minutes will disappear in a flash. As soon as the trial begins, you'll need that time to reach Seahaven. There won't be much opportunity to do any killing."

"I hope so, because I meant what I said. I won't kill innocent people just to save my own skin," Finn replied.

This time she did look at him, but it was The Shadow staring into his eyes, not Elara Cage.

"Dozens of people are risking their necks to get you out, including me," she said, her words stinging him harder than the icy wind. "You might not believe you're worth it, but it doesn't matter what you think. As 'The Hero of Metalhaven' you have power. You're a symbol that Haven can use. So what if you have to shoot someone in the leg or bash them over the head to convince the prosecutors you're one of them?"

"It matters to me, and like it or not, I'm doing this my way," Finn snapped back. "But don't worry, I'll put on a good show."

"We can't save everyone," Elara said, her frustration palpable. "It doesn't matter whether you pull the trigger or if it's Ivan or Walter or Sabrina, or any of the others. All of the offenders in your test trial will die, and if your conscience screws up this plan, countless more will suffer."

"I'm not like you," Finn said. Without realizing it, they'd both stepped toward one another, fists clenched. "I can't just kill people and carry on like nothing happened. I know your 'stats', Elara. I know how many lives you taken. But how many have you saved?"

"I don't need your judgement," Elara snarled. Her hand was reaching for her blade. "I know what I am, and I know what I've done. And I know that getting you to Haven to help tear this rotten city down won't save my soul, but it's all I can do now. So stop fucking around and do as I say! This is bigger than you; it's bigger than all of us!"

Finn stepped back so that he was on the very edge of the eighth storey but he wasn't aware of the sheer drop behind him, because he suddenly understood something that he'd missed until that point.

"You're not coming with me?"

That stopped Elara dead and her hands fell to her sides.

"I have a job to do here," his mentor replied.

"But they already suspect you," Finn said. "The evaluator robot in my loyalty interview basically said as much."

"Just focus on what you need to do," Elara replied, ignoring what he'd said. "This has all been planned, Finn. You have to play your part."

"But you're the only person who knows me," Finn said. He knew he sounded desperate and even pitiful but he didn't care. "You're the only one I trust."

"It has to be this way," Elara whispered. "I'm sorry."

Finn never imagined he'd feel emptiness again as he did when Owen died, but the news that Elara wouldn't be joining him in Haven left him feeling even more alone.

"We have to get back to the barracks," Elara said, looking anywhere but at Finn. "You have another session today and combat training tomorrow. Your foot needs rest to heal."

She set off toward the skycar, but Finn caught her arm and held her back. She flinched and her hand went instinctively to her knife, but even if she had stabbed him through the heart, there was not enough of it left to feel anything.

"I'm sorry for what I said." Finn allowed his fingers to slip away from her arm, and he looked down, too ashamed to meet her eyes. Her shock announcement was like a slap around the face, bringing him to his senses. "And I'll do whatever is needed for the plan to work. I promise you that."

Elara nodded then climbed into the pilot's seat of the

skycar, and soon the rotors were spinning, battering Finn with noise and dust, and carrying away his words, so that Elara never heard them.

"But if there's even the slightest chance I can bring you with me, I'm taking it..."

12

SUCKER PUNCH

THE PHYSICAL DEMANDS of the assault course combined with the stress of Elara's excursion to the test crucible had left Finn feeling dog tired, and for the first time since he'd arrived in the Authority sector, he slept like the dead. His alarm finally roused him at 06:25, no longer chirruping soft birdsong but blaring like an air-raid siren. He was badly behind schedule and barely had time to shower and change into a fresh uniform before the door chime sounded.

"Who that?" Scraps said, flying from the bedroom into the lounge.

"It's probably Elara, come to chew my ear off for not being ready," Finn said, hopping around the room while trying to pull on his boots. As the robot medic had promised, his foot was completely healed. "Do me a favor and let her in, will you?"

"Okay-kay!" Scraps said and zoomed off to the door.

"Oh and try to work your charm on her too!" Finn called out. "I'd rather be dealing with Elara Cage than The Shadow right now."

"How does dealing with Juniper Jones sound instead?"

Finn glanced through the bedroom door and saw his paramour standing outside, instead of his mentor. Juniper's surprise arrival caused him to lose balance and he fell over. Scraps laughed while he finally forced his boot on then jumped to his feet, trying to pretend like nothing had happened.

"Are you okay?" Juniper asked. She was smiling though it was a carefully-crafted expression that didn't suggest she was amused by his mishap, even though she probably had been.

"I'm fine, come in," Finn said, noticing that she was still waiting in the corridor.

Juniper stepped inside and the door slid shut behind her. She had a small white box in her left hand and it took Finn a moment to realize that her gold-trimmed satin suit was different to the one she'd worn at their first meeting, though no less elegant. The woman's smile broadened a touch as she looked at him then Scraps caught her attention and Juniper's face lit up, like someone who'd just noticed a puppy staring at them with big brown eyes.

"Hello Scraps," Juniper said, stroking the robot like he was a pet. "How are you today?"

"Scraps good!"

The robot shivered and giggled as Juniper continued to pet him, then he hopped into her arms and stared up at her dotingly. Finn shook his head, ruing the fact his robot had more natural charisma in his co-processor than he'd ever have.

"Hey, I thought we were meeting later?" Finn said. He was running badly late and didn't want to give Chief Prosecutor Voss or his fellow apprentices any more reasons to loathe him more than they already had.

"I know you have training, but I wanted to bring you something first," Juniper said.

She held out the box and Finn took it, with some hesitancy. He wasn't used to receiving gifts and found it hard not to be suspicious of this one.

"What is it?" he asked.

"Open it and find out," Juniper replied. Her hands were now pressed behind her back and she was twisting her hips from side to side in anticipation.

Finn opened the box, which was made from a glossy card material, and saw that it contained six perfectly round cookies. "Cookies?" Finn said, picking one out of the box. It smelled incredible and his mouth began to water.

"They'll give you energy for today," Juniper said, still swiveling her hips. "I looked up your schedule and saw that it was combat training. That can be hard, or so I hear."

"Thanks, but I don't need them," Finn said, dropping the cookie back into the box. "The breakfast counter has enough calories to keep an army moving."

It was a thoughtless comment and Juniper looked crestfallen. Scraps scowled at him to reinforce the point that he'd been a douche, not that he needed reminding.

"Sorry, I didn't mean..." Finn began, stumbling over his words. "What I meant was..."

Then he saw Scraps acting out the motion of eating with his little metal hand and he understood what his charming and more socially-aware robot was trying to tell him. Grabbing another cookie, he quickly took a large bite, and they tasted even better than they'd smelled and looked.

"Shit, these are amazing!" Finn said, shoving the rest of the cookie into his mouth.

Juniper's face lit up again and the entire room seemed to glow brighter. She skipped a step closer and delicately picked a cookie out of the box with thumb and forefinger.

"Do you really think so?" she asked, nibbling the end of the cookie. "I wasn't sure I'd gotten the recipe right."

"You made these yourself?" Finn asked, and Juniper nodded, making him feel even more of asshole for rejecting them earlier. "Well, you're a genius!" he added, taking another cookie and devouring it whole.

Juniper laughed and Finn couldn't help but be swept up in the sound of her happiness. It was like she radiated an aura that caused anyone within its reach to feel joyful and alive. He laughed along with her and Scraps giggled and waved his hands as he bobbed around in Juniper's arms. Then Elara's warning that his paramour was still a part of the Authority, no matter her current status, invaded his thoughts and Finn felt suddenly wary.

Does she really find me funny and charming, or is she just trained to make me feel that way? He wondered. Finn continued to think but he had no answers. There was no reason to believe Juniper gained anything, beyond what she'd already told him, and the truth was that she'd been open and honest about the nature of her role from the start.

"Are you okay, Finn?" she asked, perceptive as ever.

"Yeah, sorry, I've just got a lot on my mind," he replied. This wasn't a lie and so it came out naturally. "You know, training, training, training..."

"Of course, I understand." Juniper regarded him kindly, smiled again then took the box of cookies and set them down on the dining table. "I didn't mean to interrupt."

Finn was worried that he'd upset her and found that this

possibility bothered him more than he expected it to. "Maybe you can join me for breakfast?" he asked.

He immediately regretted extending the invitation, knowing that the prosecutors would not allow it, but thankfully Juniper understood the rules too.

"Thank you, Finn, it's kind of you to invite me, but only prosecutors and their apprentices are allowed in the dining hall," she explained. "It's really fine, though, so don't worry. I'll come for you later, at our appointed time."

Juniper then leaned in and kissed him, pressing her lips to his cheek for a full two seconds before pulling back. There was a floral scent on her skin that Finn found intoxicating. It was new and exotic but with delicate hints of spice and sweetness that were also somehow familiar. It left him entranced as if it were a powerful narcotic many times more seductive than the substances the Authority used to drug workers' cigarettes and beer.

"I'll see you later," she said, setting Scraps down on the table next to the cookies then opening the door.

"Not if I see you first," Finn replied. He could have died on the spot, but he continued to smile in the hope that his mortification didn't show.

Mercifully, Juniper laughed and her gaze lingered for a second or two, before she slipped outside and the door closed behind her. The scent of her lingered in the air and on his skin, though he still couldn't place it.

"You suck!" Scraps said, pointing a finger at him. "Finn got no game!"

"Who asked your opinion?" Finn snapped, folding him arms across his chest, and scowling at his robot, but Scraps was oblivious. The machine was inspecting one of the cookies from the box and looked genuinely sad that he couldn't take a bite himself. "What is that scent, though?" Finn said, unable to get it out of his thoughts.

"Labrador tea!" Scraps said.

Finn had not directed the question at Scraps specifically but his clever little robot was on the money. The scent he couldn't place was Labrador tea, a hardy evergreen that grew in the reclamation yards in Metalhaven. The plant had small, bell-shaped white flowers that had a spicy-sweet, earthy aroma.

"She's certainly done her homework, I'll give her that," Finn laughed.

Then Elara's warning again asserted itself in his thoughts and he scowled. Was it manipulative and Machiavellian for Juniper to wear such a familiar scent, or simply attentive and thoughtful? He cursed and shook his head, hating that he couldn't trust anyone other than himself and his mentor. That The Shadow, Elara Cage, one of the most notorious prosecutors in the history of Zavetgrad with dozens of kills under her belt, was his one and only ally was the most far-fetched scenario of them all. Then the door chime rang and Finn set such troubling thoughts aside.

"Did you forget something?" Finn said, opening the door and expecting to see Juniper back again, but instead it was his mentor. "Oh, sorry, it's you."

Elara scowled at him. "Were you expecting someone else?"

Her eyes narrowed further then she stepped inside and wiped her thumb across his face. It was quick and rough and it felt like an assault. Then Finn saw that Elara was rubbing something red and waxy between her thumb and forefinger and he cursed silently, realizing it was Juniper's lipstick, left over from her kiss.

"I see things are going well with your paramour," Elara said, wiping what remained of the lipstick onto the sleeve of Finn's training uniform.

His mentor then looked around the room, quickly spotting the box of cookies, before sniffing the air and scrunching up her nose as if she'd smelled a fart. Then her eyes went to the bedroom and the ruffled sheets of his unmade bed, and she put two and two together and got five.

"I hope that you still have some energy left for training," Elara said, turning on her heels and walking outside.

"Nothing happened," Finn said, chasing after her and hastily hitting the button to close and lock his door, catching a glimpse of Scraps waving at him as he did so. "She just popped over to give me some cookies."

"Are you sure that's all she gave you?" Elara replied, showing him the smudgy remains of Juniper's lipstick on her thumb.

"Yes, I'm sure," Finn said, jogging to catch up. "Anyway, I thought you said it was none of your business what we do."

"It's not," Elara admitted, though she seemed annoyed at this.

"I don't ask what you get up to with your paramour," Finn added. He felt put on and was grumpy. Then he remembered that Elara had never actually owned up to whether she had her own concubine. "You do have a paramour, right?" he asked, nervously.

"That's none of your business," Elara snapped. She was unreasonably angry with him, considering that all he'd done was eat a damned cookie.

"I thought we didn't keep secrets?" Finn said, angrier at her refusal to answer than he had a right to be. "It's not like I care, anyway," he lied.

"It sounds like you care," Elara hit back. Finn continued to scowl at her and she shook her head, giving in. "Fine, if you must know, I don't have a paramour. I chose not to."

A wave of blissful relief washed over him then he was suddenly angry again. "Hang on, if you can refuse then why can't I?"

"Because you have to fit in," Elara said. "I don't have anything to prove."

They stopped outside the dining hall and faced each other. It was like they were back on the mid-rise in the test crucible, about to come to blows.

"Look, she came around uninvited," Finn said. He didn't like being at odds with Elara and felt the need to explain himself. "What was I supposed to do? Tell her to piss off?"

Elara looked ready for a fight then she glanced inside the dining hall and saw that several of the prosecutors and apprentices were within earshot, and she clamped up tighter than a vault door.

"No, you did right," Elara finally replied, though Finn could see that it pained her to admit it. "But Juniper Jones isn't important right now. Today is combat training, and after your last performance, you need to score highly today."

Elara was referring to how Sabrina Brook had pulled him into a submission hold and forced him to tap-out, after Finn had foolishly shown the apprentice mercy and compassion. It was a not-so-subtle reminder that he'd screwed up, and it was a mistake he didn't intend to repeat.

"Don't worry, I won't go easy this time, no matter who I have to fight."

Elara nodded then entered the dining hall. As usual, all eyes fell on them and whatever conversations had been happening changed to the subject of the false-gold and her interloping mentor, The Iron Bitch of Metalhaven.

"Ignore them," Elara said, as she began loading her plate. "Your only weapon here is strength. If you show them you're strong they'll respect you, even if they'll never accept you."

"I don't care about being accepted, I only want to wipe the smug look off Ivan's face," Finn answered.

The others had returned to their previous conversations, but the Regent's son was still staring at him, perhaps trying to wish him gone with the power of his mind.

"I'd love you to put Ivan in his place but remember that he's been learning how to fight since he was a kid," Elara went on. "They all have, Walter even more so."

Finn wasn't intimidated. He glared right back at Ivan who finally looked away first. *A small victory...* he thought.

"They've been learning in a classroom, but I've been fighting for real since I was old enough to hold a laser cutter." He finished loading his plate with eggs and bacon, since his sweet tooth had already been satisfied with Juniper's cookies, then turned to his mentor. "I know how to fight better than anyone, present company excepted."

Elara nodded. She was from Metalhaven too, so she understood what Finn meant. Life in the reclamation sector was hard and if you didn't look after yourself then you'd become prey for the likes of Soren Driscoll and Corbin Radcliffe. Finn had never been prey, and anyone stupid enough to get up in his face had quickly found themselves bleeding at his feet.

Elara moved away to join the other prosecutors at the top table, perching herself on the edge, away from the others, who acknowledged her with grunts and head tilts. *They'll respect you but you'll never be one of them...* Finn thought, paraphrasing what his mentor had said. Even after all the years she'd spent as a gold, it was clear they didn't want her in the same building, let alone the same room.

He picked up his plate of eggs and bacon then carried it over to the circular apprentice's table. He sat next to Sabrina then picked up her unused fork, rather than using the one directly in front of him, and began eating. She smiled at him then reached across and stole a slice of bacon from his plate, shoving it into her mouth whole. Challenge made and accepted.

"What have you all been talking about?" Finn asked, choosing to instigate the conversation rather than wait in vain for someone to engage him.

"We were just talking about how a bad smell just entered the dining hall," Walter said, arms folded across his chest, empty plate in front of him. "It got really bad a couple of minutes ago." The bully smiled, cruelly. "In fact, it happened right about the time you walked in."

"Is that so?" Finn said, nonchalantly forking some eggs into his mouth and making a good show of not looking bothered by Walter's remark. "I thought you might be discussing other ways that you can cheat your way to first place," he said, flicking his eyes in the direction of his opponent like a snake's tongue tasting the air.

Sabrina sniggered and settled deeper into her seat,

watching Finn and Walter with eager anticipation. All she was missing was a bucket of popcorn to enjoy the show with.

"I don't cheat," Walter snapped. "Apex himself said my win was valid."

"Sure, it was valid," Finn shrugged, casually pushing a piece of egg around his plate. "I guess some of us are just more comfortable in a straight fight than others."

Walter's face went red and the man shot up from his seat, fists clenched. His powerful thighs knocked the table, causing the crockery and glasses to chink and clash, and drawing the attention of the prosecutors. Each one of them looked over and Walter was torn between his anger and his embarrassment. The dining hall was neutral ground and everyone knew that fighting, and even arguing, wasn't permitted. In the end, Ivan had to grab the sleeve of Walter's uniform and pull him down to prevent one of the mentors from intervening.

"Save it for the octagon," Ivan said, glowering at Finn. "Then we'll see if the false gold fights as well as he talks."

"Well, my money is on chromeboy," Sabrina said, drawing ireful glances from Walter and Ivan.

"Have you gone mad?" Ivan said, disgusted. "A gold-plated piece of chrome trash like him couldn't hope to compete with us. Not to mention the fact you already beat him."

Sabrina shrugged. "Yeah, but to be fair, I sucker-punched him even worse than Walter did on the assault course." The muscular man was ready to protest again, but Ivan's hand on his arm stopped him. "Now he knows we don't fight fair, and he won't fall for it again."

"We've all had years of combat training, while he was

lugging chunks of metal in the reclamation sector," Ivan said, still stunned that Sabrina would side with Finn over her own color. "What makes you think he can stand against us?"

Sabrina sat up then leaned across the table toward Ivan.

"Because he's the only one here who's already had to fight for his life," the apprentice said. "He killed to be here, don't forget that." She sat back then winked at Finn and stole his last piece of bacon. "I for one hope that it's one of you chumps who gets picked to fight him, no offence."

Finn was surprised by the unexpected vote of confidence from Sabrina, but he didn't let it go to his head, because out of everyone at the table, she was the one playing mind games best of all. She'd sown the seed of doubt into the heads of her co-apprentices and tried to make Finn believe she was no longer a threat, but he knew better. It was a well-planned gambit but Sabrina was right about one thing; Finn wasn't about to get sucker-punched again, not by her, or by Walter, or by any of the others. He was going to fight the only way he knew how, as if his life depended on it.

Chief Prosecutor Voss then stood up and the cry of "Apex" filled the dining hall. This time it was Finn who shouted the loudest.

"Apprentices, make your way to the training hall," Voss announced. "Today, we find out who amongst you is the strongest. Today, is combat training."

13

COMBAT TRAINING

Finn walked into the training hall expecting to see the octagon set out for another session of sparring, but instead the hall had been transformed into something resembling a crucible. Racks of weapons and equipment lay waiting for them as he and the other apprentices entered, and his stomach sank as he realized what 'combat training' actually meant.

"Apprentices, this session is not for you to learn how to kill, but to learn how you *prefer* to kill." Chief Prosecutor Voss stood beside the equipment racks with the mentors. "In this room is everything you need to create your unique prosecutor persona. Will you strike with a sword or crush with a hammer? Will you puncture with an arrow or pierce with a bullet? These choices are yours alone to make, and your mentors will guide you."

"Fuck..." Finn said, under his breath.

"What's up, chromeboy?" Sabrina said. She'd snuck up behind him and heard his desperate curse. "Afraid I'm gonna knock you on your ass again?" she added, nudging him.

"No, it's just that I think I left the stove on in my apartment," Finn said, quickly putting on a front and hoping that Sabrina couldn't see through his bluff. The apprentice laughed and nudged him again, and Finn breathed a quiet sigh of relief.

"For today's training, you will be fighting against one another in trial conditions," Voss continued. There were anxious murmurs from the assembled trainees and Voss held up his hands to quieten his audience. "These weapons have dulled edges and use training ammunition. Coupled with the protective armor you will all be wearing, the risk of serious harm is significantly reduced..." Voss allowed that to sink in, before adding, "... but make no mistake, this is not a game. Injuries can and will occur. You will experience pain. And the victor in each contest will only be declared when one apprentice is no longer able to continue." Voss added another pause, this time simply for theatrics. "Are you ready to prove your valor?"

The trainees chanted "Apex!" and Finn made sure to add his voice to the choir, loud and clear, though in truth he was less than eager to get started. A brawl inside an octagon-shaped ring was one thing, but a hunt was quite another. He recalled Elara's comment that his fellow apprentices had been training for situations like this their whole lives and he finally understood why his mentor had repeatedly labored that point.

"Ivan and Sabrina, step forward," Voss said.

"Fuck..."

This time it was Sabrina who had cursed under her breath. Finn glanced at her and the color in her skin had faded, like she'd just been pulled out of deep snow and was still thawing.

"You've got this," Finn whispered, looking his fellow apprentice in the eye. "Forget his name and title. He's just a man. You can take him."

Sabrina smiled at him, but it didn't seem that his pep talk had given her the boost in confidence he'd hoped for. She moved ahead and stood beside Ivan Volkov who appeared pleased with his chosen opponent. *Had he requested to fight Sabrina?* Finn wondered. She had been vocal in her support of Finn earlier, and perhaps this was his way of teaching the woman a lesson.

"Zach and Tonya, step forward," Voss continued.

Fuck... This time Finn spoke the word only in his mind. Zach being paired with Tonya was probably worse news for Tonya than it was Zack, but this wasn't the reason for his curse. With four apprentices already paired off, only two remained.

"Walter and Finn, step forward," Voss said, concluding the matchmaking part of the training.

Finn stood tall and marched to his position, making a point of looking his opponent squarely in the eyes. Walter also strode out confidently, but the look on the man's face was one of cruel anticipation, like a medieval castle torturer on his way to the dungeons to begin his day's bloody work.

"Mentors, go to your apprentices," Voss ordered. "The first contest begins in ten minutes."

Everyone dispersed and Finn found that Elara was already waiting for him by a set of weapons and equipment racks. It seemed that each apprentice had his or her own personal set so that there was no need to squabble over who got which knife or gun. *How thoughtful of them...* Finn mused.

"I thought we'd be boxing not trying to hack each other to death with axes," Finn said, drawing alongside his mentor. He picked up a curved sword, and it felt heavy enough to do serious damage. "How does this even work? Walter could take my head off with this."

"Unlikely, since it's a training blade, but I have no doubt that he'll try," Elara replied, not filling him with confidence. "Each of you gets to choose one melee weapon and one ranged weapon, plus a dagger or knife. You training uniform is fitted with sensors and implants that not only mimic pain but reproduce the physical effects of injuries too."

"So if I get shot it will feel like I've been shot?" Finn asked.

"Not only that, but you'll suffer the debilitating effects too," Elara clarified. "For example, get shot in the leg, and you'll be limping for the rest of the fight, assuming you can stand at all."

Finn nodded, understanding what the prosecutors were trying to achieve via these contests. They wanted to see how the apprentices would react and adapt in situations where panic, fear and injury were very real factors, even if the threat of death was minimal. In the end, despite what Voss had claimed, it was a game, but it was a game Finn had played before.

"Walter will likely choose a hammer, in honor of his mentor, Frost," Elara continued. She was surveying the weapons rack, trying to match something to Finn's style of fighting. "For a ranged weapon, he'll probably choose a bow or perhaps a spear. He's superb with both, but it won't be an arrow or javelin that kills you. Walter will want to get close. He'll make it personal."

"He's done that already," Finn commented. He put down the sword, which felt unwieldy in his grasp and pressed his hand to his hips. "What about me? I've never trained with weapons and all I know about guns came from the data device I kept hidden in my Metalhaven apartment."

"As I recall, you made a hash of shooting that pistol too, so I suggest we steer clear of firearms altogether," Elara mused. She picked up a weapon that resembled a rifle but was also oddly familiar to him. "This is a laser weapon, similar to the cutters that you're already used to handling."

Elara gave him the weapon and it felt comfortable in his hands, but it was memorable in more ways than one.

"This is the same weapon Corbin used to kill Owen," Finn said, and his hands suddenly trembled. He gripped the metal more tightly but not before his mentor had noticed.

"Turn your grief into a weapon too," Elara said. "Use it. Channel it."

"I'd rather forget," Finn said with a sigh, though he knew that was impossible. He slung the laser cannon then turned to the rack of melee weapons. "So what about close-combat? I doubt my fists will do much damage to Walter's thick skull."

"Try some out and see what feels right," Elara suggested.

Finn went along the rack, picking up different kinds of swords and martial arts weapons from Sai to nunchaku, but it was apparent that without a decade's worth of training under his belt, he was more likely to injure himself than his opponent. He was about to give up when he saw a metal bat at the rear of the rack. He reached through and managed to get his fingers around the handle and pull it out. It was a dull chrome color – the color of Metalhaven.

"Now this is something I can get behind," Finn said, giving the bat a few test swings. It felt natural. It felt right.

"I've never seen that before," Elara said, frowning at the weapon. "It's an odd design for a club."

"It's not a club, it's a baseball bat," Finn corrected her. "It used to be a sport before the war, where people used bats like these to hit a ball."

Elara's frown deepened to a scowl. "Why?"

Finn laughed and shrugged. "I have no idea. But I like it."

"Then use it," Elara said. "What matters most is that the weapons you choose represent you. The laser cannon speaks to you heritage, and the bat to your..."

Elara was struggling to finish the sentence but Finn knew the word she was grasping for.

"To my hard-headed stubbornness?" he suggested.

Elara smiled. It was always nice to see her smile, even though it never lasted more than a second or two at most.

"You said it, not me," she replied. Her emerald eyes were still smiling, even if her lips were not.

"Ivan and Sabrina, you're up!" Chief Prosecutor Voss announced.

There was a scuffle of boots on the ground and everyone other than the two assigned combatants withdrew to an observation lounge on the upper level of the hall-turned-crucible. Its elevation meant that Finn could see the entire arena, which was outfitted like an elaborate obstacle course. Ivan and Sabrina stood in front of the panoramic window, looking up at Voss and waiting for his order to take their starting positions.

Finn observed Ivan Volkov first. The man had a medium build but he was stronger and more agile than he looked. His confidence and arrogance shone though, however. It was like the man already believed he'd won, and Finn knew it was possible that Ivan's prestigious position meant his victory had been pre-determined. As his ranged weapon, Ivan had chosen a firearm that had the appearance of an ancient flintlock, though in fact operated like a modern pistol. His melee weapon was a glaive, a type of polearm with a sword-like blade attached to one end of the golden staff, which was six-feet long in total. They were the weapons of soldiers from two different periods of earth's history, but whether Ivan fancied himself a musketeer or a knight, it was clear the weapons were chosen to highlight his noble lineage.

Sabrina Brook had chosen a sub-machine gun and a pair of three-pronged martial arts weapons called Sai. Finn recognized them because he'd managed to stab himself with a similar weapon only five minutes earlier. He watched her practice with the Sai and it seemed obvious that she was proficient, but unlike Ivan, Sabrina did not look confident. If anything, she had the appearance of a lowly gladiator who was about to face a legion of Roman soldiers in the coliseum.

"Apprentices, take your positions!" Voss' voice boomed over speakers inside the hall.

Ivan and Sabrina saluted one another with their weapons, then ran to opposite corners of the hall. A klaxon sounded to initiate the contest and Finn watched with bated breath as the two apprentices began stalking toward one another.

"Pay close attention to the terrain," Elara said, whispering in his ear. He could smell the fruit drink on her breath and it comforted him. "Use the cover and look for ways to gain elevation. Make the crucible work for you."

His mentor continued to whisper commentary and advice into his ear as the contest between Sabrina and Ivan progressed. Initially, Sabrina gained the upper hand thanks to her longer-range weapon and higher rate of fire, and Finn wondered why Ivan would choose such a limited weapon as the flintlock. Five minutes into the battle and the Regent's son was pinned down and forced to retreat. He took a shot to the shoulder and his cry of pain was very real. A point was registered for Sabrina on a scoreboard built into the wall opposite the observation lounge, and for a moment, Finn thought she might actually win. Then he caught Sloane Stewart out of the corner of his eye. Ivan's mentor, bodyguard and paramour rolled into one was speaking softly into a comm-link. Finn scowled then looked back into the arena and saw Ivan touching his ear. *She's feeding him information! The bastard is cheating!* Finn looked to Elara, hoping that she would intervene, but even though it was clear his mentor had also seen the intervention, she shook her head at him. Finn closed his eyes and sighed, balling his hands into fists. His hunch had been right; Sabrina had been destined to lose from the outset.

Ivan started to move and thanks to his guardian angel had soon outflanked Sabrina. The man burst out of cover and fired three shots in quick succession – impossible for a real flintlock but no trouble for the modern remake – and Sabrina was hit in the back. She screamed as the bullets thudded into her body and her training uniform replicated the wounds. It was enough to class a kill, and the points were added to Ivan's total. Finn felt sick, but there was nothing he could do.

Next up was Zach versus Tonya, which on paper was an even contest. Zach had continued to keep himself to himself during breakfast and the training sessions, but Finn had been careful to observe the man as much as possible. Zach wasn't interested in making friends and he wasn't interested in prestige or fame. All Zach wanted was the opportunity to hurt and kill people without the restrictions, as minor as these were, that being a prefect had placed on him. The man had chosen an assault rifle and a serrated knife and was already on his marker, eager to begin. *Too eager...* Finn thought, and suddenly he was glad he was facing Walter rather than the sadist that was in the training hall below him.

Tonya had fastened a belt of throwing knives around her slender waist, which Finn considered to be a bold and somewhat foolish choice for a ranged weapon, especially going up against an assault rifle. For close combat she had two dirks, single-edged daggers, which Finn had overheard the red-headed apprentice saying were from Scotland – a nod to Tonya's distant heritage.

"She relies on her explosive speed and skill," Elara said, still analyzing and feeding him anything that might prove useful to his chances of survival in future contests. "She'll stay out of sight and taunt Zach, maybe even throw a few daggers in an attempt to scare him. Then, when Zach loses his cool, she'll strike."

"I can't imagine Zach being intimidated," Finn commented in reply. "If that's her strategy, I think Tonya is playing with fire, and liable to get burnt."

The arena was reset and Chief Prosecutor Voss ordered the two combatants to their starting positions, even though Zach was already there. Seconds later, the klaxon blared and

Zach and Tonya began stalking toward one another. Zach moved fast, climbing on top of obstacles and harassing Tonya to keep her on the back foot. The man had taken six spare magazines for his rifle and was not being frugal with his shots. However, try as he might, he couldn't pin Tonya down, and Zach quickly lost his temper, just as Elara had predicted.

"Show yourself!" Zach bellowed. He was standing on a crate in the center of the arena, swiveling on the spot like a gun turret. "Stop hiding from me!"

Finn thought he sounded unhinged but neither Voss nor any of the other mentors seemed concerned.

"It's all part of what will become Zach's prosecutor persona," Elara said, surprising Finn by whispering into his ear again. "He'll be terrifying in the crucible. Can you imagine him coming after you, screaming and shouting and shooting up the arena? It'll all make great TV."

Finn wanted to believe otherwise but his mentor was correct, of course. He remembered what Voss had said about the purpose of the training, which was not to practice weapons and hunting skills, but to develop their prosecutor persona. Ivan fancied himself as some sort of noble crusader, while Zach's character was a deranged madman, an unhinged psychopath who wielded terror amongst his arsenal of weapons. The difference was that Zach's persona wasn't an act.

Suddenly, Tonya leapt into view and knives flashed through the air, glinting like starlight. Zach was hit in the leg and he yelled and dropped to one knee, grasping the handle of the blade and yanking it from his flesh. Despite the dulled edged and his armor, Tonya had pierced flesh.

"Yeah! Get him Tonya!" Ivan yelled. Finn hadn't noticed

until then that the Regent's son had entered the viewing gallery. As expected, Walter was with him. "Close in for the kill!"

There was no way that Tonya could have heard Ivan, but the man's vocal support for his co-apprentice suggested more than just camaraderie. The two had made no secret of enjoying each other's company, out of training hours as well as during them.

Tonya made her move, climbing onto the crate where Zach had been perched, Scottish dirk daggers in hand, but Zach sensed her approach and sprayed bullets from his assault rifle, firing on full automatic. Tonya was hit, not badly enough for Zach to score a kill, but enough to cause debilitating pain and incapacitate the woman. She screamed and toppled off the crate, landing hard on the unforgiving floor of the training hall.

"No!" Ivan yelled, banging on the glass. "Tonya, get up! He's coming!"

Zach climbed down and drew his knife while Tonya hauled herself off the floor. One of her dirks had scattered beneath another obstacle, leaving her with only one blade to defend herself, but Zach's bowie knife was longer at twelve-inches from guard to tip, and looked like a sword in his slender hands. Knife fights were rare in Metalhaven but when they occurred they were brutal and fast, and usually left someone bleeding on the ground within seconds. Not so this contest, which highlighted the skills that both apprentices had been taught since they were children.

Tonya managed to land a punch and for a moment, Finn thought she was going to win, as did Ivan, who was still pressed up against the glass, desperately looking on. Then

Zack blocked Tonya's attack and hacked his blade across her gut. The dulled edge didn't cut but Tonya's uniform simulated the incapacitating pain of having her stomach slashed open. The red-head apprentice went down hard, screaming and clutching her simulated wound.

The scoreboard updated to show that Zach had delivered a killing blow and was the victor, but even though the klaxon sounded to signify the end of the bout, Zach was not finished. Eyes maddened with bloodlust, Zach tossed his blade then fell on top of Tonya and began raining punches into her head and body.

"Stop!" Ivan yelled, hammering the glass with his fists. "Get off her, you fuck!"

Ivan ran to the door and the prosecutors tried to stop him, but he shook them off.

"Apprentice Volkov, you will remain here!" Voss ordered, but Ivan was already out of the door and running into the arena.

14

THE FIGHT

IVAN WAS CHARGING across the arena floor toward Zach before the prosecutors had even made it into the training hall. Voss and the others repeated their cries for him to stop, but the Regent's son was blinded by rage and deaf to their cries, and moments later Ivan had torn Zach away from Tonya and thrown him to the ground.

"Bastard!" Ivan roared, hammering punches into Zach's face. "I'll fucking kill you!"

Walter and Sabrina had also run down to the arena and Finn had followed on autopilot, not wanting to be the only one left behind in the viewing gallery. By the time he reached the scene, Cleo "Garrote" McKay, Zach's mentor, was trying to restrain Ivan, but the apprentice shook him off and continued to kick and claw and punch at Zach's unconscious body.

"I'll kill you!' Ivan snarled, continuing his frenzied attack. "Bastard! I'll kill you!"

Tonya's mentor, Kurt "Blitz" McCullough, also piled in, and together with Cleo McKay, they managed to drag Ivan away, but the apprentice continued to thrash and kick like a wild man. An elbow flew into McCullough's face, splitting the man's lip, and the enraged prosecutor lashed out, punching Ivan then throwing him to the ground. Finn watched the look on McCullough's face shift from anger to regret in an instant. The prosecutor had retaliated without thinking and with the harsh realization of hindsight, he knew he'd fucked up.

"How dare you strike me?!" Ivan roared, climbing to his feet and touching his face where McCullough had struck him. "I am Ivan Konstantin Volkov, Regent Successor of Spacehaven. I should have you killed for your insolence!"

To Finn's surprise, McCullough took two steps back with his head bowed low in deference to the aristocrat. It was only then that Finn noticed Sloane Stewart, Ivan's bodyguard amongst other roles, standing toward the rear of the gathering. She had drawn a pistol and maneuvered into line of sight of McCullough. Her finger was wrapped around the trigger and Finn wondered how close the prosecutor had come to being shot dead for his heinous mistake of striking the Regent's son.

"Enough!"

Chief Prosecutor Voss pushed his way through the throng and stood in front of Ivan, who was still seething with rage and indignation.

"I remind you that in this place you are an Apprentice Prosecutor, and under my authority," Voss continued, addressing Ivan directly, head held high. "You will abide by the rules of this institution or you will be expelled, Regent Successor or not."

Ivan was still fuming but if there was one thing that

characterized all golds, it was an unwavering respect for the Authority, and within the training halls of the prosecutor barracks, there was no question that Voss was in charge.

"Yes, Apex," Ivan replied, dipping his head a fraction, as a mark of respect, though not of deference, as McCullough had shown to him. "I apologize for my rash behavior."

Voss said nothing more then turned to Tonya, who was still on the floor, but being tended to by her mentor and two medical robots that had arrived within seconds of the affray ending.

"Go with her," Voss said to Ivan, who nodded again and rushed to Tonya's side.

Finn suspected that Ivan would not leave Tonya even had Voss ordered him to stay in the training hall, and so by telling him to go, the Chief Prosecutor maintained his authority without further displeasing the Regent Successor. It was a nice touch, Finn thought. *Trials are deadly, but to the golds, politics is an even more dangerous game.*

Knuckles raw and bleeding, Ivan stayed with Tonya as she was helped to the infirmary for treatment, shadowed closely by Sloane Stewart, who had now holstered her weapon. The fact she had drawn it earlier with the clear intention of shooting McCullough should the prosecutor have continued to threaten Ivan was not even acknowledged. It was like Ivan's bodyguard and mentor was invisible. A few meters away, Zach was being loaded onto a stretcher, aided by his mentor, Cleo McKay, and another duo of medical automatons. The man was out cold and in worse shape than Tonya after Ivan's violent assault, but the scoreboard looming high above them on the wall still awarded him the victory.

"We still have one more contest," Voss said, shouting so as

to ensure he had everyone's attention. "Finn and Walter, take up your starting positions."

Walter looked at Finn contemptuously then stepped away to speak to his mentor, André "Frost" Regan. The prosecutor was carrying his apprentice's weapons, a short bow and a warhammer that was not unlike the weapon Frost himself employed in the crucible to murderous effect. A sickly, nervous anticipation gripped him and Finn searched the hall for his own mentor, whom he hadn't seen leave the viewing gallery. He was shocked to find her practically breathing down his neck, more than living up to her alias, The Shadow.

"Walk with me," Elara said, handing Finn his chrome baseball bat and laser cannon. "We need to talk strategy."

"I assume the best strategy is to hit him and don't get hit in return?" Finn offered Elara a smile, but his attempt at levity fell on deaf ears.

"Focus Finn, this is no time for games," his mentor snapped. "Remember that Walter Foster was grown from genetically-pure stock to be the perfect killer. This training and his subsequent tenure as a prosecutor is merely to prepare him for Nimbus. Once he's gained enough experience and kills, he'll be sent to the orbital platform to train the future prefects of the citadel, where he will be as a father to them."

Finn blew out a shaky sigh. "So, you're saying that he has a lot to prove."

Elara nodded and Finn understood that the stakes had just been raised.

"Walter doesn't just need to beat you, he needs to humiliate you," Elara continued. They reached Finn's starting position and his mentor grabbed the straps on Finn's training uniform and shook him firmly. "Don't let him, Finn. Don't give this bastard an inch. Show him who you really are."

Finn nodded, suddenly glad of her grip on his body, because in that moment it felt like Elara was the only thing holding him up.

"I'll give him a fight he'll not soon forget," Finn said. "Whatever he's planning to do to me, I can promise you, I've had worse." He laughed nervously. "Hell, maybe I'll even teach him a lesson or two."

"It doesn't matter if you win." Elara's voice was like ice, cold and unforgiving. "You will never be one of them, Finn. People like you and me will always be beneath their contempt. It's why this place has to be torn down, brick by rotten brick. And that starts here and now."

Elara released his straps and Finn was glad to discover that he was still standing. Voss' voice then boomed over the PA system, calling for mentors to leave the arena. The contest was to start in sixty seconds.

"I've got this," Finn said, trying to convince himself as much as his mentor. "Don't worry."

"I'm not worried," Elara replied, though Finn knew it was lie. *But is she worried about me, or worried about me failing?* he wondered. "Now get out there and show them all what it means to be Metal."

Elara slipped away and Finn was startled by the sound of the countdown klaxon blaring inside the hall. Thirty seconds... Twenty... He sucked in a deep breath and let it out slowly. Ten... Then he saw the flicker of movement in the corner of his eye and he turned just in time see a blur of gold flash by. *The cheating bastard has already started!*

The klaxon sounded again to officially start their contest,

but Walter was already on top of him, bow in hand. An arrow zipped past, so close it shaved hairs off his head, and without pausing to think, Finn was running for his life. Another arrow thudded into a container and Finn jinked and weaved, racing through the makeshift crucible without any notion of where he was headed. Another arrow grazed his arm and though the fabric of his gold uniform was not cut, the sensors in the material registered the impact and flooded his body with pain. He grabbed his shoulder and squeezed, hissing through gritted teeth, then changed course and ran harder until finally he was beyond reach of his opponent's arrows, at least for a time.

The scoreboard buzzed and registered the point scored for Walter, which only made the simulated wound sting more keenly. He readied his laser cannon and wrestled control of his labored breathing. Walter was still out there, hunting him, and thanks to his underhanded tactics and head-start his opponent had all the advantages.

Shouldering the weapon, Finn moved out, retracing his steps and hoping that Walter would run directly into a laser blast from his weapon. The cannon was heavy but it was also familiar, and while it had limited shots, he only needed one. With no other sound in the arena, the noise of his boots clacking against the metal grating underfoot was excruciatingly loud. He stopped and listened and picked up the scrape and scuffle of movement elsewhere, close and getting closer. Cursing, he shifted position, aiming his cannon though the gaps between obstacles but no matter where he looked, Walter was not there.

Where are you?... Finn felt fear rise up inside him, despite his best efforts to control it. Then there was another scuffle of noise and Finn saw him, standing atop a stack of crates, bow outstretched and string taut. He dove as the arrow flew but he was too late to evade it entirely and it scraped across his back. Finn screamed and the scoreboard registered the point, but it wasn't a killing blow, and he was still in the fight. Dragging himself into cover, he fired a blast from his cannon and scorched a groove into the crates below Walter's feet, forcing the man to move. Despite his mass, Walter was like a cat, leaping across fences and walls in stealthy pursuit of its prey.

Finn pressed his back to a wall and waited for the crippling agony to subside, but if there was one thing that he understood better than any of the apprentices, it was pain. Working shift-after-long-shift in Metalhaven, Finn had lived with pain his whole life, and had learned to control it, so that it did not control him. With his uniform's pain stimulants still pulsing, Finn pushed himself up and ran to a new position, cannon aimed at his last location. He was banking on Walter assuming that the debilitating effects of the last arrow would have left him incapable of moving, and sure enough, his opponent stalked into view, warhammer held high. He aimed his cannon but before he could squeeze the trigger, a warning cry filled the arena, alerting Walter to the danger. Finn shot the weapon but what should have been a killing blow was reduced to a glancing hit to the man's muscular thigh. Walter roared with pain but was out of sight before Finn could shoot again. He pursued, but the pulsing pain restricted his movements and his quarry got away. Cursing again he looked up to the viewing gallery and saw André "Frost" Regan staring down at them through an opened window. It was Walter's mentor who had uttered the warning cry. Intervening in the contest should have meant that his apprentice was disqualified, but if Finn's time in the Authority sector had taught him anything, it was that there was one rule for the golds and another for him.

"Keep going!"

This was another cry from the gallery but it wasn't Walter's mentor, nor was it his own. He looked up and saw Sabrina Brook's head poking through the window that Regan had opened.

"You've got this, chromeboy!" Sabrina yelled. "Kick his ass!"

Despite the pain he was in, Finn laughed. He didn't know whether Sabrina's show of support was genuine, or if it was just because she liked to stir shit up, but he appreciated it all the same, and it drove him on harder. Adopting his opponent's tactics, Finn climbed onto the crates and shuffled forward on his hands and knees to dull the sound of his advance. Then he saw Walter hiding close to small clearing, teeth gritted and eyes squeezed tightly shut as pain continued to pulse through his body. Shouldering his cannon, he took aim and had Walter dead-to-rights, then the crates he was perched on suddenly shifted like there was earthquake. He fired but the shot landed wide, then the arena began to reconfigure around him. The metal boxes sank into the ground while others rose up to create an octagon shaped arena. From having a position of advantage, Finn was suddenly exposed and Walter wasted no time in grabbing his bow. An arrow was nocked and loosed, but Walter was still shaking with pain and the shot flew wide. Finn returned fire from the hip but also missed. He held his breath and aimed again, this time waiting until the iron-sights of the cannon were pointed squarely at Walter's heart. He squeezed the trigger but nothing happened.

"What the hell?" he cursed.

Finn tried to fire again, but still the weapon didn't activate. He pulled it down from his shoulder and inspected the cannon, shaking it and pressing buttons, but it was dead, as if it had been purposefully disabled.

"You lose, scum."

Walter nocked another arrow and fired. It hit him in the dead center of his sternum, and while he felt the dull thud of the training arrow impact his body, his uniform didn't register any pain. Each as confused as the other, he and Walter looked to the scoreboard but it didn't update, still showing two points to one in favor of Walter.

"Apprentices will finish the contest using melee weapons only," the voice of Chief Prosecutor Voss announced.

Finn laughed and threw the laser cannon to the ground. Of course they would change the rules at the exact moment he was about to triumph, but even if he was destined to lose the contest, he would still go down fighting tooth and nail. Walter readied his hammer and Finn pulled the chrome baseball bat from his back-scabbard.

"You should have stayed down," Walter said, inching toward him. "Now I'm going make this hurt."

Walter charged and swung the hammer with enough force to demolish a building, and Finn was forced to dodge and roll aside, knowing that his lightweight bat would prove no defense against the heavier weapon. He was back on his feet with barely enough time to block another swing, and the power of the strike knocked him to the ground. Walter roared and swung the hammer, crashing it into the floor inches from his head. Finn scrambled away then saw the dent in the metal plates and his heart leapt into his mouth. Walter wasn't using a training weapon, but a real warhammer. He looked more closely and realized that it was André Regan's actual prosecutor weapon, a hammer that had already claimed dozens of lives.

Walter came at him again but this wasn't the first time Finn had been in a fight for his life. His instincts had saved him then and he trusted them again. Swinging his bat, he struck Walter's arm, but their uniforms were no longer simulating pain, and the man's dense muscle soaked up the impact. Walter attacked but even with his mighty strength the warhammer was a slow, cumbersome weapon, and Finn was able to dodge and hit back, chipping away at his opponent's resilience and composure with each strike of the bat.

Weakened and angry, Walter became sloppy and Finn was able to clobber the man across the side of the head. The sound filled the arena like a bell being rung and though it staggered him, the bigger man didn't go down. Walter ducked the next swing then tossed his hammer and drove his muscular shoulder into Finn's gut. Winded from the impact, he was unable to stop Walter from tearing the bat from his grasp, but instead of using it against him, his opponent tossed it aside and closed his hands into fists. Walter wanted to beat him bloody with his bare hands but by turning the contest into a street fight, the man had stepped firmly into Finn's domain. Walter may have been bred for combat but Finn had been brawling in the back alleys of Metalhaven since he was thirteen years old. He never backed down then and he wouldn't now.

They traded blow for blow, neither giving any quarter,

throwing punches and kicks, elbows and knees, and even using their teeth to bruise and puncture one another's flesh. Soon they were both bloodied and exhausted, uniforms torn and skin scraped raw, but even though Walter continued to hit harder, Finn would not go down. Owen would have asked him, "why?". Why take the beating when he knew the Authority wouldn't allow him to win?

Because fuck them, that's why.

The klaxon sounded but still they fought until prosecutors were forced to pull them apart. Elara Cage was in the thick of it, tearing Walter away from Finn and soaking up wild punches for her efforts, then Voss appeared and his voice cut through like a laser blast.

"Stop!" Voss yelled, pushing Walter back. "This contest is over!"

Finn staggered into a metal crate and used it to prop himself up. His breath was tight in his chest and blood had clouded his vision and turned the world red, yet he shrugged off the medical bots when they rushed in to treat him. Wiping his eyes, he looked at his opponent, and though battered like he was, Walter's most serious injury was not physical but to his pride. Then he looked at the scoreboard, which ready thirty points to thirty-four in Walter's favor. He'd lost the contest but from the stupefied looks on the faces of the assembled prosecutors they knew he had won the fight.

15

OUCH-OUCH

Walter was forcibly escorted out of the training hall by his mentor, though the man remained furious, snorting and stomping his feet like an enraged bull. Elara remained by Finn's side, watching Voss and the other prosecutors, who were all looking at him differently now. However, it wasn't respect so much as fear that he saw in their eyes. They were afraid of this wild man from the streets of Metalhaven who refused to go down, no matter what they threw at him.

"Report to the infirmary for medical treatment," Chief Prosecutor Voss said, addressing Elara rather than Finn directly. "Then I want all prosecutors in my office in thirty minutes. Dismissed!"

The prosecutors all chanted "Apex!", though Elara merely nodded her assent. After fighting to pull Walter off him, and taking blows in the process, Finn could see that his mentor was seething with rage and struggling to choke down her anger. Voss left and the other Prosecutors dispersed soon after, chatting amongst themselves in hushed tones. Then

Elara turned to him and studied his wounds, brow furrowed, though he wasn't sure whether her concern for his wellbeing was personal or professional. Then he noticed that her lip was bleeding, likely as a result of her struggle with Walter.

"It looks like you could use some medical treatment too," Finn said, touching a hand to Elara's chin, close to the wound. He'd done this instinctively and his mentor drew back, as if dodging a punch.

"I'm fine, it's you we need to get mended," Elara replied, continuing to inspect the damage to his body. "It's mostly superficial. I don't think anything is broken or ruptured."

"I've had worse," Finn said, shrugging off her comments. He wasn't trying to boast, he'd genuinely had far worse beatings at the hands of Metalhaven prefects. Then he smiled. "You should see the other guy."

Finn's mentor finally met his eyes and to his surprise she cracked a smile. For a moment, The Shadow had moved into the background and he was looking at Elara Cage from Metalhaven.

"Walter won't forget *that* in a hurry," Elara said, still smiling. "And neither will the other prosecutors and apprentices. They'll treat you differently now."

"Differently, as in better?" Finn wondered, but Elara shook her head.

"Not really, but they'll be more careful about what they say, to your face at least," she replied.

Finn nodded. If it meant taking less shit from Ivan and Walter then he considered that a worthwhile outcome in itself. Then he pointed to the scoreboard, which continued to display the result of his contest with Walter.

"I still lost though," he said.

"On points, maybe," Elara said. "But no-one expected you to last two minutes against Walter, and you fought that asshole to a stalemate, despite his supposed superiority. That's a victory, and don't for a second think otherwise."

"I wish Voss would have let it go on a little longer," Finn said, flexing his arms and shoulders, which were starting to throb and ache as the numbing effect of adrenaline wore off. "I'd have loved to put that guy on his ass at least once."

"You might still get your chance," Elara replied.

The two medical robots were still standing by and one of them had its fingers pressed into a steeple, drumming them against one another gently but still loud enough to get Elara's attention. The other machine then simulated a polite cough, as if to reinforce the point that they were waiting.

"Come on, let's get you fixed up," Elara said.

She pressed her hand gently to the small of Finn's back and led him away. The medical robots followed in a procession behind them both but they'd barely made it out of the training hall before he spotted another foreman-class machine stomping toward him. The imposing, armor-clad robot was accompanied by a special prefect, opaque visor pulled down and sub-machine-gun in hand.

"My appointment isn't until tomorrow," Finn said, trying to head off the robot interrogator before it began its spiel.

"That is correct, Apprentice Prosecutor Brasa," the evaluator robot replied, cheerfully. It then turned its mechanical eyes to Elara. "I am actually here to remind Prosecutor Elara Cage that she is late for *her* appointment."

"Elara? What the hell do you want with her?" Finn said, unable to hide his shock.

"It's okay, Finn, I still have to undergo yearly loyalty

evaluations," his mentor explained. "Today's training simply overran, that's all."

"I was not notified of this delay," the evaluator said, still in an annoyingly cheerful tone.

"Well, I'm notifying you now," Elara answered in a perfectly passive-aggressive way.

The machine smiled and nodded before extending a hand along the corridor and inviting his mentor to join them. "Assuming your duties permit, we can begin now," the robot said.

Elara sighed and nodded. "I'll be there presently."

"I am happy to escort you…"

"I said I'm coming, okay?" Elara snapped, cutting across the robot. "Just go to the interview room and I'll see you there in a few minutes."

The special prefect flinched when Elara raised her voice and were it not for the cool reaction of the evaluator robot, Finn thought that the officer might have actually leveled his weapon at her.

"Of course, Prosecutor Cage," the evaluator said, nodding respectfully. "I will see you soon."

Elara waited for the robot to stomp away with the special prefect in tow then she blew out another sigh and pressed her hands to her hips.

"Are you okay to take yourself to the infirmary?" his mentor said, looking deflated. "As you can see, I have another matter to attend to."

"They're still testing you, even after all this time, and after all the trials you've been a part of?" Finn asked.

"Like I told you, we're not one of them, Finn, and we never will be," Elara replied. She patted him on the arm and smiled; it was the closest to a "well done" he'd gotten from his mentor, and it felt good. "I'll come and find you later, okay?"

Finn nodded and smiled. "Okay."

Elara headed off down an adjacent corridor and Finn waited until she was out of sight before turning to the two medical robots that were following him like lost puppies.

"You two can buzz off," Finn said. He had no intention of being poked and prodded by the machines. "I'll sort myself out, thanks."

"But we have been instructed to give you medical attention," the foremost of the two machines said.

"Do you have any painkillers on you?"

The robot's metal eyebrows twisted into a scowl. "Yes, but..."

"And do you have some disinfectant and dressings?" Finn said, cutting across the machine.

"Yes, but..."

"Then just give me those and get lost," Finn said, again cutting the robot short. "That will fulfill your directive of giving me medical attention."

The robot turned to its companion who merely shrugged and for a second or two the machines conversed in the silent language of data transference. Finn could practically hear the transistors fizzing inside their electronic logic processors. Then a compartment opened in the center of the lead robot, and the machine held out a tray containing painkiller tablets, ointments and dressings.

"Are you certain that you would not like us to apply these dressings?" the robot asked.

"I'm certain, thanks," Finn said, snatching the tray then

flipping the compartment shut with the back of his hand. "Good job guys, you can go now."

The machines frowned at one another but it seemed clear that the situation was not one they had been programmed to handle, and thus defeated they trundled away. *At least I won that battle...* Finn thought, before turning on his heels and heading in the opposite direction, towards what he thought was his apartment. However, after five minutes of walking up and down corridors that all looked the same, he realized he was lost.

"Shit, I was sure my apartment was down here," he muttered.

"It is."

Finn's heart leapt and he turned to see Juniper Jones standing behind him, hands pressed together in front of her bare midriff. The suit she was wearing was another new cut, more revealing than the last, including the golden crop top that showed the tanned skin of her stomach.

"My God, what happened?" Juniper said.

While Finn had been distracted by his paramour's tailored flawlessness, it seemed that Juniper had also washed her eyes over him, though what she'd seen was clearly far less appealing. She ran to him and began pawing over his torn and bloodied jumpsuit and delicately touching his face, turning it gently from one side to the other to look at the wounds. Then she saw the tray with its meagre contents and she shook her head.

"This just won't do," Juniper said, taking the tray from him. "Go back to your room and lie down, I'll be back soon." She hurried away then hesitated and turned back. "Your apartment is next right, fourth door on the right," she added, before leaving for good.

Finn was grateful for the directions, though he'd wished his paramour had left the tray of first aid items, but she'd snatched it away and vanished before his pain-addled mind could interject. Hobbling along the corridor, he followed Juniper's instructions and found his apartment, though it took four attempts for the door to recognize his thumb pattern. Stealing inside, he loped through his plush apartment and collapsed on the bed, which had been neatly made-up by the cleaning robot during his absence.

"Ouch-ouch!"

From the flat of his back, Finn couldn't see Scraps but then he heard the whir of the robot's rotors and within seconds the machine had landed on his chest.

"Finn hurt!" the robot said, little hands pressed to his head in shock and confusion.

"It's okay, buddy, it looks worse than it is," Finn said, though he didn't actually know this for a fact. "But I could use a few pints of Metalhaven beer to numb the pain."

He laughed at his own joke and shooting agony paralyzed his body, compelling his eyes to shut and making him hiss air through his teeth like a punctured tire.

"Seriously, you should see the other guy," Finn added, repeating the joke comment he'd made to Elara earlier, knowing that Scraps would find it funny too.

"Finn tough!" Scraps laughed, flexing his non-existent biceps. "Finn good fighter!"

"You'd better believe it!" Finn replied, patting his robot's head.

Putting on a brave face was not just a macho reaction.

Everyone in Metalhaven, man or woman, talked down any injuries sustained during a fight. It was simply part of bar-brawl etiquette.

The door chime sounded and Finn managed to wheeze the word, "enter" just loud enough for the sensor to pick up his voice. The door swooshed open and Juniper breezed inside, carrying a heavy-looking black case, instead of the tray she'd taken from him. He tried to get up but had barely lifted his shoulders off the newly-blood-stained satin sheets before his paramour had slid onto the bed beside him and pushed him down again.

"Stay there and let me tend to these injuries," Juniper said, clicking open the latches on the box, which was also now on the bed beside him. "And no complaining. I know how stubborn you can be."

Finn scowled at her. "I'm not stubborn," he protested.

Scraps laughed heartily at this, which swept the rug out from beneath his argument in one fell swoop. He considered fighting his corner but he'd done enough fighting for one day and so simply relaxed on the bed and let Juniper work. He didn't feel a thing as his paramour cleaned, stapled and bandaged his wounds with as much skill and attention as any medical robot, and with a far more agreeable bedside manner too. Then he noticed a used injector resting on the lid of the medkit with an empty phial of painkiller still inside it. She'd administered the jab without him even noticing.

"I didn't know you were also a trained medic," Finn said, already feeling a thousand times better, most likely due to the drugs flowing through his bloodstream. He smiled at her. "Is there anything you can't do?"

Juniper smiled right back at him, which was a more

effective tonic than anything her medical kit might have contained to soothe his body's weary muscles.

"I'm sure there must be, but honestly nothing comes to mind," she replied, playfully.

Juniper continued to work for several minutes until every cut, bruise, scratch and bite on his body had been tended to and the blood was wiped from his skin. He sat up and saw that she'd also cut away sections of his training uniform, making it look as though he'd been set upon by a swarm of giant moths. Then he noticed the Finn Brasa-shaped bloody mark that had been left behind on his sheets and winced.

"I don't suppose this apartment has built-in laundry facilities?" he said, rubbing at the stain, but it was already ingrained and mostly dry.

"Yes, it's called the cleaner robot," Juniper replied, clicking the fasteners shut on the medical kit. "I'll notify housekeeping, so just throw the whole lot on the floor in the corner, and it'll be taken care of."

"Thanks, Juniper, what would I do without you?" Finn said.

"Let me think..." Juniper pressed a manicured finger to the corner of her mouth in a contemplative pose. "Probably bleed out and die?" she said.

They both laughed and it felt natural. Then she leaned in and kissed him gently on the lips, which took Finn by surprise and he recoiled from her.

"I'm sorry, I didn't mean to startle you," Juniper said, head tilted down.

"No, it's okay, really," Finn replied. He could still taste the kiss, a hint of raspberry and vanilla from her lipstick. "I just wasn't expecting it."

She looked up and inched closer but Finn slid off the bed and walked toward the door, knowing that if he stayed and let her kiss him again it would progress to something more. He liked Juniper and found that he liked her more each day, but she had still been assigned to him as a paramour, and he struggled to believe that whatever was happening between them was entirely organic. Elara's warning sounded in his mind. *She's still a part of the system. Remember that...*

"I should probably shower and get changed," Finn said, rapidly changing the subject. "I don't think Chief Prosecutor Voss will appreciate my current standard of attire."

Juniper slid off the bed and stood in her customary pose with her hands in front of her stomach. She was smiling but beneath it he was astute enough to tell that she had been hurt by his rejection.

"Yes, you're probably right," she said, though the brightness in her voice sounded more forced. "It seems that you are the talk of the town though."

Finn frowned. "Really? What have you heard?"

Juniper shrugged. "I only caught the back of a few whispered conversations as I collected the medical kit from the prosecutor's stores, but whatever you did to acquire those injuries made an impression, that's for sure."

"Good or bad?" Finn asked.

Juniper considered the question carefully before answering. "I'm not sure. They are not sure."

"Not sure about what?" Finn said.

Juniper again thought carefully before answering and Finn was left wondering why. *Was she trying to spare my feelings or was her caginess down to a fear of betraying the Authority?*

"They're not sure whether you are a problem," his paramour finally replied. "It seems that they underestimated you."

Finn laughed weakly. "Why wouldn't they? I'm a lowly chrome from Metalhaven."

Juniper shook her head. "That's not what I see when I look at you."

She took a step toward him but was careful not to come too close. Even so, Finn still felt like running.

"There's more decency in you than in any of the true-born golds," Juniper continued. "I've never been to Metalhaven, but if everyone there is like you, then it's a far richer place than this sector will ever be."

Finn laughed and Juniper looked at her feet. It seemed that no matter what he did, he couldn't fail to cause the woman distress.

"I wasn't laughing at you," Finn explained. "It's just that if you had seen Metalhaven, you'd know it's not rich with anything but sweat, toil and hardship."

"Who knows, perhaps one day, I will see it for myself," she replied, still looking at her feet.

"What does that mean?" Finn said. It was a strange answer, since there was no reason he could think of why Juniper would ever have cause to visit his old sector.

"Oh, nothing, I was just thinking out loud," Juniper said. It was accompanied by another forced smile, but she seemed agitated too. "I should let you shower and get changed."

She picked up the medkit and hurried to the door before Finn could stop her. He was about to press her further when the door slid open. He was conscious that the bug-killer devices Elara had planted in his room didn't extend into the hallway outside, and that he had to be more careful about what he said.

"I'll see you tomorrow, maybe?" Juniper said from the corridor outside his door. "Assuming you've healed up okay, that is. I'll check to make sure first."

She smiled again then the door whooshed shut leaving Finn alone in the middle of the room with his mouth open. He was used to pushing people away, which was why in his entire life only Owen, who had been as much a brother as a friend, had ever remained by his side, but the speed at which he'd turned Juniper against him was a record even by his standards.

"Juniper sad," Scraps said.

Finn hadn't noticed that his robot had flown onto the dining table and was standing with his little metal hands pressed to his oil-can hips.

"Yeah, and it's my fault, as usual," Finn said, pulling up a chair and sitting down. "I seem to have a knack of pissing people off and making them hate me."

"That not it," Scraps said, brushing off Finn's comment with a waft of his hand. The robot waddled closer and sat down facing him. "Her job go bad."

"But her job is me?" Finn replied.

"Yes-yes!" Scraps said.

Finn rubbed his temples. His head had started hurting again, but this time it was from stress rather than because of Walter's punches.

"But you just said I'm not the reason she's sad," Finn asked. "Which is it Scraps?"

Scraps thought for a moment, trying to piece together how best to explain what was fizzing around his modified

Foreman Logic Processor, but the door chime sounded before he could speak.

"Maybe she came back and I can just ask her myself?" Finn wondered.

He hurried to the door but the slab of metal whooshed back to reveal his mentor instead of his paramour.

"Expecting someone else?" Elara said, reacting to the look of disappointment on Finn's face.

"Yes. Well yes and no," Finn answered, unhelpfully.

Elara scowled then stepped inside without waiting to be invited and closed the door behind her. She looked at his bandages and stitches, all neatly tended to, and seemed impressed.

"Those robotic monstrosities actually did a good job on you," Elara said. She picked at his sliced-up uniform. "You'll need a change of clothes, though."

"I'm not really up for another bout of combat training just yet," Finn said.

He could have mentioned that Juniper had tended to his wounds instead of the robot medics but for some reason he chose not to.

"I just came to check on you, like I said I would," Elara said. "Oh, and my loyalty interview went fine, thanks for asking."

"Shit, I forgot, sorry." Finn cursed under his breath. It seemed that it was his day for pissing people off. "It's just been a bit of a whirlwind few hours."

His mentor appeared to accept his apology then scanned the room with her emerald eyes before they finally came to rest on his face, narrowing as they did so. She wiped a thumb across his bottom lip then tasted it.

"Why didn't you mention she was here?" Elara said, hot with anger. *Or was she jealous?*

"I didn't think it was relevant," Finn replied.

They stared into each other's eyes for a few seconds, neither one blinking. He didn't want another fight but it seemed that he was getting one whether he liked it or not.

"Be careful," Elara finally said, breaking the stalemate.

"I am," Finn replied. He was getting tired of being lectured. "Was there another reason you dropped by, or was that it?"

"As it happens, yes," his mentor said. "Tomorrow is a day off from training, because a trial is taking place, and we're all attending. Call it a field trip, if you like."

Finn didn't appreciate the dark humor since their field trip would involve innocent people being slaughtered, but he let it slide. He didn't want to stoke any more animosity.

"Where is this trial?" Finn asked.

Elara's eyes sharpened. "It's in Metalhaven. We're going home."

16

A PINT AND A FIGHT

THE SKYCAR FERRYING Finn and the other apprentices to the trial in Metalhaven passed over the perimeter wall of the Authority sector and it was like they had travelled into a war zone. After the clean streets and grand architecture, Finn was now staring down at narrow lanes covered in trash and dirty snow with grime-blackened mid-rises to either side, like claustrophobic prison walls. And this was just Makehaven, which by all accounts was one of the better work sectors, especially compared to Stonehaven and Metalhaven, which were known to be the hardest to survive in.

"Apparently, the trial is in reclamation yard one," Tonya said. She sat beside Ivan, hand on his thigh. "Anyone know what that means?"

"Who cares what it means?" Walter grunted, his powerful arms folded across his chest. The man's face still bore the bruises from their fight the day before. "They're all stinking chromes, so what does it matter which yard the trial is in?"

All the apprentices were travelling in a single skycar, while their mentors had their own transport. They sat three to a bench, with Tonya, Walter and Ivan on one side, and Zach, Sabrina and Finn opposite, though Zach had chosen to scrunch himself into the corner. The seating arrangements neatly summed them up as a group. Zach the loner, Ivan, Walter and Tonya thick-as-thieves, and Finn with an unlikely ally in the form of Sabrina, prefect honor graduate. If anyone had told him a few weeks earlier that he would be friendly with a prefect, he would have laughed in their face, yet here they all were.

"The yards are numbered according to how hazardous their contents are," Finn said. Walter hadn't asked, but he was going to educate the man whether he liked it or not. "Yard one is the most dangerous, since it contains salvaged nuclear-powered naval vessels, along with missiles and a ton of unexploded ordnance. If the radiation doesn't kill you then an unexploded bomb or landmine probably will."

"Sounds like a delightful place," Sabrina said. Her legs were crossed and her right foot was waggling, impatient for them to arrive. "It's a wonder they don't all blow themselves up."

"They do. Quite often, in fact," Finn replied. Then he looked at Walter again. "But people from Metalhaven are tough. They can handle a little danger."

"Which yard did you come from?" Tonya asked.

"I worked in yard seven, which was mostly old tanks, armored personnel carriers, and downed combat airplanes from the war," Finn replied. "There are thirteen yards in total."

"Seven?" Walter snorted. "So, not so tough then?"

Finn smiled and pointed to the bruise on Walter's cheek. "Tough enough, I'd say."

Walter unfurled his arms and tried to stand, but the seatbelt around his waist held the man firmly in place, and his attempt to rush Finn ended in comic failure. Sabrina laughed, which only enraged Walter more, then Ivan calmly spoke into his ally's ear, no doubt reassuring him that Finn would have his day, soon enough.

"It looks like a good crowd," Sabrina said, leaning across Finn so that she could look out of the window. Her hair smelled faintly of leather and mineral oil, like the back of an armored prefect car, but without the added stench of sweat and stale beer from that night's arrests. "Does anyone know who the prosecutors are?"

Ivan laughed and shook his head. "Death Echo is one of them. How can you not know that your own mentor is taking part in this trial?"

Sabrina sat back and shrugged. "I didn't ask, but it'll be good to see her in action again. It also means that you chumps can see how a real prosecutor operates."

The comment was issued with a playful smile, though for once neither Ivan nor Walter took the bait and jumped to the defense of their own mentors.

"Who is the other prosecutor?" Finn asked, hoping that it wasn't Elara. He had no desire to watch another trial, especially not one where the only person in the world that he trusted might end up getting killed.

"Frost is the other," Walter said, looking altogether too pleased at this fact. "My mentor will break a hundred and fifty kills today, the second highest kill total in prosecutor history."

"You must be very proud," Finn said, sarcastically.

"I am, why wouldn't I be?" Walter replied. "Are you not

proud of your mentor's achievements, like any true gold would be?"

Finn had spoken his acerbic reply without thinking and he had to remind himself to rein in his antagonistic urges. "Of course I am," Finn lied. He was getting better it. "But quantity isn't everything. The Shadow kills with style, whereas Frost is just a blunt instrument, like his apprentice."

"Sheesh!" Sabrina cut in, wafting her hand in front of her nose as if someone had just broken wind. "The smell of testosterone is getting a bit strong in here, so how about you boys save your dick measuring contest until we're on the ground and the doors have been opened?"

Tonya laughed and Finn did too. His years spent drinking in Metalhaven's recovery centers meant he was accustomed to crude humor and its ability to break the tension in almost any situation. Walter, however, was not amused, and sat with his arms folded for the remainder of the journey, which was mercifully short. Before long the skycar had touched down inside the local law enforcement hub, which was a short walk from the crucible. Finn could see that an entire street had been cleared of workers specifically so they could progress to the spectator stands without having to mingle with the great unwashed of Metalhaven.

"Welcome home, chromeboy," Sabrina said, slapping Finn on the backside unreasonably hard before skipping ahead. "Don't forget to come back after the trial, or I'd miss you," she added, blowing him a kiss, before winking and running over to her mentor, Death Echo, who was already in full prosecutor ensemble.

"No-one will miss you, worker scum," Ivan said, breezing

past and barging into him on purpose. "If you know what's good for you, you'll stay here, where you belong."

Tonya followed, practically arm-in-arm with Ivan, then Walter walked past and intentionally blanked him. Not that Finn minded. He'd rather be ignored than have to smile and put up with Walter constantly belittling his lowly origins, as the man had repeatedly done during their flight over. Despite this, Walter had failed to get a rise out of him, and Finn considered this another minor victory.

"Is it how you remember?"

Finn suddenly noticed that Elara stood waiting for him by the fence. Whether wearing her chameleonic armor or not, she had an incredible talent for sneaking up on people.

"I honestly didn't expect it to feel so strange," Finn admitted. "It feels colder here, even though we've only travelled a few miles, and the air smells different." He filled his nostrils with icy Metalhaven air and though the acerbic, smoky flavor was familiar, it was no longer what he was used to. Then he looked up and allowed the snow to gently caress his face. "Hell, even the sky looks different."

"Burned metal, ale and cigarettes," Elara said. She was also drinking in the atmosphere of her old home. "None of those exist in the Authority sector and you've gotten used to their absence."

Finn frowned then inhaled deeply again, and this time the perfume of strong, hoppy beer and powerful cigarettes was so obvious he couldn't believe that he hadn't noticed the first time.

"You're right!" he said, sucking in another lungful of Metalhaven air. "Shit, it makes me want a pint and a cigarette, and I never even used to smoke." He laughed and shook his head. "I used to berate Owen for smoking so much. I thought they would be the death of him, but…"

His voice trailed off in the hope that not finishing the sentence would help him to ignore the memory he'd inadvertently dredged up, but now all he could think about was sitting in a bar with Owen, drinking and talking shit.

"Keep that locked up, especially while you're here," Elara said. It was a cruelly unsympathetic reaction but he understood why she had chosen to be so unforgiving. "You're a gold now, and you need to act like it. Make no mistake, this is a test. Everyone will be watching you."

"I understand," Finn said, resolutely. "It's just hard not to be reminded of him, especially here."

Finn took another look at the grimy buildings outside the razor-wired fence that surrounded the law enforcement hub and watched the even shabbier workers of yard one shamble toward the public viewing areas and recovery centers in readiness to watch the trial. Many of them were already dead on their feet from a hard day's toil, while others were clustered into groups, swaying from one side of the road to the other in a drunken perambulation, fueled by beer and cigarettes, the smell of which Finn now couldn't get out of his head.

"So what happens next?" Finn asked, turning back to his mentor. "Is it champagne and canapés in the VIP area?"

He was making a joke but the look on Elara's face suggested that he'd hit the mark pretty much dead on.

"Shit, really?" Finn said, and Elara nodded, still unsympathetic. "Can't I just loiter outside the VIP area until the trial starts?"

"Why would you want to do that?" Elara asked.

Finn shrugged. His reason had been to avoid having to politely rub shoulders with obnoxious VIPs, but now that he thought about it, he liked the idea of seeing his old sector one last time.

"I never got a chance to say goodbye to Metalhaven, before I was whisked away to the prosecutor barracks and dumped in front of you," Finn said. "I can't say that I have any real love for this place, but it wasn't all bad. There were good people here. Honest folk."

Elara nodded, and naturally she understood. "There's technically no law against a gold walking around one of the work sectors, it's just that no-one would ever want to," she replied. "It would be like choosing to wade through a rat-infested garbage heap instead of walking across a bridge."

Finn scowled at his mentor. "Is that how you see us now? Rats in a garbage heap?"

"It's how the golds see all workers," Elara answered. "And you keep forgetting that you're not one of them, anymore, Finn. You're a gold and that's how everyone here will see you. If you're hoping to be welcomed back with open arms, you can forget about it."

"I don't expect that," Finn said. He was still working through his reasons in his own mind, but the urge to see his old home remained strong. "I don't know what it is. Maybe, I just want to make my peace with this place. Does that make sense?"

"Prosecutor Cage, a moment, please?"

Chief Prosecutor Voss was waiting by the gate leading out of the enforcement hub. He was with Metalhaven Head Prefect, Captain Viktor Roth, a man whom Finn had no desire to speak to again. Even the sight of the sadistic officer made his blood boil. Then he spotted the scar on the man's face that he had caused and was reminded of the fact that Roth likely wasn't overjoyed to see him again, either.

"Make your peace but stay in the designated VIP areas and try to behave like a gold," Elara said. "We can't afford you to fuck things up, not here. Do you understand me?"

The harsh dressing down from his mentor stunned Finn into silence and Elara was gone before he'd recovered enough to speak. Then he realized he was the only one left in the law enforcement hub and was compelled to move because of an intrinsic fear he might be arrested for loitering. The road to the VIP area had been swept of snow and trash and lined on either side with an eight-foot, razor-wire-edged fence to keep the workers out. Most had already made their way to the crucible or to their local recovery center so there were few people on the streets, and those that were out and about were careful not to look at him. His gilt-trimmed uniform singled him out as a member of the Authority, and unlike himself when he was a chrome, few Metalhaven workers would risk invoking the wrath of the Prefecture for the crime of looking at a gold the wrong way.

Soon he could hear the musical chink of crystal glasses and smell the canapés being served beneath the heated marquee where the VIPs had assembled, and he stopped dead in the middle of the road. Despite the delicious smell of the food, his stomach turned at the idea of making merry with the Zavetgrad aristocracy, while twelves workers waited to be executed in the arena. He contemplated turning back and waiting in the skycar until the trial began when he noticed that a section of razor-wire was missing from the fence to his right. Beyond it was a narrow street that led to the back of a recovery center. He could see the beer barrels piled up in the courtyard.

Don't do it, Finn... he told himself, as the kernel of an idea germinated in his mind. *Listen to your mentor and behave...* He knew it was a bad idea, but at the same time, he knew he was going to do it, anyway. Wrapping his fingers through the wire mesh, Finn scaled the eight-foot fence with ease and dropped down into the trash-covered street on the other side without making a sound. Approaching the rear courtyard of the recovery center, he found a jacket slung onto a pile of empty barrels, left there by a worker who had likely stripped it off while toiling to unload the mass quantity of beer needed to fuel a trial-night bender. He pulled it on and it stank of stale sweat, ale and cigarettes. The smells of his old home.

The back door was open and he stole up to it and peeked inside, but the recovery center was full to bursting and so busy that he could have danced naked and none of the staff would have noticed him. Sneaking inside, he worked his way around the bar and into the main saloon, squeezing past other workers, who were either heading to their tables, pints in hand, or heading to the bar for refills. No-one gave him a second look. *Why would they?* he mused. Besides a prefect, no gold would ever been seen dead inside a recovery center. To the patrons of the bar, he was simply one of them.

Resting against the far edge of the counter, Finn pressed his back to the bar and watched as a few good-natured brawls kicked off. It was nothing serious, just the standard post-shift 'pint and a fight' that every Metalhaven worker enjoyed, some more than others. The TVs were already tuned into the trial channel, where the commentary and analysis teams were running through the stats for Death Echo and Frost. There were good odds on Frost achieving the second highest kill total in history, and had Owen been with him, he had no doubt his friend would have bet heavily on a successful outcome. The giveaways had also started and for those willing to brave the crushing crowds and icy evening air, the opportunity to win beer and cigarette chits, and even time off work, was too good to miss. It was all crushingly familiar to him and he both loved it and despised it in equal measure.

"You want a beer, mate?" a man said.

Finn turned to the worker, who was an old hand by Metalhaven standards, probably thirty-five, though he looked sixty.

"Here, have a beer, and fag too," the man continued, not waiting for Finn to answer. "I scored me some extra chits in a giveaway earlier, so I'm feeling flush!"

"Thanks, pal," Finn said, accepting the drink and the cigarette, which the man lit for him. The drink was ice cold and deathly strong while the cigarette made his head rush, as if he'd just stood up too quickly.

"Who are you bettin' on?" the man said, nodding toward one of the TVs. "That Frost guy is a right bastard, but everyone is bettin' on him, so I'm banking on Death Echo to make the first kill. Long odds, but if I'm right, then I get four hours off work. Think of that! Four whole fucking hours extra I can stay in bed!"

The man laughed and Finn laughed along with him, then they chinked glasses and Finn downed half of the pint in one go. It was delicious and revolting, brain-numbing and invigorating all at once, but most of all it tasted of home. Suddenly, he was jolted and he spilled some of his beer onto the sleeve of a man to his left. The worker swore bitterly and shook his arm, spraying some of the spilled liquid into Finn face and eyes.

"Oi, watch what you're doing!" the man said. He was a lot younger than the old hand, maybe only twenty-two, but the scars on his face suggested he'd already survived a number of close shaves with death. "You clumsy fuck, I'm soaking wet!"

"Sorry, pal, my mistake," Finn said, accepting the blame even though it wasn't his fault.

"Yeah? Well, you fucking will be soon!" the man said, getting up in Finn's face.

"Calm down," Finn growled, shoving the man back then pointing a finger at him. "Don't be a fool. Just walk away and enjoy your drink."

The man already had backup in the form of two other guys, both as young and scarred as the agitator was.

"No-one calls me a fool and gets away with it!" the man roared, surging forward, fists flying, but his punches were so telegraphed that Finn could have counted to three and still avoided them. Embarrassed, the worker swung at him again but Finn blocked then jabbed the man in the nose, drawing blood.

"That's enough!" Finn yelled. *A pint and a fight. Just like old times...* "Go back to your seat before I put you on your ass."

Their scuffle had drawn a little crowd, as bar fights of this sort always did. Instead of the trial, people were now betting on whether the worker, who was apparently called Dave, would even be able to land a punch on the stranger. The trio then came at him in unison, and Dave's accomplices grabbed his coat sleeves, intending to hold him while the third man unloaded punches, but Finn was wise to this tactic, and slipped out of the coat before the ploy could be executed. A swift right hook felled one accomplice and an uppercut knocked Dave onto his ass, just as Finn had promised, before the third member of the trio held up his hands in submission.

"Fair play, mate!" the surviving member said, backing away. "No worries! My mistake!"

Finn popped him on the nose anyway, and the man went crashing through a table, sending half-drunk pints flying. A cheer went up from the crowd but it was quickly silenced as the baying throng saw the glint of gold on his uniform.

"Fuck, he's a gold!" someone shouted, and there was a swell toward the exit.

"Hang on, I know you!" someone else said. "That's not just any gold, it's Finn fucking Brasa!"

The mass exodus stopped and suddenly everyone in the recovery center was staring at him.

"Hey, you're the Hero of Metalhaven!" the old hand who'd bought him the beer said. "You're him, aren't you? You're Finn Brasa."

Finn considered lying and he considered vaulting the bar and fleeing, but in the end he simply nodded and shrugged and said, "Yes."

The old hand then raised his arms and the bar quietened down. "It's only the Hero of Metalhaven, drinking in our bar!"

The room erupted into raucous cheers and chants of "Bra-sa! Bra-sa!", and Finn was jostled and jockeyed from all sides, as people rushed in to shake his hand. Questions and compliments were fired at him too fast to answer. *How did it feel to knock-out Bloodletter? How did you know where the weapons stash was? Did it feel good to fuck over the Authority? What happened to the girl from Spacehaven? My mate said she got out? Did she get out?* Then they all stopped cheering his name and chants of "Metal and Blood!, Metal and Blood!" rose up, so loud that Finn thought the windows would blow out.

Suddenly, the doors were flung open and prefects burst inside the room, demanding that the chant be stopped. From feeling positively euphoric, Finn suddenly realized the trouble he'd inadvertently caused, and he knew he had to get out. If he was seen then the prefects would assume it was him inciting sedition against the Authority, and Voss and the Regents would have all the reason they needed to execute him and be done with the troublesome false gold. He tried to climb over the bar, but the swelling crowd made it impossible. The chants of "Metal and Blood!" continued over the crackle of electrified nightsticks and the thump of fists and table legs slamming into prefect armor. It wasn't just a fight. It was a riot.

Finn didn't know which way to turn when he was grabbed and pulled through a side door, which was rapidly slammed shut behind him. A single incandescent bulb above his head illuminated the face of Elara, one half in sharp relief and the other in shadow.

"What did I tell you?" Elara shouted, shoving him hard in the chest. "I told you to stay out of the sector. I told you not to fuck things up, and yet here you are?"

"I'm sorry," Finn said, at a loss for anything better to say. "I didn't think anyone would notice me."

More prefects were piling into the bar and Finn could hear the sound of armored ground cars rolling up outside.

Elara grabbed his arm and dragged him through the corridor and out of another door that opened into a back street, close to where he had snuck into the recovery center in the first place. Still pulling him along behind her, she lifted up a section of fence and ducked under it, practically dragging Finn through after her, before resetting the fence and smoothing down her uniform. Prefects began rushing into the side streets and climbing into the courtyard to enter the bar from the rear. Finn could already see workers being beaten and thrown into waiting ground car as two more vehicles drew up to cart away other rabble-rousers. Despite the ruckus, the chant of "Metal and Blood!" was still being sung loudly.

"You were right, Elara," Finn said. He knew he'd screwed up but being in the recovery center and seeing how the workers looked at him had been a revelation. "These people see me as a symbol of hope, maybe even rebellion." He turned to his mentor and held her shoulders tightly. "I'm something to these people, Elara. Maybe I *can* help them after all?"

"That's what I've been telling you!" Elara shrugged him off and for a second he thought she was going to reach for her dagger. "But you can't help them from inside the city, and you sure as hell can't help them if you're dead!"

She turned her back on him and kicked a loose stone across the road, hands pressed to the back of her head. He'd never seen her so angry and it made him feel like shit.

"The Authority knows you're a danger to them, Finn, they've known it all along," Elara said, turning back to him, her anger barely contained. "And the only reason they haven't executed you is because it would make you a martyr. Better to turn you into one of them, if they can, but make no mistake, if they start to see you as a figurehead for rebellion, they'll put a bullet in your brain, and you'll never see it coming."

Finn didn't know what to say so he simply said nothing. He'd screwed up enough for one day.

"Come on, I can get us back to the VIP area without being seen," Elara said. She took his wrist and was about to lead him away, when she stopped and looked into his eyes, but it wasn't Elara Cage staring at him, it was The Shadow.

"Disobey me again... put *me* at risk again... and we're done, do you understand?"

Finn swallowed hard and nodded. "I understand."

17

DEAR DIARY

Training Week Nine, Tuesday.
Personal Diary – Encrypted (Scraps Cipher V3)

IT'S BEEN MORE than two months since I arrived in the Authority sector and began my training to become a prosecutor of Zavetgrad. I very nearly didn't make it past the first week thanks to my stupid stunt at the trial in yard one. If Elara hadn't rescued me from that recovery center when she did then maybe my head would still be rotting on a pike in the central square, and hers would have been right alongside it. Since then, I've kept my nose clean, done what Elara tells me to do, and been a good little gold. And the training is going well. So well that, in a few short weeks, I'll undertake my test trial and hopefully get out of this godforsaken place.

In some ways, I'll miss the barracks, though I feel nauseous for admitting that. I like the daily routine, and learning how to use different weapons and equipment, and I like the physical training too. Working in the reclamation yards made me hard, but thanks to the regular gym work and assault courses, not to mention the food, I can see and feel my body getting stronger every day. Something tells me I'll need the extra fitness and stamina for what's still to come.

My relationships, if that's even the right word to describe my association with the other apprentices, have improved in some ways and worsened in others, but generally I'm tolerated now. I'm like sensitive teeth – persistent, often annoying, but generally nothing to get too worked up about.

Sabrina and I continue on good terms, though she still teases me mercilessly and refuses to stop calling me 'chromeboy', despite her promises. I've gotten used to it, and to her, and she's the closest thing I have in this place to a genuine friend. Elara doesn't count, since she's my mentor and in many ways my protector, and Juniper doesn't count either because... Well, because that's complicated.

Tonya largely tolerates me, and is friendly enough when Ivan isn't around, but as soon as those two get together, she changes to reflect the Regent Successor's mood. If Ivan is a dick to me then she's a dick to me. If he ignores me, she ignores me. It's sad, really, but I've come to expect it.

Walter has gotten worse. I thought I might have earned some respect from standing toe-to-toe with that meathead but it's only made him bitter and more resentful of me. The fact I've also gotten stronger and more skilled means that I'm more capable than ever of holding my own against him. I can see that he's desperate to put me down, to dominate me and prove to everyone, especially himself, that his pure-bred status matters, but I won't let him beat me.

Then there's Zach, who is even more of an outsider than I

am. He rarely speaks and the others don't try to engage him, but from time-to-time, I've managed to spark up a conversation with the man, even if only for a few seconds. He's a dark one, that's for sure, only interested in learning better and more efficient ways to kill. Training with him is like juggling a live grenade and hoping to God that you don't accidentally pull the pin. At least once or twice every week, Zach's darkness has gotten the better of him, as if there's a demon inside him that takes control, but the prosecutors are wise to it now, and a situation like what happened with Tonya hasn't been repeated. I can see the desire to kill in Zach's eyes and it terrifies me. I've seen similar looks in the eyes of prefects as they beat workers to death in the streets then laughed and joked about it afterwards. The difference is that Zach doesn't hurt people for fun, but for some other reason. I'd like to say I wish I knew what that was but I suspect I'm better off not knowing. It would be like glimpsing Cthulhu and being driven insane due to its incomprehensible and overwhelming unknowability.

Thankfully, I'm much better with tasks than I am with people, and regularly come first or second in the assault course challenges that round off each week of training, much to the annoyance of Ivan in particular. It's usually either me or Walter who comes first, depending on how Chief Prosecutor Voss has set out the course for that week. Sometimes, he favors agility over power and stamina, and that's when Sabrina does well. She's usually third or fourth. Walter still tries to trip me up or cheat me out of victory in some other way, but I'm wise to his tricks and that pisses him off. We come to blows most weeks and it's always Walter who instigates, and always Voss who lets him get away with it, chalking it up to mere 'spirited competition'. What a bunch of self-serving hypocrites. If it was me that started the fight, you can bet your ass that Voss would reprimand me and give Elara a hard time for not controlling her apprentice.

Of all the training sessions, weapons training continues to be my weakest area. I think it's understandable given that the other apprentices have been learning martial arts since they were kids, but according to Voss, I simply don't apply myself correctly to the task. What a dick. I'm beginning to hate Voss more than anyone, Walter included, and that's saying something! I still look forward to weapons training, though, because more than any other session, it highlights the sort of prosecutor that each of us is becoming. Our choice of weapons and combat styles play into the 'personas' that everyone has been developing, like acting students learning new roles.

Walter is following in Frost's footsteps, focusing on brutality, power and intimidation. He stuck with the warhammer that he almost killed me with, but instead of a bow he now uses javelins as his ranged weapon. At first I thought this was a dumb move, since they have limited range and even Walter can't carry more than five or six, but that meathead can throw a spear like a Greek god. I'm sure it will be a crowd pleaser when he finally skewers someone for real inside the crucible.

Ivan has been honing his skill and finesse with pistol and sword and is leaning heavily into his aristocratic background. I remember reading The Three Musketeers by Alexander Dumas on my illegal data device, and I can't help but think of Ivan as a King's Musketeer from seventeenth century France.

However, I suspect he would serve Cardinal Richelieu rather than Louis XIII.

Sabrina has cleverly harnessed her speed and agility and molded those attributes into a predator persona, like a jaguar or cheetah. She still uses a crossbow pistol but prefers to set traps that allow her to get close enough to kill with her Sai, which she wields with mesmerizing skill. Like Walter and his javelins, I'm sure she'll be a crowd pleaser.

No doubt encouraged by Ivan, Tonya has also leaned into her heritage and created a persona as a Celtic warrior. Personally, I doubt she actually has any ancestors from Scotland but with her fiery red hair and dirk daggers, she certainly looks the part. The only change to her weaponry is the addition of a hunting rifle for ranged combat, which I argued didn't really fit her character, but she's terrible with a bow and so my opinion was dismissed.

Then there's Zach and the less said about his 'persona' the better. He favors weapons that maim rather than kill, but his choice of a garrote for close-quarters fighting was too gruesome even for his mentor to allow. I heard the prosecutors talking one afternoon, and they're concerned that Zach is simply too barbaric, and that his style of killing will make for poor TV. Whenever I start to forget what I'm actually training for, it's moments like those that snap me back and make me want to tear down the Authority all the more.

As for myself, I've stuck with my laser cannon and baseball bat, much to the amusement of the other apprentices, who consider my choices as crude and unsophisticated as I am. They don't really know what to make of me and I like it that way. I like being the outsider on the inside, because that's who I am. Besides, Elara approves of my choice of weapons, and that's all I care about. If she's happy then I'm happy. Ivan, Walter, Voss... they can all go to hell.

Soon, they'll give us our prosecutor names and assign us the tailor-made weapons, equipment and armor that we'll become synonymous with. I have no idea what they'll make me look like or what they'll call me and I'm not looking forward to finding out.

Outside of training, my life is no less interesting and challenging. Pritchard continues to be annoying but well-meaning and in truth I'd be lost without his help. I also happen to like the guy, which is perhaps the most surprising development of all. I never thought I'd meet a gold I didn't hate but there he is. I'd like to think there are more people like Pritchard in the Authority sector but the cynical side of me doubts it. He's a better man than me, that's for damned sure. He does anything and everything to make my life better, and he does it with a smile. I've never even asked him his first name. Does he have a wife? Kids? I have no clue. Shit, sometimes I wonder if I'm really any better than a gold.

Then there's Juniper Jones... Man, what do I say about her? She's funny and charming and beautiful, and on top of all that she seems to actually like me. Other guys walk past us on our 'dates' in the cultural quarter, all more handsome and better-dressed than me, but she doesn't even look at them. When we're together, I'm her entire world and that's more intoxicating than drugs. Sure, it could all be an act but I'd like to think I'm sharp enough to tell the difference. Or maybe I'm just like every other guy, blinded by good looks and attention.

Well, almost. Eleven weeks in and we still haven't slept together, not that she hasn't tried and not that I haven't wanted to. Man, have I wanted to... But every time my resolve weakens, Elara seems to notice and reins me back in and reminds me to trust no-one but her. I know she's been watching my paramour, and checking into her, but after eleven weeks there's still no suggestion that Juniper Jones is anything other than what she says she is. She's just a bronze working as a paramour to pay for genetic corrective surgery that will allow her to book passage to the Nimbus Space Citadel. I'm a means to an end, and I need to remember that.

Even so, the look on Juniper's face when I spurn her advances kills me every time. I don't like hurting her, because I enjoy her company and I miss her when she's not around. I sometimes wonder if it's love, but honestly, how would I know? Chromes from Metalhaven don't get to experience love. And even if I was in love with Juniper, it wouldn't make a difference. Elara is right that I have to stay detached. I almost ruined everything with my stunt in the recovery center, and that wasn't the first time I put her and myself in danger. I won't do that again. I won't risk her life. She means more to me than anything, and I'd rather die than be the cause of her discovery and capture.

If that wasn't already enough drama for one week then there are the regular interrogations conducted by the Special Prefect branch to test my loyalty and determine whether I'm truly gold. It's the worst part of my week by a long distance. I'd rather suffer Ivan's scorn and derision for the rest of my life than have to endure more painful, personal questions from that fucking evaluator robot. I swear that one day I'll rip its square head off its shiny neck and pummel its logic processor to dust with my bare fists.

The line of questioning never changes, always picking on my past transgressions and highlighting my many slights against the Authority, and I always give it the same damned answers. It doesn't matter what I say or how well I lie, that piece-of-shit robot always ranks me as an eighteen-carat gold and stamps my paper file, 'Under suspicion'. I fucking hate that robot.

Then last week they went easy on me and I thought the worst of it was over, but the bastards were just trying to lull me into a false sense of security. The next session was brutal and though they didn't physically beat me, I walked out of room 616 on shaking legs, feeling like my brain had turned to mush. I almost broke at the end of week eight and told them everything, but Elara pulled me back, like she always does.

You see, they'd figured out that Owen is my Achilles' heel and they used his death as a lever to apply unbearable pressure. Every time I think I'm over his death, it hits me again like a tidal wave. The guilt. The shame. I remember why I'm alive and he's not. Sometimes I'll lie awake at night thinking about what I could have done differently to save him. I confide in my mentor and she gives me the tough love that I need, but despite this she's not heartless and I see glimpses of the old Elara Cage from Metalhaven. When they shine through it's like she's a different person. I like that person. A lot.

It makes me wonder how she knows about dealing with loss. Did she lose someone when she left Metalhaven? I ask her but she avoids my questions and just says that what she lost was her 'soul'

– the person who she was. I get what she means. Elara chose to become a gold by winning her trial, and it cost her everything. That's what she says, anyway, but I don't believe it, not fully. I know the old Elara is still in there, somewhere. But after all the people she's killed, is there ever a way back for her? Does she even deserve it? Selfishly, I'd like to think so because that old Elara Cage from Metalhaven is someone I'd like to know better.

Scraps suddenly bleeped an alert and Finn blinked his bleary eyes and stopped dictating his diary to the machine.

"Time-time..." Scraps said, tapping his little wrist where a little watch would be. "Finn sleep."

Finn scowled at his robot then at the clock on his bedside, which read 02:03. "Shit, I guess time got away from me, huh?" Finn said, patting his robot on the head. "Thanks, Scraps."

"Scraps end recording and save?" the robot asked.

"Yes, pal," he replied, yawning. "Everything is fully encrypted, right? No-one other than me can access these recordings."

Scraps nodded. "Encrypted, yes-yes!"

Reassured, Finn plumped up his pillow then shuffled under the covers and wriggled to get comfortable, causing Scraps to giggle as he bounced around on the bed. He was about to turn out the light when the little robot jumped onto his chest and looked at him with curious eyes.

"Finn-Finn?"

"Yes, pal," he replied.

"Elara not lady-bad-man no more," Scraps said. "Elara good. I like!"

Finn laughed and the robot bobbed up and down again, giggling.

"Yes, pal, I like her too," Finn said.

He reached over and turned out the light but his mind was still racing and sleep didn't claim him for another two hours.

18

ANOTHER WOMAN

FINN TURNED the ornate brass handle to shut off his shower then stepped out onto heated floor of his bathroom and grabbed a cotton towel that was so soft it practically melted in his hands. The day's training had been rough but nothing he wasn't used to, and despite the fresh bruises on his skin, he felt good.

"Ouch-ouch?" Scraps asked, pointing to a mark on Finn's shoulder.

"Nah, it's okay," Finn said, though he admitted the graze looked pretty gnarly. "I'll put some of that healing ointment that Juniper gave me on it."

Scraps nodded then flew outside and returned a moment later with the jar held in his hands. The robot placed it next to the sink then sat on the toilet cistern and smiled at him.

"Thanks, pal," Finn said.

He opened the lid then dug his fingers into the jar, scooping out a generous amount of the medicated ointment before applying it liberally to his new wounds. The ointment smelled like Juniper's hair, which Finn knew she'd done on purpose to ensure he was reminded of her at every possible opportunity.

The door chime sounded and Finn wrapped the towel around his waist then went to fetch the fresh training uniform that was hanging from the back of the door. Checking the computer screen built into the garment's wrist, he saw that he wasn't due to meet with his paramour for another thirty minutes.

"She's keen today," Finn said.

"Not Juniper," Scraps replied. Finn hadn't intended his comment for Scraps, but the little robot had answered anyway.

"Then who is it?" Finn asked.

Scraps' eyes lit up and he threw his hands into the air in celebration. "Elara-good!"

"Really?" Finn said, heading out into the lounge, still only wearing a towel. "I only left her ten minutes ago."

Scraps shrugged and Finn called for the door to open, which it did with a customary 'whoosh'. Elara walked in, casually at first, before stopping dead as the sopping wet, half-naked form of Finn Brasa confronted her.

"Aren't you forgetting something?" Elara said, folding her arms. "Like pants, for example?"

"I haven't forgotten them, I just haven't put them on yet," Finn replied. "Someone rudely interrupted me, you see…"

Elara raised an eyebrow at him then sat on the arm of his sofa and gestured toward his bathroom. "Please, don't let me stop you," she said.

"It's okay, I'm good like this," Finn replied, smiling. "I like how it makes you squirm."

"I'm not squirming," his mentor said, also smiling. "I am, however, a little nauseous…"

"Fine…" Finn laughed, relenting and returning to his bathroom to get dressed. "But if you ask me, I think you're just intimidated by my new, chiseled physique."

"I didn't ask," Elara called out. "And I already told that I'm nauseated, not intimidated."

Over the weeks, he and Elara had developed a strong rapport as mentor and apprentice, but their relationship had also mellowed and they had grown accustomed to one another's company. He wouldn't quite call them friends, since their association was still formal in nature, but Elara was much more than just a colleague, and he cared about her.

"Was there a reason you dropped by?" Finn asked, pulling on his training uniform. "I'd have thought you'd had enough of me for one day."

"I have, especially after seeing you in a towel, but this is important," Elara replied.

Finn recognized that her tone had become more earnest and he hurried getting dressed so he could hear what she had to say. "What's up?" he asked, heading back into the lounge, arms folded and brow furrowed.

"The test trial has been moved up to tomorrow," Elara replied, getting straight to it.

"Tomorrow? But we're not due to finish training for almost four weeks."

"I know, but this happens sometimes," his mentor said, with a fatalistic air. "It's tradition that the Mayor watches the test trials of each new prosecutor intake, and his schedule has been forced to change."

Finn shuddered at the mention of the Mayor of

Zavetgrad, a position that was currently occupied by Maxim Volkov, Regent of Spacehaven and Ivan Volkov's father.

"Volkov divides his time between here and Nimbus," Elara explained. "He was due to travel in four weeks, just after the trial, but because of a changing long-range weather forecast, the launch has been set for tomorrow night instead. Volkov won't be back for another three months, which means the trial has to be moved up too."

Finn puffed out his cheeks and blew a sigh. It was a shock but in some ways it was also a relief because it meant that he was getting out sooner. Then he had a terrible thought.

"Will the Metals be ready to spring me out by tomorrow?" Finn asked.

Their plan hinged around escaping through a disused drainage tunnel system in the Seahaven sub-sector, but if the test trial had been moved up, the plan might have to change.

"Word has already been sent and they'll be there," Elara said, putting his mind at ease. "The plan hasn't changed, just the timescale."

Finn nodded. He felt nervous but also excited and his stomach fluttered. Perhaps noticing his anxiety, Elara moved closer and held his shoulders. Her grip was pincer-tight against his fresh bruises but he didn't show any pain. He'd gotten used to hiding it.

"You're ready for this," Elara said, confidently. "Everything will go according to plan, and by this time tomorrow, you'll be in Haven, drinking a cold beer."

Finn laughed, though while his mentor had painted a pleasant fiction, it was missing one key element. "But you'll still be stuck here," he said, dryly.

"Yes," Elara said, not trying to sugarcoat that fact. "But that's the plan and we stick to it, okay?"

Finn sighed again and nodded. "Okay."

Elara's wrist-computer chirruped an alert and Finn saw that it was a message from Voss to all prosecutors, calling them to his office for a meeting.

"Duty calls," Elara said, releasing him and smiling. "I'll see you tomorrow."

"Not if I see you first," Finn replied, hammily, and he was pleased to get a polite laugh from his mentor.

Elara left and he suddenly felt very alone. He looked for Scraps and noticed that his robot was peeking out from behind the bathroom door. He looked anxious too and it was clear that he'd been listening in on the conversation.

"Don't worry, pal, everything will go according to plan," Finn said, trying to convince himself as much as his robot.

The door chime sounded again and Finn scowled.

"She must have forgotten to tell me something important," Finn said, hustling to the door and opening it. He expected to see Elara in the corridor outside but it was another woman, one he'd not seen before. "Oh, sorry, I thought you were someone else," Finn said, trying to explain the shocked look on his face.

"That's okay, Finn, I know I'm a little early," the woman said, smiling warmly at him. "But I thought since this was our first time, we could spend an extra twenty minutes getting to know one another better."

Finn shot the woman a confused frown then noticed she was wearing a satin-white skirt-suit with gold trim to match her lustrous eyeshadow and nail varnish. She was standing with her hands in front of her bare stomach, just like Juniper did, and she even wore the same perfume.

"I'm sorry, but who are you?" Finn asked, wondering if he'd just been transported to an alternate dimension.

"My name is Serenade Williams, I'm your new paramour," the woman said.

"My new what?" Finn blurted, startling the woman. He held up his hands and took a breath. "I'm sorry, it's just that I already have a paramour, Juniper Jones."

"You perhaps missed the memo on your computer, but Juniper was reassigned," Serenade replied. She looked apologetic and embarrassed. "I am your replacement."

"Reassigned? Why?" Finn said. He was conscious that everything he said to Serenade sounded like an accusation and tried to calm himself.

It seemed obvious that Serenade hadn't expected to be the one informing Finn of the change and it took her a moment to compose herself too, wetting her cherry-red lips before speaking.

"All paramours must successfully seduce their assigned partners within a set period of time," Serenade began. She was looking at her feet as she said this. "It is our primary responsibility, and Juniper failed in this regard."

"What the hell does 'successfully seduce' even mean?" Finn said, throwing his arms out wide. Despite his best efforts to remain calm he was frustrated and angry.

Serenade lifted her chin and finally looked Finn in the eyes, though it seemed that she would rather look anywhere else.

"It means take to bed," she explained, and Finn's heart almost stopped beating. She wet her dry lips again. "It means that because you two didn't have sex, she failed in her duty and has been reassigned. I am your replacement."

For several seconds Finn just stood there, staring at the paramour, mouth agape. At first he thought it was a joke, a prank by one of the other apprentices, most likely Sabrina, but his gut told him otherwise. He recognized the look in Serenade William's eyes, because he'd seen the same look in the eyes of wellness center workers in Metalhaven. It was a look of utter resignation. It was a look that said, "I don't have a choice."

"Where is she now?" Finn asked.

"I don't know," Serenade said. What she didn't say was, "and even if I did, I couldn't tell you."

"I have to find her and sort this out," Finn said, pushing past Serenade into the corridor. "It's not her fault, it's mine."

"It doesn't matter now," the paramour called after him. "It's already decided. There's nothing you can do."

"We'll see about that," Finn growled. He then looked behind Serenade to his still open door. "Scraps, come on pal, I need you," he called.

The little robot zoomed out of the apartment and the door whooshed shut behind him, leaving Serenade alone outside, like a jilted bride. He felt sorry for the woman, who had done nothing wrong, but he couldn't worry about that now.

"I need you to find Juniper, pal," Finn said, throwing himself around corners then cutting through the kitchen area, which was the quickest way out of the barracks block. "I need you to tell me where she is, right now."

Finn hurtled through the kitchen, knocking over pots and pans and startling the kitchen staff, including three chef robots, before barging open the emergency exit door and bursting out into the street. Scraps was with him every step of the way, his sensor dish spinning like it had gone haywire.

"Found-found!" Scraps said, landing on his shoulder. "Check 'puter."

Finn looked at the screen built into his training uniform and saw that Scraps had uploaded an address. It was a building at the edge of the Authority sector closest to the border with Seedhaven, in a zone he'd never seen before. He plotted a route and set off again in the direction of the closest monorail.

"Do you know why she's there?" Finn asked the robot, walking fast but not running so as not to draw undue attention to himself. "What even is this place?"

Scraps thought for a moment, his eyes scanning from left to right so fast his mechanical pupils were a blur.

"Scraps hack 'puter," the robot said, sounding distressed. "Secret-secret. Not much data!"

Finn read the new information but his robot was right that there was little to go on. All it said was that Juniper was under house arrest in her apartment block, pending reassignment. There was a conformation code, Authority-11X-TT25, and nothing more.

"Do you know what that code means?" Finn asked, but Scraps shrugged.

"Nope-nope," the robot said, sounding angry and sad. "Big encryption. Even Scraps no crack."

"Then I'll just have to ask her myself," Finn said.

He knew he was risking a lot by trying to find his paramour, especially with the test trial only a day away, but he remembered something that Juniper had told him on their very first date. Finn had asked what would happen if she didn't perform her 'duties' and Juniper had told him she would be reassigned. He sensed even then that 'reassigned' had a darker connotation, but Juniper had evaded his questions about what it meant, and he kicked himself for not pushing harder for an answer at the time. Now, he prayed it wasn't too late.

The monorail journey felt like it lasted for hours, despite nowhere in the Authority sector being more than five- or ten-minutes travel in any direction. He darted out of the car and checked his computer screen, which was guiding him to the building where Juniper was being held. He followed the directions carefully, noting that the zone was far more modest than the other parts of the Authority sector he'd seen, especially the opulent cultural quarter. The streets were still clean and the buildings well-maintained, but it was staid in comparison to what he'd grown accustomed to, like a scrubbed and polished version of the residential district in Metalhaven.

Soon he was standing in front of the building where Scraps had said Juniper was being held under house arrest. He approached the front then saw that two special prefects were standing guard in front of the main doors, and he instantly turned away, careful to ensure that the prefects couldn't see his face.

"What the fuck are they doing here?" Finn whispered.

Normal prefects were one thing, and he felt sure he could bluff his way past a regular officer, but special prefects were a law unto themselves. He'd learned the hard way during his loyalty evaluations that they couldn't be swayed and that they were not nearly as gullible as the rank-and-file officers.

"Pal, is there another way inside this building?" Finn asked, diverting down the side of the apartment block, which was cordoned off behind a two-meter brick wall. "A service door perhaps, or a maintenance entrance?"

"Yes-yes!" Scraps replied, excited. "Follow Scraps!"

The robot leapt off his shoulder and flew ahead, leading Finn to the rear of the building before zooming over the top of the wall, which was lined with razor wire. *Why the fuck does this place have razor wire on the walls?* he wondered, looking for the best place to scale the barrier. *What the hell is this place?*

Suddenly, Scraps reappeared carrying a cardboard box that had been folded flat, ready for recycling. The robot placed the cardboard over the top of a section of wall, covering the razor wire.

"Here-here!" Scraps said.

The robot vanished again before Finn could say anything, then a rope was thrown over the wall, where the cardboard had been positioned. He grabbed it and saw that it was not a rope but a bunch of bedsheets tied together.

"Thanks, Scraps," Finn said, tugging on the makeshift rope, which had been anchored somewhere on the other side of the wall. "Keep a lookout, will you?"

Finn climbed and reached the top of the wall then found himself staring into the lens of a security camera. His heart raced and he considered jumping back down, but Scraps waved at him to stop.

"Scraps hack!" the robot said, pointing to the security device. "Camera spoofed."

Finn laughed and shook his head. "You'd make one hell of a good spy, buddy."

Scraps shrugged and giggled then Finn climbed down the other side of the wall and into the courtyard. It was dirtier than he expected, with overflowing bins and the first items of trash that he'd seen since arriving in the Authority sector. Scraps was over by a service entrance and Finn could see that the robot had already hacked the lock, because the door was ajar. He stole inside, with Scraps again sat on his shoulder so that the sound of his rotors wouldn't give them away.

"Floor four," Scraps whispered into his ear. "Room Four-D."

Finn nodded and made his way up the emergency exit staircase to the fourth floor of the building. Inching open the door, he peeked into the corridor and saw another special prefect standing guard outside one of the apartments. Referring back to the map on his computer, he saw that it was Room Four-D. Juniper's room.

"Can you distract the guard?" Finn said, turning again to his resourceful robot to save the day.

Scraps nodded then sprouted the sensor dish from the compartment in his back. A few seconds later, Finn heard the muffled sound of voices speaking on the special prefect's comm-link. The man listened intently then nodded and acknowledged whatever message had been received, before drawing his sidearm and running along the corridor, out of sight.

"What did you do?' Finn asked.

"Spoof call," Scraps said, smirking. "Man outside ask for help."

Finn laughed again. "You're a genius," he said, causing the robot's oil can body to swell with pride. "Keep a lookout, I'll try to make this quick."

Finn ran into the corridor, feeling like a thief in the night, and rapped his knuckles gently against the door of Room Four-D. He waited for a second then knocked again, heart thumping in his chest. The handle turned and the door was pulled open, only a little, but enough for Finn to see Juniper's face. It was wet with tears.

"Finn?" she said, the word catching in her breath. She peeked through the gap, noticing that the guard was gone, then pulled him inside. "What are you doing here? How did you even know?"

"Never mind that, we don't have a lot of time," Finn said, holding her hands. They were trembling and clammy. "I came as soon as I heard what happened. I need to know how to fix this, Juniper. I need you to help me fix this."

"You can't," Juniper said. She broke free of him and stepped back. It was only then that Finn realized she wasn't wearing her white and gold suit but a bronze-colored one-piece. "It's already too late."

"Why didn't you tell me this would happen?" Finn said. He knew it was unreasonable to be angry with her, but he couldn't stop himself. "I could have done something."

Juniper turned to him and shook her head. She was furious and hiding it badly.

"You knew what we had to do. You've always known. But I respected you and waited, and waited, and waited, hoping you would want me too, and then it was too late."

Finn recoiled at the accusation but he had no comeback because Juniper had hit him with the truth. "You still should have told me," he said, responding like a wounded animal and lashing out. "I never wanted this." He looked at the apartment, which was meagre like the accommodation in

Metalhaven. The only difference was that it was clean and warm. "What even is this?"

"This is my punishment for failing," Juniper said, bitterly. "I've been reassigned."

"To what? To where?"

Juniper scowled at him. It didn't suit her face. "You don't know?"

"No, I don't," Finn said, feeling desperate. "Fuck, Juniper, what's going on?"

The former paramour's shoulders sank and she looked at her feet before finally drawing the courage to meet his eyes again. "They're making an example of me," she said, softly. "Tomorrow, I'm being sent to trial. Your test trail."

Finn couldn't believe what he was hearing. He refused to believe it and for a time he just shook his head in denial.

"There must be something I can do," he eventually said, repeating this over and over to himself, though he knew that saying the words wouldn't make it true.

"There isn't," Juniper said, flatly. She'd accepted it, he realized. She was resigned to her fate. "It's decided, Finn."

"No," Finn said.

Shock was giving way to anger, and a fierce resolve to fix his mistake, but there was only one way he could do that, and it would mean risking his own survival too. He'd made his decision, come what may.

"I'm going to get you out of here, Juniper," Finn said, taking her hands again, and this time she let him. "Tomorrow, in the test trial, I'm escaping. It's all been arranged."

"Escaping?" The word trembled from her lips. "To where?"

"To Haven," Finn said. "It's real and that's where I'm going. That's where we're going."

Juniper shook her head; it was too much for her to take in but he didn't have time to explain. Then Scraps darted into the room, frantic.

"Time-time!" the robot said. "Guard coming!"

Finn cursed then fixed his eyes on Juniper's and waited till he was certain she was focused on nothing but him.

"Listen to me, Juniper," he began. "Tomorrow at the trial, go the Seahaven mini-sector and hide in the boathouse by the waterside. Don't do anything else, just go there and hide."

"Why? I don't understand?"

"There isn't time," Finn said. He looked at Scraps and he was waving for him to follow, jumping up and down on the spot, like the floor was lava. "Just go there and hide. I'll find you and we'll get out together."

Juniper was shaking like a leaf but he needed to know that she'd heard him.

"Juniper, please," Finn said. "Trust me. I know I don't deserve it, but please trust me."

Juniper nodded then their lips were pressed together and he pulled her into an embrace. It felt desperate but real.

"Finn-Finn!" cried Scraps.

Finn pulled himself away, tasting the salt of her tears on his lips, then stole one last glance at Juniper's face, strained with fear but hopeful, and ran.

19
COMING CLEAN

Finn was already awake and dressed by the time the door chime rang to announce Elara's arrival. He'd barely slept, despite knowing the importance of being rested for the test trial, but the fits and starts of sleep he had achieved were interrupted by twisted nightmares. He would find himself back in yard seven, smiling up at Owen who had just killed Bloodletter and saved his life, then Owen's face and body would morph into Juniper's before a spear was thrust through her heart by Walter Foster. Finn would wake screaming with that image in his mind, terrified that it wasn't just a nightmare but a premonition. The door chime sounded again and Finn pushed himself out of his desk chair and stood as tall as the pressures weighing him down would allow.

"Come in," Finn said.

Elara walked into his apartment wearing her full prosecutor armor and without the smile he'd grown accustomed to being greeted with. The burdens of the day ahead were weighing on her too. She waited for the door to close behind her then diligently checked that the bug-killer devices were operating before speaking a word.

"Are you ready?" she asked.

Finn nodded. "I'm ready." He knew he needed to tell Elara about Juniper but he didn't know how, and he also knew that once he left his apartment, the opportunity to do so would be gone.

"Training today is cancelled for obvious reasons," Elara said, perching on the arm of his sofa. "The first order of business is your confirmation ceremony, where you and the other apprentices will receive your prosecutor aliases and equipment."

"What's the betting they name me, 'chromeboy', just out of spite?" Finn said, attempting some dark humor, which fell on deaf, serious ears.

"Once you've all been confirmed and fitted with your new armored uniforms, skycars will take us to the test crucible, where the offenders will be paraded in front of you," Elara continued. "It's another part of the ceremony and you'll have to suck it up, I'm afraid."

Finn sighed and shook his head. The idea that the condemned men and women would be further tormented by being shown their executioners was cruel but on brand for the Authority.

"Hopefully, my new uniform includes a mask so no-one can see my face," Finn replied.

"It doesn't," Elara said. "So, it's important you look the part."

Finn nodded. "I can play my role for a little while longer. Then I won't have to pretend anymore."

"Usually, there are twenty-four offenders in each test trial but today there are twenty-five," Elara went on, reading the screen of her C.O.N.F.I.R.M.E. device. "It looks like there's been a late addition."

Finn's stomach knotted as his mentor scanned the list of offenders, brow furrowed. Then her expression hardened, her eyes widened, and he knew she'd read the name.

"Juniper Jones is on this list," Elara said, glancing at the screen again to double-check she'd read the information correctly. "Your Juniper Jones..."

Finn swallowed hard and nodded.

"You knew?"

"I found out last night," Finn said.

"And when were you going to tell me this?" Elara said, practically yelling at him. Then she cursed and shook her head. "You've done something, haven't you? I can see it in your eyes, Finn, I know you too well now."

"It's my fault this happened," Finn said. "I pushed Juniper away and kept pushing her away, just like you asked, and that's why the Authority 'reassigned' her. They're sending her to trial as a punishment because I rejected her."

"I told you not to trust her, I didn't say anything about not bedding her!" Elara snapped.

Finn staggered back a pace as if a strong gust of wind had just smacked him in the face.

"But you were always there, like a goddamn walking chastity belt!" Finn yelled. "You told me not to get too close or too intimate, because she was still part of the Authority and a risk. I thought this was what you wanted?"

"What I want is to get you out of here," Elara said. She then pressed her eyes shut and hissed another curse. "What did you tell her, Finn?"

"Why do you think I told her anything?" he replied, suddenly on the defensive.

"You knew Juniper was on trial before I did, and you're not kicking and screaming at me to do something, which means *you* already have," Elara said.

Finn considered lying to her but he couldn't bring himself to do it. They'd been through too much and he owed her the truth.

"I went to her last night," Finn admitted, and Elara turned her back on him. "I found out where they were keeping her, under house arrest in some shitty condo at the ass-end of the sector. I told her I was getting out today and that I was going to take her with me."

"You might have ruined everything," Elara said. She was eerily calm. "If she talks then the last nine weeks will have been for nothing, and you'll have gotten us both killed."

"It won't come to that," Finn said. He had no right to make such an empty promise but he had to believe it was true. "The plan stays the same. All that changes is that two people escape through the drainage tunnel in Seahaven, instead of one."

Elara said nothing in reply and remained with her back to him. The silent seconds felt like hours but there was nothing he could say that would soften the blow or undo what he'd done. He knew he'd compromised the plan and he hated himself for putting Elara at risk, but he couldn't turn his back on Juniper, not when he was the reason she'd been marked for death. Then she turned but the woman who met his eyes was The Shadow, not Elara Cage, and she was furious.

"You've compromised us for a hooker you've known for all of three months," Elara snapped. Finn was shaken by the malice in her voice. "She's just one person. You should have let her die."

"I can't do that, I'm not like you," Finn said, reflecting Elara's spite back at her. "Your soul might be broken beyond saving, Elara, but mine isn't."

Elara Cage was the toughest person he'd ever met but his words cut her more deeply than any blade could have.

"You told me once that my selflessness is rare and that it makes me special. That it makes me Metal," Finn added, anger getting the better of him. "But if I turn my back on Juniper now, and let her be slaughtered in that crucible, then I'm no better than you are."

Elara gasped and turned her back on him again so that he couldn't see her face. Even so, he couldn't stop himself from twisting the knife. He was too incensed.

"If I condemn her then the Finn Brasa who enters Haven won't be that same man you saved," Finn said. "And if I'm broken too then what's the point of any of this?"

Even before he'd finished speaking he'd knew he'd said too much. Some of it he'd meant and some of it was spoken in anger and haste, but the words were out there and he couldn't take them back. He wanted Elara to come at him and kick and punch him to the ground, because he deserved it for betraying her, but instead she just shook her head and left.

20

THE REDEEMER

"All prosecutors and apprentices will gather in the training hall at once," said the voice of Chief Prosecutor Voss booming over the barracks' PA system. "The confirmation ceremony will begin presently."

Elara had left the door to his apartment open and Finn could hear the sound of boots scrambling across the polished tile floor as his fellow apprentices rushed to the training hall, but he remained numb. Then Sabrina appeared outside and screeched to a halt.

"What the hell are you doing, chromeboy?" she said, clinging onto the door frame and swinging her head and shoulders inside. "Didn't you just hear the announcement? We're getting our prosecutor aliases!"

Finn's head was a mess and though he tried to compel his addled brain to speak, it was demanding all of his effort just to keep from crumpling into a fetal position on the floor. Sabrina darted inside and grabbed his arm and the decision was made for him.

"Come on, Finn, we don't want to be the last ones there,"

she said, switching to his actual name, which she only did on the rare occasions that she was being serious.

Sabrina guided Finn to the training hall and he let himself be led. Behind him, he could hear the whir of rotors and he spotted Scraps tailing him, a worried expression contorting the robot's delicate metal features. Then before he knew it, Finn was being dragged into the training hall and propped up beside the other apprentices, with Sabrina to his right, fizzing with energy and excitement, like she was about to be awarded a prize. Scraps also stole inside and hid in the rafters, so that Voss couldn't see him and order the robot out.

"Though I regret that your training must be cut short, I am confident that you have all learned the skills required to succeed as prosecutors of Zavetgrad!" Voss announced to a resounding cheer of "Apex!".

Finn barely managed to mumble the word, but the volume of the other shouts shook him out of his daze. He looked for Elara amongst the other prosecutors and saw her at the rear of the pack, eyes down to the floor. He desperately wanted to go to her, to make her understand, but it was impossible. The few meters that separated them were as impassable as Zavetgrad's towering electrified fence.

"Each of you will receive your prosecutor aliases and the weapons, equipment and armor that will come to define you inside the crucible," Voss continued. "In accordance with tradition, your test trial will be witnessed by the Mayor of the Authority, and Regent of Spacehaven, the most honorable Maxim Volkov!"

Ivan Volkov stood taller as Walter and Tonya cheered and jostled his shoulders. Finn resisted the urge to shake his head, and Sabrina rolled her eyes. After nine long weeks, even she was sick of Ivan's bullshit and the sycophants that pandered to him.

"I know you will all do us proud," Voss continued, allowing the interruption only because of who Ivan was. Anyone else would have been told to shut up in no short order. "Now, we shall begin."

Voss and the other prosecutors walked to a dais that had been set up where one of the fighting octagons usually stood. Finn was always amazed at how the cleaning robots were able to remove the blood stains from the floor without a trace.

"Zach Spencer, step forward!"

Zach moved out of the line and stepped onto the dais. Racks of weapons, armor and equipment then rose from beneath the floor and Zach's mentor, Cleo "Garrote" McKay, stepped forward.

"Zach Spencer, you have proven yourself ruthless in the pursuit of justice and worthy of the title, Prosecutor of Zavetgrad," McKay began, delivering the line with ritualistic grandeur. "In sight of those assembled and with the power granted to me by the Chief Prosecutor, you will henceforward be known as, Scourge!".

Everyone in the room chanted, "Scourge!" loud enough to shatter glass.

Finn watched as Cleo McKay continued with the ceremony, beginning with presenting Zach with his custom-made armor.

"May this armor protect you as you dispense justice in the name of Zavetgrad and the Authority."

"Scourge!"

McKay presented the armor to Zach's body and it snapped into place as if attached by magnets or some other mystical force. There was a torso-section followed by separate pieces for his legs and arms, which added a sense of bulk to Zach's slender build. Gauntlets with razor-sharp serrated blades along the forearms were then slid over his hands, before the suit of armor was completed with a head covering resembling a Spartan helmet with a long faceplate tapering to a point.

"These weapons are the means through which you will deliver righteous judgement to those who forsake the law."

The room chanted, "Scourge!"

Zach was presented with a self-reloading harpoon gun with a vicious barbed tip that was designed to rip and maim human flesh, like his gauntlets. For close-quarters fighting, he was given a handheld chainsaw the size of a machete. Zach sparked the weapon into life and it roared with the promise of violence.

"Together with these weapons and armor, you are more than a man and you are more than gold," McKay continued. "You are a Prosecutor of Zavetgrad. Say his name!"

"Scourge!"

Voss stepped onto the dais and shook Zach's hand before inviting him to join with McKay and the others.

"Welcome, Scourge," Voss said, leaning into his role a little too theatrically for Finn's liking. "Now take your place amongst the other prosecutors."

Zach "Scourge" Spencer stepped off the dais but the man didn't rejoin his fellow apprentices, because he was no longer a trainee. Zach was a fully-fledged Prosecutor of Zavetgrad, about to embark on his first trial, where he would sanctify his new weapons with the blood of innocents.

Finn forced down a dry swallow, knowing that Voss

would soon call another name. In one sense, he wanted it to be him, so he could get the farce of his ceremony over with, but he was also afraid that they wouldn't call him forward, and that his dreams of escape and rebellion would end before they'd even begun. He thought about Juniper, and Elara's warning of what might happened if she talked, and a surge of crippling remorse gripped him.

"Sabrina Brook, step forward!"

Sabrina's eyes lit up and she beamed a smile at Finn before practically skipping onto the dais. Her mentor, Ayla "Death Echo" Price also advanced and cleared her throat.

"Sabrina Brook, you are resourceful and relentless, and no-one will escape your judgement," Price began. "In sight of those assembled and with the power granted to me by the Chief Prosecutor, you will henceforward be known as, Ruin!".

A chant of "Ruin!" filled the hall.

The ceremony continued, beginning with Sabrina's armor, which was more subtle and stealthy than Zack's warrior-inspired ensemble, to suit her quiet style of assassination. For a ranged weapon she was given a crossbow pistol, along with a variety of traps and mines, before her trademark Sai were presented to her. The weapons were designed and built with exquisite detail and Finn noted the crimson tint to the blades, which suggested poison.

"Together with these weapons and armor, you are more than a woman and you are more than a gold," Price continued. "You are a Prosecutor of Zavetgrad. Say her name!"

"Ruin!"

Sabrina winked at Finn then jumped down off the dais

and joined the other prosecutors. She looked magnificent, Finn thought, and he was proud of her. Then the crushing reality of what she had been trained to do – what she was soon about to do – hit him and he felt like a traitor to his own people.

"Walter Foster, step forward!"

Ivan slapped his friend on the back and Walter strode toward the dais like a prize bull going to market. The pure-bred gold was stronger, leaner and meaner than he'd ever been, and he still hated Finn with every fiber of his being.

"Walter Foster, you command the full power of the law and strike with the authority of the gavel," André "Frost" Regan began, chest swelling with pride as he addressed his apprentice. "In sight of those assembled and with the power granted to me by the Chief Prosecutor, you will henceforward be known as, Vigor!".

The chant of "Vigor" was the loudest so far, and Ivan almost deafened him.

The ceremony continued in the same vein as with Zach and Sabrina, and Walter was clad in something resembling fourteenth century Brigandine armor. The suit was focused on protecting his upper body, adding even more bulk to his muscular frame, while also giving him a warrior look. Weapons came next and it was no surprise that Walter was presented with a set of five golden javelins held in a back scabbard. Then, in a rare twist to the usual ceremony, Frost presented Walter with his own personal warhammer, a weapon that had claimed more lives than Finn cared to count.

"Together with these weapons and armor, you are more than a man and you are more than a gold," Regan bellowed. "You are a Prosecutor of Zavetgrad. Say his name!"

"Vigor!"

The chant was deafening and Finn felt sure that it would only be beaten by one other. He side-eyed Ivan, wondering when they would call the Regent Successor's name.

"Tonya Duke, step forward!"

Kurt "Blitz" McCullough hopped onto the dais and smiled at his apprentice, though Tonya only had eyes for Ivan.

"Tonya Duke, you are the flame of justice, a cleansing fire that rids Zavetgrad of those who dare defy our laws," McCullough announced. "In sight of those assembled and with the power granted to me by the Chief Prosecutor, you will henceforward be known as Inferno!".

The chant of "Inferno!" wasn't as loud overall as it had been for Walter, but Ivan's shout left Finn's ears ringing.

Tonya's armor was supposedly inspired by Celtic warriors, though it was a mishmash of styles, blending chainmail, leather and furs to create an outfit as striking as the woman herself. Her main weapon was a shotgun that fired Dragon's Breath rounds, capable of incinerating hapless offenders from a range of up to fifty meters. The dirk knives that had become her signature weapon were then presented, and Finn saw that an image of dragons had been etched onto each blade.

"Together with these weapons and armor, you are more than a woman and you are more than a gold," McCullough said. "You are a Prosecutor of Zavetgrad. Say her name!"

"Inferno!"

Finn blew out a sigh and tried to calm his jangling nerves. He expected to be called next, knowing that Ivan Volkov would want the limelight shone on him last. He looked for Elara again, hoping to draw strength from her emerald eyes, but she was still hidden behind the others, either by chance or on purpose so that she wouldn't have to look at him.

"Ivan Volkov, step forward!"

Finn felt sick. *What does this mean? Am I not to be called? Has Juniper talked?*

Sloane Stewart, Ivan's bodyguard and paramour, was in the room, but since she was not herself a prosecutor, it was Voss who stepped forward to conduct the ceremony.

"Ivan Volkov, you are the noble embodiment of the law and a pure-gold son of Zavetgrad," Voss began, raising his voice loud in honor of the duty he was performing. "In sight of those assembled and with the power granted to me by the President and Voice of the Authority, Gideon Alexander Reznikov, you will henceforward be known as Herald!".

Everyone chanted the word, "Herald!" as if their lives depended on it, so it didn't matter than Finn was too stunned to make sound.

Ivan's armor was brought to him and it was unlike anything Finn had seen before. It flowed like leather but shone like gold and was accessorized by a black and yellow cavalier shoulder cape that give Ivan a regal appearance, like a seventeenth century noble warrior. A flintlock-style pistol was then presented to him along with a glaive, but Ivan was also given an ornate, bejeweled rapier that appeared to be an antique, perhaps a treasure from the Volkov family's vault.

"Together with these weapons and armor, you are more than a man and you are more than a gold," Voss said. "You are a Prosecutor of Zavetgrad. Say his name!"

"Herald!"

This time, Finn made sure to chant Ivan's new alias, knowing that the eyes of the room would now be on him, assuming he was to be called and not condemned. Ivan stepped off the dais and joined the others, who were waiting to congratulate him like good little sycophants. Voss then turned to Finn and he pressed out his chest and pushed back his shoulders, hoping for the best. He waited and waited and didn't even take a breath until Voss spoke again.

"Finn Brasa... step forward."

The order was made with no enthusiasm but Finn didn't need to be asked twice. He marched to the dais and turned to face the others, hoping that his expression did not betray the fear that still gripped him. Then to his relief Elara Cage advanced and climbed onto the dais. She met his eyes though it hurt her to look at him, and an aftershock of shame and regret hit Finn hard.

"Finn Brasa, you were born chrome, not gold," Elara began. Her voice was strong and filled the room. "Shedding blood and tears you endured the crucible and were re-forged. Now you stand amongst us, as one of us. You were redeemed, so in sight of those assembled and with the power granted to me by the Chief Prosecutor, you will henceforward be known as Redeemer!".

His name was chanted though only in muted and apologetic tones, apart from Sabrina, who sang it loud. Elara then began to fix his armor, which was chrome with gilt edging. It resembled the armor of an ancient samurai warrior, though Finn likened himself more to a Ronin, an undesirable without the favor of his masters.

"This armor will protect you while delivering justice in the name of Zavetgrad and the Authority."

"Redeemer..."

The chant was muted and begrudging.

Elara brought out his weapons and continued the ceremony, though she would no longer meet his eyes. The ranged weapon was a modified version of the laser canon he'd become proficient with, while for close-quarters fighting he was given a black baseball bat, a crude weapon symbolizing his humble origins.

"These weapons are the means through which you will deliver righteous judgement to those who forsake the law."

"Redeemer..." was chanted, though even more feebly.

"Together with these weapons and armor, you are more than a man and you are more than a gold," Elara continued, her voice still strong despite the subdued response. "You are a Prosecutor of Zavetgrad. Say his name!"

No one spoke and Voss didn't interject to force their compliance. Finn was about to step down but Elara drew her black roundel blade and scraped it across Finn's armor. Sparks flew and the banshee screech of metal on metal turned all eyes toward her.

"Say his name or dishonor us all!" Elara shouted, punching the blade above her head. "He is a Prosecutor of Zavetgrad. *Say his name!*"

"Redeemer!"

The chant was the quietest of them all but it was still loud and even Ivan and Walter had been shamed in to speaking his name. Once again, as she had always done, Elara Cage had fought for him. He turned to her, ready to thank her, but Elara had already stepped down off the dais, and then her chameleonic armor shimmered and she was gone.

21
JUST SAY IT

Finn looked at the crucible though the skycar window as the vehicle began its descent to land. The arena was already powered up like a macabre fairground house of horrors but on a massive scale, which meant that the electrified fence was deactivated below ground level. If all had gone to plan, the Metals from Haven would be on their way through the subsurface tunnels to the Seahaven mini-sector. Perhaps, he wondered, they might already be there, waiting for him.

"It's bigger than I expected," Sabrina said, leaning across him to get a better look. "I like how they've split it into all the different sectors."

Sabrina sat beside Finn, huddled tightly to his side, as she had been for the entire flight. She was putting on a brave face for the others but Finn could sense her anxiety, which had built the closer they'd come to the crucible. The other new prosecutors were also passengers in the skycar, but the vehicle was large enough that they could all spread out. Even so, Ivan and Tonya were sitting together like a couple of lovestruck teenagers, while Walter focused on the crucible, warhammer in hand and foot tapping impatiently on the deck. Finn didn't know whether the man was nervous or just keen to get the killing started. Zack was calmest out of everyone and Finn knew why. The man was finally getting what he wanted, the opportunity to kill with impunity, and be rewarded for it too.

"What's it like?" Sabrina asked, lowering her voice so that the others couldn't hear. "Killing someone I mean?"

Finn turned to the newly-minted prosecutor and frowned, surprised by the question.

"Why are you asking me that now?" Finn said. "You'll know yourself soon enough."

Sabrina shrugged. "Up until now it's all been academic, you know? We've just been learning how to kill. Now we actually have to do it and I just wondered how it felt."

"I honestly don't remember," Finn said, looking back out of the window. It was a lie, he could remember every microsecond of what he'd done to Corbin Radcliffe, but he didn't want to talk about it, because talking about it only reminded him of Owen. "Everything happened so fast and I acted on instinct," he added.

Sabrina nodded and slumped back into her seat, though she remained tightly tucked in beside him. He looked at the woman's face and, if he didn't know better, he'd have thought she was the one being sent to trial, rather than the one prosecuting it. He didn't want to feel empathy for her, given what she would inevitably be compelled to do inside the arena, but in the three months they'd spent together, he'd grown to like Sabrina "Ruin" Brook. The woman beneath the mask was not a bad person, not yet, but the crucible would change her, as it would change them all. As it had already changed him.

The skycar landed in the center of the test crucible and Finn disembarked along with the others. He caught his reflection in the mirror-polished finish of the flying vehicle and didn't recognize himself. In full gear and with his weapons in hand, he looked powerful and intimidating, like a comic book super-villain; the perfect tool to assert the Authority's unyielding will. Then something else caught his eye and he smiled. Scraps had attached himself to the roof of the skycar and hitched a lift along with them. His little robot was now airborne and headed toward the Seahaven mini-sector. Many things were uncertain in the hours that lay ahead, but he knew one thing for sure, which was that he wasn't leaving Zavetgrad without his robot buddy. Scraps was simply too important to him, even more than saving Juniper.

Each of them had been given trackers prior to embarking, similar to prefect C.O.N.F.I.R.M.E. computers, and the device on Finn's left wrist suddenly sparked into life. Twenty-five signals appeared on the screen, all moving toward him. Then he saw Chief Prosecutor Voss, together with Frost and Death Echo, marching the offenders out to meet their executioners. The men and women were arranged into a single long line, then the former mentors split off to speak to their protégées for one last time. The intention was to talk strategies and techniques, and reinforce the rules of the game, which were simple – complete their training by scoring as many kills as possible.

Sabrina tore herself from Finn's side to confer with Death Echo, rapping her knuckles against his armored shoulder as she did so. Then he saw Elara and his stomach did summersaults. There was so much he wanted to say to her, and he knew it wasn't the time or the place, but it was also his last chance. If he did escape to Haven, there was no guarantee he'd ever see her again, and as Elara walked toward him the crushing reality of that fact struck him dumb, and his chance to speak his heart was gone.

"Take this, but keep it hidden," Elara said, pressing a small phial into Finn's hand. If she had noticed his tormented expression, she did not let on.

"What is it?" Finn asked, casually slipping the capsule into one of the webbing pockets in his armored uniform.

"It's a fast-acting sedative," his former mentor explained. "Get this into an offender's bloodstream and it will knock them out and slow their heart rate to almost nothing. The tracking devices will read it as a kill, and Voss will be placated."

Finn nodded. With everything else that had gone on, he'd forgotten that he would be expected to kill at least one or two offenders in the test trial, and that not doing so would draw suspicion to him. Elara hadn't forgotten though. As usual, she had his back, even though he'd betrayed her.

"Thank you, for what you said in the training hall at my commencement," Finn began, making sure to speak before the moment was lost and Elara derailed his efforts at reconciliation. "It meant a lot to me..." He faltered and blew out a shaky breath. *Just say it, you coward...* "You mean a lot to me."

"I need you to focus on the mission," Elara replied. She was looking down, pretending to adjust a component of her armor, but Finn could see that it was already attached flawlessly. "Concentrate on getting where you need to be. I'll handle the other problem."

Finn frowned. "What the hell does that mean?"

"All mentors shadow their former apprentices inside the crucible, observing at a distance in case anything goes wrong," Elara explained. "That gives me a chance to fix your mess."

Finn had gotten used to Elara speaking in riddles when outside the safety of his apartment, but it still took him a moment to work out what she meant.

"You'll help Juniper?" Finn asked, taking a chance and speaking plainly. "You'll help get her to Seahaven?"

Elara finally looked at him and she was still furious and struggling to keep a lid on it.

"It does neither of us any good if you charge off trying to be a fucking hero," she spat, pouring her anger into her words. She wanted to hurt him and he couldn't blame her. "So you stick to the plan and let me worry about the other problem."

Finn nodded. "I seem to be saying this a lot, but thank you, Elara."

"Don't thank me," she replied, gruffly. "I have a job to do, that's all."

"A job?" Finn said, reeling back a touch. "Is that all I am you to?"

He accepted that he deserved her vitriol but this was too much. Never in their time together had he believed Elara simply looked at him as a task on her to-do list. They had grown close, or at least that's what he'd thought.

"What did you think this was, Finn?" Elara said. She'd found a soft spot in his armor and was attacking it. "Do you think we're friends? Do you think I'm doing this out of the goodness of my heart?" She shook her head. "When will you wise up? You're an asset, nothing more. Haven believes they can use you to destabilize the Authority, and it's my job to deliver you to them."

"An *asset*?" Finn said. This was somehow even worse than being labelled a 'job'. An asset was just a thing to be bought and traded. "So you don't give a fuck about me at all, is that what you're saying? You'll post me off to Haven and never think about me again?"

"Don't pretend that you really care about me," Elara said. She grabbed Finn's arm and moved them further away from potentially prying ears. "You hate what I am, you've never made a secret of that. And I warned you that if you compromised me for a second time that we were done, so we're done. I'll deal with your little girlfriend then you two can go to Haven together and live happily ever after, and never have to think of me again."

Elara turned to leave but he caught her arm and pulled her back. The Shadow took control and Elara's black roundel dagger was pulled from its sheath and pressed into his armpit. He felt the knife cut his skin but he didn't release her, not until he'd said his piece.

"I like Juniper and I won't apologize for not wanting her to be murdered, but if you think I don't care about you then you're out of your goddamn mind," Finn said. He released her arm, but the roundel blade remained tucked into his flesh. "You're the only person in the world who knows me, and if it was a choice between you and her, I'd pick you in a heartbeat."

Elara shook herself free and stepped back, head turned away. He had no idea if he'd reached her or even if she could be reached.

"Haven isn't for people like me," Elara whispered, her

emerald eyes staring into the distance toward the Davis Strait. "I'm beyond saving. You said it yourself."

Elara walked away and Finn tried to go after her but the other prosecutors were watching them now and he had to let her go. He wanted to explain that he'd been angry when he'd spoken those words and that he didn't mean them. He wanted to tell her that she *was* worth saving, because that's what he believed. And he wanted more than anything for Elara to come with him to Haven. But she was gone and so was his last chance to make things right.

22

THE TEST TRIAL

"Prosecutors of Zavetgrad, here are your offenders!" Voss bellowed, gesturing to the line of twenty-five men and women exhibited before them. "Each one has broken a fundamental law of Zavetgrad and will face justice at your hands!"

Voss's delivery was bombastic and hammy and done for show, since it wasn't only prosecutors, new and old, who were in attendance but also the Mayor of Zavetgrad and Regent of Spacehaven, Maxim Volkov. The aristocrat stood with his son, arm gently resting over his shoulder so as to denote affection, but neither Ivan nor Maxim appeared particularly comfortable in one another's presence.

"As is our law, these offenders will be given an opportunity to prove their innocence by surviving a trial inside this crucible," Voss continued, strutting up and down in front of the line of trembling, broken workers. "But should they die inside this arena their guilt is proven!"

"Apex! Apex! Apex!"

The chant, accompanied by the clash of weapons against

armored chests, was so loud and ferocious that many of the offenders broke and collapsed to their knees. Several were unable to hold onto the meagre contents of their stomachs while others lost control of their bladders, but Finn was only subliminally aware of their ordeals, because his attention was focused only on Juniper. She was at the far right of the line, closer to Finn than any of the other prosecutors, but she dared not look at him, and he didn't want her to. He was afraid that seeing the terror in her eyes would reveal a chink in his new chrome armor. He had to be resolute. He had to be a Prosecutor of Zavetgrad for another hour, and then he would be free.

The twenty-five offenders were herded like cattle to their starting positions in the center of the crucible. The prosecutors were grouped into pairs, as they would be in a normal trial, and to his relief and hers, Finn was paired with Sabrina. Ivan got Tonya, not by chance Finn suspected, and Walter was paired with Zach. Compact skycars then airlifted the three groups to different starting positions within the arena. Finn and Sabrina were dropped off in the Metalhaven mini-sector. He jumped out of the vehicle and it flew off just as another skycar deposited Elara and Ayla "Death Echo" Price a hundred meters behind them. Their former mentors would observe their performance from a distance, judging how they dispensed bloody judgment on the offenders.

"You must feel right at home, chromeboy," Sabrina said, jostling him on the shoulder. She delivered the joke with her usual zing but Finn could still tell she was anxious. "Maybe this is Voss's idea of a joke?"

"More like Ivan's," Finn grunted. It had occurred to him that their starting position was a subtle dig at his origins. "I'm sure that he and his asshole father thought it would be funny to start me off here."

"Well, you've got me as backup, so don't worry," Sabrina replied, jostling him again. "Though this is only my second time ever in Metalhaven, or anything resembling it, so I suggest you lead the way."

Finn agreed since him taking point made it easier to steer them toward Seahaven, which is where he needed to be.

"Metalhaven is a tough crucible, so I suggest we head out of the sector and hunt elsewhere," Finn said, playing his card. "There are too many narrow streets and places to hide here. We want somewhere more open where it will be easier pickings."

Sabrina looked at him, surprised. "I didn't expect you to be so eager to make a kill," she said. "Honestly, I still don't even know if I can do it."

A less wise Finn Brasa would have further discouraged Sabrina, but he knew that the prosecutors would be watching, and he had to make sure there was no doubt in their minds he was one of them.

"You'll be fine," Finn said, stalking ahead. "When the time comes, your instincts will kick in and you won't hesitate. In that moment, you'll be Ruin, not Sabrina."

A scream floated across the crucible, as shrill and icy as the wind that carried it to his ears, then it disappeared just a quickly. His tracker vibrated softly and he checked the screen.

"Walter has a kill already," Sabrina said, already a step ahead of him. "Shit, if he keeps going at this rate, there won't be anyone left for us to kill."

Finn forced himself to laugh while he checked the list of names to make sure that Juniper was still alive. She was but a woman from Seedhaven was dead. She had been twenty-two years old and her crime had been accidently ruining a crop of algae.

"Where should we go?" Sabrina asked. "If Metalhaven is difficult then where is easy?"

"We go to Seahaven," Finn said, pointing the way then taking the lead. "Much of it is open water, which means the offenders will cluster inside boat huts and other buildings. It will make them easy targets."

"Fine, whatever," Sabrina said, then she blew out a shaky breath. "I don't care where we go so long as you're still with me, okay?"

"You got it, Ruin," Finn said, smiling at her. "We're a team."

"We're the *best* team," Sabrina corrected him. "And I don't care if Walter racks up half the kills all by himself, so long as we beat Ivan and his doxy, Tonya. I hate how she always sucks up to him."

Finn laughed again, though this was genuine. "On that we are very much agreed…"

He picked up the pace, conscious of time. There was a limited window in which he could escape, and he didn't intend to be late, but he also knew that the chances of Juniper reaching the boat house reduced in line with the number of offenders that died ahead of her. Twenty-four were alive at that moment, but with each worker that fell, the target on her back would get bigger.

By the time Finn and Sabrina had reached the edge of the Metalhaven mini-sector the offenders had clustered together into groups, based on their home sectors. Workers from Metalhaven, Seedhaven, Volthaven, Seahaven, Spacehaven and Stonehaven were all represented. Chrome, green, red, blue, white and orange. There was a solo offender too, colored bronze on Finn's tracker. Juniper. She was out on her own, heading straight for Seahaven, and making rapid progress.

"Look at this one, out on its own," Sabrina said. Finn saw that she had highlighted Juniper on her tracker and he cursed under his breath. "I've never seen bronze before. Which sector is that?"

Finn shrugged. "No idea," he lied.

"Well, I say we take this one down first," Sabrina said, taking over the lead. "That blip is headed right where we're headed, and it'll be an easy kill to get us on the scoreboard."

"No, we should focus on the groups," Finn said, jogging ahead and blocking Sabrina's path. She didn't look impressed. "Hear me out, okay. One kill gets us nowhere fast. We need to put in a good showing today, as our kills determine our starting ranks as prosecutors. You don't want to be last, do you, behind Ivan and Tonya?"

Sabrina scowled at him and he knew he'd hooked his fish.

"You know I don't," she snapped. "So what's the play, chromeboy?"

"Look, four offenders from Stonehaven have just crossed over the edge of this sector," Finn said, showing Sabrina his tracker. "We take them out and maybe rack up two kills apiece."

"Two against four sounds a lot worse than two against one," Sabrina said.

"But they're unarmed and look at us," Finn said, fighting his corner. "Hell, I'm sure that the formidable 'Ruin' could take them all out by herself."

"You smooth talking bastard," Sabrina said, smiling and nudging him.

He returned her smile and for a second or two he forgot where they were and who she was. They were just a couple of trainees back in the barracks, bantering with one another as they always did. He wished he didn't like the woman because that would have made everything easier, but it would also have been a lie. Then more screams echoed around the crucible and Finn focused on his tracker. Ivan was also now on the board, as was Zach. Finn felt sick as he checked the names. Astrid, Hector, Jonas. *No Juniper. She's still alive...* Then his screen updated again and the quartet of Stonehaven offenders were closing in on them fast.

Cursing under his breath, he signaled to Sabrina to move into cover then readied his laser cannon. The phial that Elara had given him was still safely in his pocket, but to use it he would have to get close. Sabrina's training kicked in and she stalked ahead, crossbow aimed with a steady hand. Then the workers broke cover and came at them, screaming and yelling like berserkers, with blocks of stone and crude metal bars in their hands. Finn aimed and fired his laser cannon, blasting objects in front of the group and landing shots at their feet in an effort to scare them. Surprised and dazzled by the blazing laser light, the group's charge faltered and two fled, tossing their makeshift weapons in the process.

Finn drew his baseball bat, resigned to the fact he'd have to crack skulls in order to subdue the offenders and administer the sedative, but before he could advance, Sabrina darted out of cover. She fired her crossbow, striking one of the Stonehaven workers in the thigh. The man screamed and went down but the final worker charged past his associate, twisted metal bar raised high. Finn couldn't just stand by and let Sabrina be clubbed to death but he also didn't want to murder the man, so he fired the cannon and wounded the worker in the shoulder, forcing him to drop the bar. Then Finn charged out, baseball bat drawn back and yelling like a madman, forcing the worker to flee in terror.

"Fuck, thanks," Sabrina said, dropping to one knee, hands shaking. "For a second, I thought that bastard was going to get me."

Three of the Stonehaven workers had fled, but the injured man was still on the ground. The worker was trying desperately to claw himself to safety, but the crossbow bolt was buried deep and there was no escape.

"What do we do now?" Sabrina said, getting to her feet and pointing to the injured man. "Do I let him bleed out or does this already count as a kill?"

"No, it doesn't."

Finn spun around and aimed his cannon into the darkness as Death Echo stepped out of the shadows. She had been watching and evaluating their performance. Finn looked for Elara but he couldn't see his mentor or the shimmer of her chameleonic armor.

"Now, you finish him," Death Echo added, looking at the worker through dispassionate eyes as the man cried and pleaded for his life.

Sabrina nodded then drew one of her Sai and approached the offender, blade angled toward the man's throat.

"No, please don't!" the worker begged. "I didn't mean to damage that forklift. It was an accident! I'll work extra shifts to pay for it, please!"

Finn desperately wanted to intervene on behalf of the

worker but he knew he couldn't, just as he couldn't stop Sabrina from killing the man. If he did then he'd expose himself, and by extension Elara, and they'd both end up dead. Instead, and under the attentive gaze of Death Echo, he forced himself to watch Sabrina stab the Sai into the worker's chest and drive the blade into his heart. The man didn't die instantly and Finn could see how each tortuous second of the worker's death throes were carved into Sabrina' brain, like grooves on a record.

"Well done, Ruin," Death Echo said, as Sabrina sheathed her blood-stained weapon. It took three attempts because her hands were shaking so much. "The first kill is always the hardest. The next will be easier."

Death Echo then turned to Finn, and spared from the scrutiny of her mentor, Sabrina hunched over the side of a wall and vomited.

"Now it's your turn, Redeemer…" Death Echo said, speaking his name with disdain. "Let's see if you really are one of us."

23

BEST TEAM

Sabrina took a knee behind one of the dozens of vertical farming units in the Seedhaven mini-sector and checked her tracker. Finn covered his partner and surveyed their surroundings, spotting Death Echo watching them from the roof of an algae processing building. He looked for Elara but he couldn't see his former mentor, either because of her shadowy armor or because she was elsewhere. He hoped that she was helping Juniper, and while this thought gave him comfort, he also felt guilty that Elara was again risking her neck because of something he'd done.

"The three Stonehaven offenders who fled are moving into the Autohaven mini-sector," his partner said, scrutinizing the readings. "But they're still the closest. Should we go after them?"

"No, they'll be like cornered animals now, dangerous," Finn said, trying to discourage Sabrina from diverting them off course. "We should keep heading toward Seahaven. The tracker says there are another three offenders hiding out in there, close to the sector perimeter, so we can take them out enroute."

Sabrina checked her tracker, frowning. The three Stonehaven offenders were closer, as she'd pointed out, but Finn was banking on his partner accepting his made-up argument that they were more trouble than they were worth.

"Fine, we go after this new trio," Sabrina said, switching from her tracker to her crossbow. "So long as we stick together, I really don't give a shit."

"I'm not going anywhere," Finn said, stalking to her side. "After all, I'm playing catch up, and these new contacts are my ticket onto the scoreboard."

Sabrina laughed but it lacked her usual verve and Finn could see that was still in a state of shock. The kill she'd made was up-close and personal and it had shaken her to the core. She was putting on a brave face but it was obvious that the act of taking another person's life had split her in two. One half of Sabrina Brook was fighting to hold her nerve, and to keep Ruin alive, while the other was traumatized and sickened at what she'd done.

"Let's move out and get this over with," Sabrina said.

She pushed herself up but her legs were like jello and Sabrina was forced to grab a hold of the farming unit to anchor herself. She had tried to disguise her unsteadiness as a simple misstep but the act hadn't fooled Finn and she didn't try to bluff him.

"I bet Walter or Zach didn't lose their lunch at the sight of their first kills," Sabrina said, angry and embarrassed. "Some prosecutor I am."

"That just means you're a better person than they are," Finn replied. "Taking a life shouldn't be easy."

"At least he was a convicted offender," Sabrina said, rationalizing her action and trying to make herself feel better. "And it's our job to uphold the law. That's all I did. That's all we're doing, right?"

"That's right," Finn lied, as they resumed their hunt. "We're just upholding the law."

Finn wanted to tell Sabrina that she was wrong and that the trials had nothing to do with justice and everything to do with the Authority exerting fear and control on the worker population. He wanted to tell Sabrina that she'd killed that man for no good reason because he'd committed no crime that any sane society would recognize, but he didn't. He played his part and told her a comforting lie, and he hated himself for it.

"I guess this must be hard for you," Sabrina said, filling one of the awkward silences. "I mean, not long ago you were a worker too."

"That's all in the past, I'm a gold now," Finn said. He was good at telling this lie since he'd fed it to the evaluator robot every week for the past nine weeks. "Redeemer is my name. Finn Brasa died in a crucible, not unlike this one."

Sabrina nodded but it was clear that his answer had surprised her.

"You're handling this better than I expected," Finn's partner said. She then laughed weakly. "Shit, you're coping better than I am, that's for damned sure."

Finn's tracker vibrated and he signaled for Sabrina to stay quiet and take cover. He moved into hiding a few meters apart from her then leopard-crawled forward until he spotted the location his tracker had highlighted. It was an algae testing station near the edge of the sector, small enough to be innocuous but large enough to hide three or four workers. He pressed his hand to the webbing pouch where the phial was stored, feeling the cylinder push back against his skin, then instigated his plan.

"They're in there," Finn whispered to Sabrina, while pointing to the testing station. "Wait here and I'll ambush them. With any luck, I'll take out one quickly and flush the rest in your direction."

"I have some snares," his partner said, unhooking one of the devices from her webbing. "If I can trap the offenders as they run out, I can tag them with crossbow bolts, quick and painless."

"Good idea," Finn replied. He sensed that the 'quick and painless' part was important to her. "Let's get to it."

Sabrina nodded but her body was trembling again, causing the snare trap to rattle in her hands like a loose bolt. The prospect of taking another life was weighing heavy and Finn wondered whether the prosecutor alias that had been bestowed upon her was a curse rather than a gift. Instead of being the scourge of Zavetgrad's criminal population, the burden of becoming a prosecutor may end up being the ruin of Sabrina Brook instead.

"Hey, this time we make the kills cleanly, okay?" Sabrina added, pressing her hands tight to her body to stop them from shaking. "I'm not Zach. I don't enjoy seeing people suffer."

Finn nodded. He was glad that Sabrina was showing some compassion, because he knew that the others would not, but it didn't change the fact she was a killer, and he found it hard to have much sympathy for her.

Sabrina set out her snares, though Finn had no intention

of driving the offenders into her trap, then got into position, using part of a farming unit to support her aim. Finn gripped his baseball bat and was about to begin his approach when his partner called to him.

"Make sure you take one down if you can," Sabrina said in a hushed voice. "Death Echo wasn't messing around earlier. She doesn't believe you're a gold and neither do any of the other prosecutors. If you don't prove yourself they'll send you back to Metalhaven or even execute you."

Sabrina's concern for his welfare appeared genuine and it took him by surprise. Of course he knew that the prosecutors didn't trust him and never had done, but it had always remained unspoken, a truth that everyone knew but no-one said out loud.

"Why do you care?" Finn asked, interested to find out how long Sabrina's sudden bout of honesty would last.

"I kinda like you, chromeboy," she replied with a shrug. "Is that a crime?"

Finn laughed. "A few months ago, it probably was," he replied, and Sabrina laughed too. "Now, stay here and keep a steady aim. I'll be back before you know it."

Finn took off using the skills he'd learned in the training hall to move fast and without making a sound. He reached the rear of the outbuilding and peeked through a window, spotting three offenders huddled inside, shivering with cold and fear. There was a woman and two men, none of them any older than twenty-six or twenty-seven, he figured. All of them had injuries that suggested close scrapes with the other prosecutors but one of the men was more seriously hurt than the others. He had a makeshift bandage wrapped around his head, covering his left eye, and it was soaked through with blood.

Finn took a deep breath then stalked to the door furthest from where Sabrina was hiding, so that she wouldn't be able to see him enter, and wrapped his fingers around the handle. Releasing the air in his lungs, he threw open the door and darted inside, swinging the bat at the closest offender before any of them had even looked up and seen him coming. The clang of metal on bone was sickly sweet and the woman went down without making a sound. The man with the bandaged head cried out and dove under a table but the third offender held his ground. His jumpsuit was stained with blood but Finn recognized the color of the fabric because it was the same color as his armor.

"Fuck you, prosecutor pig!" the Metalhaven worker yelled, rusted metal bar in hand. "Metal and Blood!"

The man attacked but it was clumsy and rushed and Finn was able to swat the rusted bar away with ease. Even so, the offender didn't run and Finn recognized the grit in the man's eyes. He was a chrome from Metalhaven, just like him, and chromes didn't back down from a fight.

"Metal and Blood!" the man yelled again.

The chrome came at him, swinging punches at Finn's head and body like he was in a bar brawl, but Finn's guard was too strong and his armor was too tough, and before long the man had punched himself out. Finn retaliated, landing a measured combination of punches that dropped the exhausted man to his knees.

"At least kill us quickly," the worker said, mumbling like he had a mouthful of marbles. "You can give us that much, you fucking sadist."

"No-one is dying here," Finn said. Even beaten the chrome had guts enough to look him in the eyes. "At least, not right now."

"You're Finn Brasa?" the worker said, though he sounded uncertain.

"I am," Finn replied. "And I need your help."

"My help?" The man laughed, but it quickly became a painful wheeze. The chrome pointed to his companions, one barely conscious and the other still trembling beneath a table. "I don't think we're in much of position to help anyone."

Finn knelt beside the man and he shrank away, fearful that a dagger might soon be thrust into his neck, but Finn stowed his bat and held up his hands to show he was unarmed.

"We don't have much time, but I need you to trust me."

"Trust you?" The man snorted. "I was there in the recovery center for the yard one trial, when you snuck in and stirred shit up. Finn Brasa, the fucking Hero of Metalhaven, drinking in my bar..." He smiled as best he could as the memory crystalized. "You gave me hope that day. You gave us all hope." He laughed again. "And we also gave those prefects a good fucking hiding!" Finn laughed too; he remembered it well. Then the man rested a hand on his shoulder and sighed. "For a few glorious minutes, we were all free. It was a good feeling. Then it was gone and so were you."

The man coughed bitterly and blood oozed over his lips from where four teeth had been smashed out of his mouth.

"I remember," Finn said, also resting his hand on the man's shoulder. "I was proud of you all. Proud to be chrome."

"Metal and Blood, do you also remember that?" the man

mumbled, cradling his broken jaw. "I thought you were different, Finn. I never thought you'd end up like them."

"I haven't forgotten," Finn said, with feeling. "And I'm not one of them. Not now, not ever. I'm Metal and I'm not going to kill you, but I need to make it look like I have.

The man scowled at him. "How?"

Finn removed the phial from his webbing pouch and showed it to him. "This is a sedative," he explained as the man eyed the canister with interest. "It will lower your heart-rate to the point where the prosecutor tracking devices will register you as dead. After that, no-one will come for you, because no-one will know you're still in the crucible.

"Then what?" the man said. "We'll still be stuck here."

Finn hadn't thought this far ahead and he was torn over what to do next. If he told the man about the Metals and his escape plan, it might comprise his own chances of escape, especially if word spread. At the same time, if he lied then he was condemning the workers to death through an act of omission. It would be no different to him slitting their throats then and there.

"I'm getting out of here, today," Finn said, making his choice, for better or worse. "There's a way out in Seahaven, a tunnel system accessed under the water line. So long as the crucible is powered up, the electrified fence doesn't reach below ground. You can get out with me, to Haven. You all can."

The worker smiled at him but to Finn's surprise there was no suggestion he was intending to act on the information.

"So, you really are a Metal," the worker said. He grabbed Finn's arm and squeezed it in solidarity with him. "But I can't come with you. None of us can. We'd get you caught."

"No, it'll be okay," Finn said, stunned at the refusal. "I can't just leave you here, not when there's a chance..."

"There's no chance, not for us," the man said, cutting him off. He took the phial from Finn's hand, removed the lid and knocked a few drops onto his tongue. "Do the others too. At least then no-one else will come after us and maybe we can hide out in here." He laughed, though his eyelids were already fluttering and drooping. "It's better than working the fucking yard..."

"What's your name?" Finn asked. Already the man's eyes were glassy.

"Erik," the man replied. "Though call me Trip, everyone does."

Finn smiled. "Why?"

"Because when I go to the bar, I get a pint for my pal and three pints for me!"

Trip tried to laugh but the man's legs suddenly gave out and Finn barely managed to catch him before his head hit the metal floor. The phial fell from the workers hand and he picked it up, salvaging its contents. Finn lay the worker down and at the same time the man with the bandaged head shuffled out from beneath the table. He took the phial and tapped three drops onto his tongue before moving over to the woman Finn had clubbed and doing the same to her. Within seconds, all three offenders were out cold on the floor, and not long after their signals had disappeared from Finn's tracker. He checked the scoreboard on his wrist-mounted device and it confirmed his kill. The number three was listed beside his name, "Redeemer".

Suddenly, Sabrina burst through the door armed with her

Sai, and Finn was so surprised that he almost blasted her with his laser cannon.

"You did all three?" Sabrina said, dropping her hands to her side.

Finn nodded. "Piece of cake."

Sabrina laughed, though it was a nervous laugh.

"Shit, Finn, I don't know whether to be impressed or fucking terrified of you," Sabrina said.

Finn got to his feet and grinned at his shaken partner, remembering to play the role of Redeemer, Prosecutor of Zavetgrad.

"If I were you, I'd be both," he said, slapping her on the back and jolting her out of the door.

The joke broke the tension and she shook her head at him. "It looks like I'm the one who needs to make up my kill numbers," she said. "So, I guess we'd better get to Seahaven."

Finn nodded and invited Sabrina to take the lead, then when she'd gone, he picked up the phial of sedative from the unconscious worker's hand and returned it to his webbing. He took one last look at the worker from Metalhaven who had refused his offer to escape, a man braver and more selfless than he had ever been, then left and closed the door behind him.

24

THE BOATHOUSE

SABRINA RECOVERED her snare trap from outside the algae testing station then hooked the device to her armor and jogged back to Finn's side. In the meantime, he'd checked his tracker device, noting two key points. The first, which was the least relevant but most irritating, was that Walter "Vigor" Foster was at the top of the kills leaderboard with six victims to his name. Fourteen offenders remained, which meant that Walter had claimed more than half of the kills so far.

The second and vastly more concerning point, at least so far as Finn was concerned, was that Juniper's signal had disappeared from his tracker. He'd been following her bronze marker on the scanner display as she headed through the Makehaven mini-sector toward Seahaven, then it had vanished. For a heart-wrenching moment he thought she was dead but the scoreboard that tallied each prosecutor's kills hadn't increased. It was like Juniper had vanished without a trace, and without any information to go on, he assumed – he hoped – that this was Elara's doing. In any case, Finn had no choice but to continue to the boathouse, where he would hopefully find Juniper waiting for him, and they would escape together. However, in order for that to happen he had to perform the unhappy duty of ditching Sabrina.

If his mentor were with him, Elara would have no doubt suggested that Finn simply kill her, but he wasn't going to do that. It wasn't his place to act as judge, jury and executioner. That would make him no better than a gold. Besides, he liked Sabrina, as much as he wished he didn't. One day, perhaps, there would be a reckoning and the golds of Zavetgrad would pay for their crimes, but that was not this day. Today, his mission was to survive and escape.

"We should split up a little as we enter Seahaven," Finn said to his partner. They were approaching the end of the Seedhaven mini-sector and he needed to lose her soon. "We're a bigger, easier target huddled close like this, and Seahaven is much more open. The offenders could see us coming and lay an ambush."

Sabrina frowned at him. "You're not trying to get rid of me, are you?"

Finn laughed, hoping that it would hide any tells that might give away his true intentions, which were exactly as his partner had just described.

"No, I just don't want to get ambushed by an angry mob," Finn replied. He grinned again, or rather, Redeemer did. "Besides, I want to claim more of the kills for myself and add to my tally."

"What happened to us being the best team?" Sabrina said, playing along.

"We are the best team," Finn replied, still grinning. "But every team has a star player and that's going to be me."

"Bullshit!" Sabrina snorted. "We'll see who has the highest number of kills by the time this is over."

Finn began to inch away from Sabrina but she grabbed his sleeve before he was out of reach. "Hey, don't go too far, though," she said. Suddenly, the game wasn't funny anymore. "I need you, chromeboy. I can't do this on my own."

"I'll be watching you the whole time," Finn said, squeezing the armor plating on her shoulder. "As soon as I spot an offender, I'll signal you and we take them together, okay?"

Sabrina nodded. "Okay," she said, reassured.

Finn smiled then released his partner and snuck away, using the towering vertical farming units for cover. Sabrina watched him go, growing more anxious and afraid as the distance between them increased. He waited until she took her eyes off him to move ahead, then dove into cover and hid. Rolling onto his back, he lifted his arm and removed the tracking device from his armor before tossing it as far away as he could manage. Wasting no time, he shifted onto his stomach and crawled in the opposite direction, toward Seahaven, and pulled himself up behind another algae testing station at the perimeter of the sector.

"Finn!" The hushed call was barely audible but it was loud enough for him to hear the anguish in her cry.

"Finn, come on, this isn't funny!" Sabrina risked a louder call, which only emphasized her fear. "Stop fucking around, I mean it!"

Finn blew out a heavy sigh then set his jaw and moved out. He reminded himself that Sabrina was not his friend, not really, and that she was not someone to feel sorry for. She was a Prosecutor of Zavetgrad and a killer. That he liked her didn't change anything.

"Finn, please!" Sabrina shouted.

This time the shout was unrestrained, despite the risk of giving away her position. The stab of guilt Finn felt rose proportionate with the increased volume of her cry. He cursed under his breath then stole away, quickly crossing the boundary between the Seedhaven and Seahaven sectors, before making a run for an abandoned smokehouse that would keep him hidden from view. Without his tracker, he had no idea where the offenders or other prosecutors were located and was forced to rely on his senses and his training to guide him. Laser cannon charged and baseball bat held firmly in his grasp, he stalked deeper into the sector, eyes locked onto the stretch of water where he would make his escape.

"I hope you're out there, Juniper…" Finn whispered, knowing that if she wasn't already hiding inside the boathouse, he wouldn't be able to wait for her.

An anguished cry floated across the crucible from the direction of the Makehaven mini-sector but it wasn't Sabrina this time. Instead, it was the death cries of another worker being executed, probably by Walter or Zach. Fourteen had remained the last time he'd checked his tracker, with each further death acting like a doomsday clock counting down. Once all the offenders were dead the test trial would end, and Finn knew he had to be long gone before that happened.

Moving into cover behind a rusted, snow-covered fishing boat that was in drydock, Finn steeled himself to make the final dash to the boathouse when he heard a sound like the scuffing of boots. He froze and listened intently, then the noise came again and he aimed his laser cannon in the direction of the sound. Someone was approaching from the opposite side of the stranded fishing boat, trying to sneak up behind him. He dropped to a crouch and waited, ready to ambush his attacker before they had chance to strike first. Then he felt cold steel at his neck and his muscles tensed up like he'd been gripped by an electric current. He managed to catch a glimpse of the blade as it protruded past his chin and saw that it was jet black, like the water he was working his way toward.

"You're dead," Elara said, removing the roundel dagger from his neck.

"How the hell did you do that?" Finn said, turning to face his mentor. "I heard you coming, but from the other direction."

Elara removed a puck-shaped device from her armor and activated it. The object began to vibrate and make a scuffing sound, exactly like the one he'd heard.

"You never taught me that trick," Finn said, embarrassed but also impressed.

"A woman needs some secrets," Elara replied, pithily. "Besides, if I taught you everything I know then you'd know everything you needed to kill me."

Finn scowled at her. "I never wanted to kill you."

Elara raised her eyebrows and Finn accepted that this was a lie.

"Okay, in the beginning maybe I did, before I knew who you were, truly," Finn explained. "But surely you must trust me now?"

"I trusted you with my most dangerous secret," Elara said, biting back anger. "And you threw that trust back in my face."

Finn knew it was neither the time nor the place for them

to have an argument so he bit his tongue and accepted his mentor's disappointment.

"We have to make our move now," Elara continued, switching gears so that The Shadow was back in control. "I see that you've already ditched your tracker and Sabrina, and I've taken care of her mentor, so we're good to go."

"How exactly have you taken care of Death Echo?" Finn wondered.

"I didn't kill her, if that's what you mean, not that I wouldn't like to," Elara said. Finn noticed that her tracking device was missing too. "I just knocked her out and ditched her body. When Ayla comes around, she'll think it was an offender that got lucky and not say a word to anyone about it. She'd never admit to Voss that she was bested by a lowly worker. He'd strip her of her prosecutor title and put her on trial herself."

"What about Juniper, is she safe?" Finn asked.

Elara's jaw tightened and her eyes sharpened and Finn realized he was pushing his luck to the limit.

"I only ask because her marker vanished from my tracker, but the device didn't register her as dead," Finn explained, trying to ease Elara's tensions. "I was hoping you had something to do with that?"

"I should have put a damned crossbow bolt in her head, but I disabled her tracker, yes," Elara said. Finn blew a sigh of relief, though this only seemed to irritate his former mentor further. "After that, I don't know what happened to her. I gave her advice on how to reach Seahaven unseen, but I left it up to her to make it."

"Thank you," Finn replied. He knew there were no certainties but Elara had at least given Juniper a fighting chance. "You're a good person, Elara, despite what you may think of yourself."

"Don't try to mollify me," Elara snapped. "I only did it so you wouldn't risk the mission trying to save her yourself."

"So you already told me," Finn said, though he knew in his heart there was more to her decision than simple logic. "But I don't believe it, not for one second."

"We're wasting time," Elara said, tuning her back and walking away.

Finn hurried to her side. He knew this might be the last chance he got to speak to her and he wasn't going to waste it. "I'm sorry for what I said before," Finn continued, staying close by his old mentor's side so that she had no choice but to hear him. "I don't believe your soul is lost. In fact, I know that the old Elara Cage is still in there somewhere, and despite everything you've done, you deserve a second chance."

Elara stopped dead and faced him. She looked more tired than angry.

"They're just words, Finn," Elara said. "We both know that I'm rotten, and we both know that if it was me on trial instead of Juniper, you wouldn't risk your neck to save mine."

Finn recoiled from her. He didn't know whether she'd intended to wound him or whether she truthfully believed what she said, which was far worse.

"I'd give my life for you, if that's what it took," Finn said, holding her emerald eyes without blinking. "Without you, I'd already be dead. I owe you everything, Elara, and I'd give everything to keep you alive."

Elara tilted her head to one side and her eyes, usually so unwavering, flickered like candlelight in a breeze. She opened her mouth to speak then turned away so that he couldn't see her face.

"We're wasting time," she said again, walking away.

Finn followed, still intent to say more, but each time he was about to draw level, his mentor quickened her pace so that Finn remained always a few steps behind her. Then they were at the boathouse and the urgency of their mission overrode everything else. The time for words was over and he hoped he'd said enough.

"I have to go into the water to open the gate," Elara said, pulling two cigar-shaped objects out of a pocket in her armor and fixing them to a mouthpiece. "This is a rebreather, it will allow me to stay underwater for several minutes."

"I don't suppose you have one for me?" Finn asked. He was looking at the water in front of the boathouse, which was still and black like the night sky. "As you can probably guess, I have no idea how to swim."

"Once the hatch is open, you won't need to," Elara said, screwing the cylinders into the mouthpiece. "You just jump in and pull yourself inside. The inner chamber is only partially flooded. There's enough headroom and air for you to make it through."

Finn nodded but he was still uncertain. They had reached the part of the plan that required a leap of faith, literally.

"Wait here, and stay out of sight," Elara said. She moved to the water's edge then glanced back at him. "And see if you can find your precious paramour. If she's not here by the time I return, you either leave without her, or don't leave at all."

With that, Elara crashed through the surface of the black water and vanished, leaving nothing more than a swirl of bubbles behind, which rapidly dissipated to nothing.

Suddenly, alone, Finn backed inside the boathouse, and tightened his hold on his baseball bat, seeing every shadow and dark corner as a possible hiding place where an offender could leap out at him. He wouldn't even put it past Walter and Ivan to be stalking him. A quick hammer blow to the head would be all it took to take him down, then "Vigor" could simply push his body in to the water and make up any story he wished.

A scuffle of feet snapped Finn out of his macabre daydream and set his senses on high alert. Remembering how Elara had so easily tricked him, he backed into a corner so that no-one could flank him, and raised his bat, ready to swing. The sound came again followed by the flicker of a shadow from further inside the boathouse. He tried to get a look at whoever was sneaking up on him, but his view was blocked by a mass of worn fishing nets that stank of stale water and mold.

"Juniper?..." Finn whispered, taking a chance that the other person was his paramour. "Juniper, it's Finn. If that's you, then step out into the light."

The shadow moved then a figure walked into the open; a woman with golden yellow hair wearing a bronze jumpsuit. Finn practically threw down his baseball bat and ran to her, wrapping his arms around Juniper and squeezing her so tightly that she squealed.

"I was worried you wouldn't make it," Finn said, releasing his hold on her and drawing back.

"There was never any doubt," Juniper said, smiling at him. "I'm glad you made it too."

Considering how broken she had been when Finn had found her in her tenement building, Juniper appeared unreasonably calm and composed, as if the horrors of the trial were little more than a forgotten dream. She looked exactly as he remembered her in the line-up before the trial had begun, with not even a hair out of place, while her jumpsuit looked clean and fresh, like she'd only just put it on.

"Are you okay?" Finn said. He felt like she should be panicky and breathless, as he was. "Did something happen?"

"A lot has happened, Finn," Juniper said.

She stepped back and pressed her hands in front of her stomach in the quietly-reflective pose that she always adopted. It was only then that Finn noticed an addition to her humble outfit; a C.O.N.F.I.R.M.E. computer wrapped around her left wrist. There were more scuffles of feet and flickering shadows, and three special prefects in black and gold armor emerged into the boathouse behind her.

"Juniper watch out!" Finn yelled, aiming his cannon at the officers, but he couldn't get a clean shot, not without risking Juniper.

"It's okay, Finn," Juniper said, smiling sweetly like the first time they'd met. "It's over now."

More special prefects burst into the boathouse, three from each side, all armed with sub-machine guns and riot batons, and Finn was surrounded.

"Lower your weapon, Finn," Juniper said. "You can't win."

"You're one of them?" Finn gasped, and Juniper nodded.

Finn felt like his world had fallen apart but he was still armed and he still had a choice. He could be captured by the woman who had played him for a fool and become the Authority's latest trophy, or he could fight and die and give them nothing. In the end, it was no choice at all.

"Maybe I can't win," Finn said, aiming his laser cannon at Juniper's heart. "But I can die and take you with me."

He squeezed the trigger, expecting to burn a hole into Juniper Jones' deceitful, black heart, but the cannon didn't fire. Gritting his teeth he hammered the trigger again and again, willing it to shoot, but still nothing happened. Then three special prefects grabbed his arms and twisted them behind his back, immobilizing him and forcing him to his knees.

"I disabled your cannon, I hope you don't mind," Juniper said.

She stepped forward, hands still in place, smile intact, then crouched in front of him. He tried to grab her, but there was no chance. He was her captive and she knew it.

"I hope you're looking forward to tonight's date, Finn Brasa, Traitor of Metalhaven," Juniper said. The smell of her perfume washed over him and it made him sick. "I've picked out a special cell, just for you."

25

MEETING CANCELLED

Finn was hauled to his feet by special prefects and marched in front of Juniper Jones. She had unzipped her bronze jumpsuit to waist level, revealing skin-tight black amour, like a scorpion's carapace. The emblem of the Authority, gleaming in polished twenty-four-carat gold, adorned the left chest section of the armor, while a special prefect badge sat opposite. She wore no discernible rank but it was clear from how the other officers deferred to her that Juniper was superior to them all.

"I trusted you," Finn said, watching as Juniper slipped out of the jumpsuit then kicked the garment into the water, like it was trash. "I thought you were my friend. I thought you liked me. Loved me, even."

Juniper laughed and suddenly any affection he felt for the woman was gone, like a mist burned away by the morning sun.

"Of course you trusted me," Juniper said, attaching her C.O.N.F.I.R.M.E. computer to the black shell of armor that covered her body up to the neckline. "I know how to make men and women trust me. And I know how to make them love me too."

She tilted her head to one side and took a step closer to Finn, drawing the back of her hand down the side of his face. "I wonder, did you love *me*?" she asked.

"No," Finn replied. He spoke cruelly in the hope his bluntness hurt her somehow, though he doubted Juniper had ever cared for him at all. "There was a time I thought I might have loved you, but I realize now that it was nothing, just like you and I are nothing to one another."

"A shame," Juniper said, straightening her head. "Most men love me in the end. It's easy once I get them into bed, but you held out. It seems that Elara kept you honest."

Finn laughed. "Or maybe I just didn't find you attractive."

Juniper's eyes hardened but her Mona Lisa smile remained as she moved her lips close to his ear, allowing her hair to brush Finn's face, filling his senses with her intoxicating scent.

"I know you wanted me, Finn," she whispered, and her breath on his neck sent shivers down his spine. "But I also knew you felt more for her than you ever could for me."

Juniper drew back, still hiding behind her perfect smile, but Finn had spent enough time with his fictional paramour to recognize the cracks in her once flawless repertoire, and he knew he had wounded her. He could see it in her eyes, the humiliation and indignation of rejection.

"I suppose I can't blame you," Juniper said. She shrugged and began to circle around him, like a wasp trying to get at something sweet. "She is beautiful in a crude sort of fashion, like an uncut gemstone, and she's strong too."

Finn scowled at her. "What the hell are you talking about?"

Juniper feigned surprise. "Oh, come now, Finn, let's not pretend you don't have feelings for your precious mentor? Why else would you reject me?"

Finn was about to protest when the words suddenly caught in his throat. Juniper was right. Elara had always been there, right in front of him, but her shadowy façade had hidden the truth. Now, he saw it clearly and it was so obvious he felt stupid for not noticing sooner.

"I should have foreseen that a chrome from Metalhaven would fall for one of their own," Juniper continued, as Finn stared into space, trying to process the jumble of emotions that were bombarding him. "That's why, in the end, I had to revert to a different playbook."

Juniper stopped behind him and leaned in close again. "Finn Brasa, the knight in shining armor come to rescue the helpless maiden..." She laughed. "I should have gone with that from the start. It would have spared me weeks of our tedious dates."

Finn stood tall. He knew what came next and he wanted to make sure Juniper knew that his ability to resist didn't stop at her charms.

"You're sick, all you golds are," Finn said, eyes straight and level. "And you must know that I won't tell you anything."

"You all say that in the beginning," Juniper said, circling around to face him again. "But you'd be surprised at how persuasive pain can be."

A voice crackled on Juniper's C.O.N.F.I.R.M.E. computer and Finn recognized the speaker right away.

"Skycar Juniper P-1 on final approach," said the evaluator

robot, cheerful as ever. It could have been a different model to the one who had spent weeks interrogating him but Finn didn't think so. "Is the offender in custody?"

"I have him," Juniper replied, flashing her eyes at Finn. "Land at once. I want to get started right away."

"Affirmative," the robot replied.

Finn heard the roar of the skycar's rotors before he saw the jet-black vehicle descending through the cloud-covered sky. It landed a few hundred meters away, in a clearing between the perimeter fence and the edge of the Seahaven mini-sector. Then, as he was watching, he caught the glint of something metallic on the roof of an adjacent building. He narrowed his eyes and focused on the point then saw the object wave a delicate metal hand at him. It had an oil-can for a body, painted chrome and gold.

Scraps... Finn thought, clamping his jaw tight shut so that the sudden swell of emotion didn't color his grim expression. He had no idea what his little robot had in mind, but he knew that Scraps had a plan, and he needed to stall Juniper to find out what it was.

"Was this test trial set up just to trap me?" Finn asked, stealing his captor's attention away from the computer. "Am I that important?"

"You're not important at all," Juniper said, harshly. She was insulted by the mere suggestion that Finn mattered. "But the Metals seem to think you are, which makes you important to me. You are my way into the spy network that has invaded Zavetgrad like a cockroach infestation. With your help, we'll find these Metals and force them to expose their entire operation. Then, once we're sure the rot has been eradicated, we'll attack Haven and kill every last man, woman and child inside."

Finn wasn't prepared for the level of vitriol and hate that had spewed from the woman's mouth. He'd only ever known Juniper Jones as a vivacious and caring human being without a bad bone in her body, but the ugly truth was now laid bare. The Authority was a hive of zealots and fanatics obsessed with their own superiority, and in amongst that hive, Juniper Jones was a queen.

"Even your meagre estimation of my worth is exaggerated," Finn said, determined to remain strong and unwavering. A Metal. "I don't know anything about Haven, other than that it exists. And I don't know any Metals. So torture me all you like, but I can't give you anything of value."

Juniper shook her head and snorted a laugh at him, determined to mock and denigrate him at every turn. "Do you think we don't know that?" she sneered. "You may not know anything, Finn, but your mentor and arch-conspirator does."

Finn felt his throat tighten and his stomach harden but he tried not to let Juniper see his weakness.

"Elara Cage will tell us everything," Juniper continued, reveling in her victory over him. "She'll tell us everything because if not, we'll hurt you. She'll stay strong for a time, knowing that you can handle a beating, but once we start sending her little pieces of you, she'll crack. It may take a few fingers and toes, or maybe a whole hand to break her, but I promise you that she'll break, because whether she admits it or not, you matter to her too."

"You underestimate Elara," Finn said, the words scratchy

in his throat. "She's tougher than anyone I've ever met. She won't break."

He expected Juniper to laugh again and mock him, but instead her expression hardened like magma cooling in an icy ocean, and she looked like a different woman. Cruel, jagged and unyielding.

"She'll break," Juniper whispered, and the words carried with them the anticipation of violence. "One way or another, Traitor of Metalhaven, I always get what I want."

Suddenly, a rock sailed past Finn's face and struck Juniper on the side of the head. She cried out, more from shock than pain, and reeled back, pressing her hand to the wound. She looked at the fresh blood wetting her fingers with a mix of anger and confusion, then another rock whistled past and struck her above the left eye, knocking her off her feet.

"There, look!" one of the special prefects yelled, then all eyes were on Scraps, who sat on the roof the boathouse, with a line of rocky ammo at his side.

"Shoot it!" Juniper yelled, shrugging off the offer of help from another officer. "Shoot it but watch the traitor! I need him alive!"

Five officers opened fire with their sub-machine guns but Scraps had already moved, using his rotors to dart from place to place, too fast for the special prefects to track. Three officers then electrified their nightsticks and surrounded Finn, but even outnumbered he bet on himself to win the fight. The Authority had trained him well and his armor was strong.

A nightstick was thrust at his neck, but he dodged the weapon then crushed the attacker's nose with a brutal strike from his armored forearm. The nightstick was now in his grasp and he knew how to use it better than the officers facing him. Blocking and evading two separate assaults, he waited for an opening then seized it, ramming the nightstick under one officer's armpit and sending thousands of volts coursing through his body. The man dropped like a stone onto the concrete floor and Finn stepped over the convulsing body, launching a flurry of strikes at his remaining opponent. The man was skilled, all special prefects were, but Finn was a Prosecutor of Zavetgrad and twice the fighter he was. He crushed muscles and snapped bone, not even bothering to use the nightstick's paralyzing shock-prongs to defeat his enemy. His anger was raw like an exposed nerve and even more charged than the electrical tension pent up inside the baton. The man fell at his feet, but nine special prefects remained, and even with his new skills, he couldn't hope to beat that many.

"Enough!" Juniper yelled.

She was back on her feet, blood streaking down the left side of her face like racing stripes, and the men stopped firing at her command. Finn scanned his eyes across the roof of the boathouse, now pockmarked and perforated with bullet holes, but there was no sign of Scraps, dead or alive.

"Bind his hands!" Juniper added. She came across unhinged. "Fall back to the skycar!"

Three more officers approached him and Finn steeled his body and mind, ready to fight them to the death if necessary, but before they reached him the lead prefect was shot in the neck by a crossbow bolt and sent down. A shimmering blur floated past, like a burst of steam from the nozzle of a kettle, and a black blade flashed, opening the throats of the two other men. The officers dropped to their knees, croaking and spluttering as they died, leaving the rest of the special prefect unit in shock. Finn felt no surprise. He knew what had happened, and he knew exactly what to do next.

With his laser cannon still disabled, Finn grabbed one of the prefect's sub-machine guns and clicked the weapon to automatic. Squeezing the trigger, he poured all of his rage into every bullet that escaped the barrel of the weapon, until the remaining six prefects lay dead on the ground. Then the shimmer resolved into the shape of Elara, roundel dagger in hand, dripping with blood and pointed directly at Juniper.

"You!" she roared, advancing toward the woman. "You and me. Now!"

Finn expected Juniper to run but to his surprise she held her ground. Pulling a knife off the body of a dead prefect, she discarded the scabbard and met Elara's challenge.

"We should have killed you the moment you set foot in the Authority sector," Juniper said, juggling the knife in her hand. "Even then, we knew you were trouble."

"You have no idea how much trouble I can be," Elara snarled, "but you're about to find out."

Elara was poised to attack when the stomp of heavy boots behind Juniper caused her to hesitate. A figure entered from the rear of the boathouse, at first in shadow, until it reached Juniper's side and was revealed by moonlight. It was the evaluator robot that had interrogated Finn, smiling its same soporific mechanical smile, as if they were about to have another interview session.

"Hello, Finn, it's good to see you again," the robot said. "I found it very interesting that you were able to defeat my tests, and I am very interested to learn how you achieved this."

Finn had never seen the machine out of its chair in Room

616 but now that he had, the robot was massive. Bigger even that a foreman, it was at least seven feet tall and possessed the strength to tear his arms off. Juniper's smirk said it all. Knives and crossbows were no use against this mechanical behemoth, which was as much assassin as it was interrogator.

"Take them, both," Juniper said, slinking behind the machine. "Break bones if you have to but I need them alive."

"Affirmative," the evaluator robot replied, cheerfully.

The machine stomped forward, then out of nowhere, Scraps dropped onto its head like a dive bomber. The evaluator's mechanical eyes narrowed and it tried to grab Scraps, but the little robot had already stuck something into the machine's ear hole and flown away. Confused, the evaluator yanked the probe out of its ear and scowled at it. Then its body convulsed and rattled like a car driving over cobblestones before its power core shut down.

"Evaluator, activate!" Juniper yelled, but the machine didn't response. "Evaluator, protect me, that's an order!" Still nothing.

Finn laughed and strode over to where he'd discarded his baseball bat after Juniper had first appeared to him.

"I think today's evaluation has been cancelled," Finn said, returning to the machine and tapping it with the bat. It made a hollow sound, like an empty oil can. "What a shame, I was growing to really like this bucket of bolts."

He swung the bat as hard as he could and the evaluator robot's head sailed off its neck and landed, crashing and shrieking across the concrete floor, at Juniper's feet. The woman cried out then charged at Elara, wielding her knife with the skill of a prosecutor. Blades clashed and scraped across armored bodies, each woman landing blows and taking them. Juniper's C.O.N.F.I.R.M.E. computer was cut from her wrist and skidded across the floor, coming to rest beside the evaluator's head. Then another slash of the roundel dagger cut through Juniper's carapace armor and sliced through her flesh. She yelped and backed away, cradling the wound to her shoulder.

"This isn't over," Juniper growled, speaking to Finn rather than her opponent. "It's only a matter of time before we find all the other Metals and Haven falls."

Elara darted forward but Juniper dodged then landed a foreman strike to her throat. It wasn't enough to put her down but it gave Juniper the precious seconds she needed to escape. Finn gave chase but Juniper was faster and more agile and soon he had lost sight of her. He stopped and listened but even the sound of her footsteps was absent, as if she had vanished into thin air.

Juniper Jones, if that was even her name, was gone for now, but whatever came next for Finn in the days, weeks and months that he hoped still lay ahead, he knew that he would see her again.

26

THEN DON'T

"Should we go after her?" Finn said, running back to Elara. She had recovered from Juniper's attack but looked as mad as a bottle of wasps that had just been shaken.

"No, forget her, we need to get you out," Elara said, rushing to the water's edge. "The water outlet is open and the Metals will be waiting. There's no time."

"Fine, but you're coming with me," Finn said. Elara shot him a look that could have cracked diamond, but he stood firm. "Don't give me any shit, Elara. Juniper knows you're with the Metals, which means you're compromised. If you stay, they'll arrest and torture you."

Elara looked ready to argue but Finn was right and she knew it. He used her moment of hesitation to drive the point home in a way he knew she couldn't refuse.

"You're either coming with me, or neither of us leave," Finn said. He wasn't bluffing. "So what's next? How do we escape?"

"It's like I told you, already," Elara said, looking into the black water. "We jump in and pull ourselves into the drainage tunnel and keep going until we're outside the gate."

"Fine, you first," Finn said. He had his fish on the hook and wasn't going to let it escape.

"When we're clear of the city, you and I are going have a little talk," Elara said.

Finn had a special talent for pissing people off, but no-one had ever looked like they wanted to punch him more than Elara did in that moment. His former mentor then took up position and was about to jump into the water when Scraps zoomed in front of her, waving his arms.

"Wait-wait!" Scraps yelled. "Tunnel closed. Metals gone!"

"What?" Elara said, inching back from the edge. "Are you sure?"

"Yes-yes!" Scraps replied. "Prefects alerted. No way out!"

Elara cursed and stormed away from the water, fingers pressed to her temples, thinking hard, but their plan was sunk, just like their escape route.

"Then it's over," Elara said, turning to face Finn. "All we can do now is fight."

"It's not over until we're dead," Finn said, refusing to give in. "We find a way out of the crucible and make our way to Metalhaven. There are people there who can harbor us until we get word to the Metals. We just have to be patient, smart."

Elara considered his idea but shook her head.

"They might hide you, the Hero of Metalhaven, but not me," she replied. "I'm not a chrome anymore. To the workers of Metalhaven, I'm part of the Authority."

"I'll vouch for you and tell them who you really are," Finn insisted. He moved closer, but she backed away, as if she was radioactive and feared she might taint him. "You're with me and that's all they need to know."

Elara thought some more but Finn knew that she wasn't going to agree. He also knew the reason why, which had nothing to do with the logic of his argument. It was simply because Elara had convinced herself that she wasn't worth saving and deserved to be punished for what she had become.

"Wait-wait!" Scraps said, suddenly zooming in and landing on Elara's shoulder. "Scraps has plan!"

"What is it, pal?" Finn said, experiencing a rush of anticipation. "Anything has to be better than what we've got now."

Scraps leapt off Elara's shoulder then landed on the head of the evaluator robot. "Scraps reprogram bad-robot," Scraps said. "Make robot friend!"

"But it's just a head, pal, what use is that?" Finn asked.

"Skycar!" Scraps said, climbing to a hover and pointing to where the evaluator had landed the special prefect skycar. "Scraps make bad-robot fly skycar!"

Finn picked up the head of the evaluator and couldn't help but smile as he examined the enormous dent his baseball bat had put into the machine's metal cranium.

"But even if you can hack the evaluator and make it fly the Skycar, we can't use it to escape," Elara said. "All skycars are limited to an altitude of a hundred-and-ninety meters from ground level, ten meters below the top of the fence."

"Scraps can re-program," the robot said, shrugging casually.

"Really?" Finn asked. "You can reprogram the skycar to fly over the fence?"

"Yes-yes!" Scraps replied. "Scraps clever. Finn made him so!"

Finn looked at Elara and she looked back, eyebrows raised, and for once not looking entirely cynical.

"It could work," she said.

"It *will* work," Finn corrected her.

He picked up the C.O.N.F.I.R.M.E. computer that Elara had cut from Juniper's wrist and attached it to his own armor using magnetic clasps, figuring it might come in useful. Then he clipped the head of the evaluator robot onto his webbing, picked up a sub-machine gun from the ground and stood ready.

"Let's do this," Finn said. "Haven awaits."

Scraps led the way, flying just high enough that he could keep a lookout and alert them of any dangers, but despite the interruption by the special prefects, the trial was still ongoing, as if nothing unusual had happened. Reaching the perimeter of the Seahaven mini-sector, Finn was finally able to take in the boundary fence in its full majesty. Rising two-hundred meters into the air, and loaded with enough electricity to fry a dragon, it had stood for centuries, an impenetrable barrier keeping the workers of Zavetgrad locked inside the city walls. No-one had scaled it since the very first Metals escaped to found Haven. Finn intended to be next.

"Wait-wait!"

Scraps' alert cry flipped a switch in Finn's brain and his training kicked in. Moving fast and low, he snuck into cover with Elara close by and also concealed. Then he looked across the narrow plain between them and the fence and saw the reason for his robot's warning. There was not one skycar parked on the snow-covered concrete but two. The first was jet-black, like Juniper's carapace armor, while the other was gold.

"That's a prosecutor's skycar," Elara said, observing the scene. She looked at him, anxious but still determined. "It's Voss' skycar. They must know what happened."

The gull-wing doors of the golden vehicle swung open, then men and women dressed in shining armor and armed to the teeth filed out. Finn recognized them all: Sabrina, Walter, Tonya, Ivan and Zach, new prosecutors, all. Then their mentors alighted, but Finn counted only three. There was Andre "Frost" Regan, Cleo "Garrote" McKay and Kurt "Blitz" McCullough, but no Death Echo.

"Are you sure you didn't kill Ayla Price instead of just knocking her out?" Finn said, frowning.

Elara shrugged. "I'm not exactly certain, no," she said, cagily. Finn continued to scowl at her and she threw up her hands. "Okay, I might have killed her. She was a pain in the ass."

Finn huffed a laugh. "Don't be sorry. If what I think is about to happen, happens, you'll have done us a favor."

A final figure emerged from the skycar, and advanced to the head of the pack. It was Apex himself, Dante Voss, Chief Prosecutor of Zavetgrad. He had a pistol in his right hand but was otherwise unarmed and still wearing his regular uniform.

"Despite his rank, Voss is just a regular gold," Elara said. "His loyalty is to his prosecutors, but the special prefects are above the law. Even Voss will do what they say."

Finn nodded. "Which means we'll have to fight our way out."

"It will mean fighting the people you trained with," Elara

said. She looked at him to make sure he understood. "It will mean killing them."

"I know," Finn replied, speaking the words as part of a stoic sigh.

Ivan, Walter, even Tonya he could rationalize. They would all kill him in a heartbeat given half a chance, but Sabrina was another matter.

"Don't forget who they are," Elara said, sensing his unease. "Don't forget what they are. And don't for a single second think that they are your friends."

"We know you're out there!" Voss cried. Even without an amplifier, the man's voice carried to them like it had been blared through a PA speaker. "And we know what you are. Traitors... Metals!"

"He really does love the sound of his own voice," Finn muttered, wishing he was close enough to put his fist through Voss' teeth.

"Now, you will pay the price," Voss continued. "New prosecutors, bring them to me alive for interrogation. Earn your names and you will honor us all!"

There was a resounding cheer of, "Apex!" then Ivan Volkov stepped forward with Finn's other classmates in tow, each of them brandishing the weapons that had recently been bestowed upon them. Ivan had his flintlock pistol, glaive and ornate rapier at his hip. Walter held a golden javelin in his right hand and his steel warhammer in the other. Tonya's shotgun was crude and short-range, but she also had her knives and her speed. Then there was Zach, who only wanted to kill, and didn't care who fell at his feet. The man hadn't even bothered to carry his harpoon, and simply waited, impatient, chainsaw growling like an angry beast.

"Care to give me one final lesson?" Finn said, as his classmates advanced. "Because I don't know how we get past those five, let alone Voss and the other prosecutors."

"I have an idea," Elara said. She was carefully loading a poisoned bolt into his crossbow. "It should buy us some leeway, but there's no getting away from this. We're outnumbered and we're going to have to fight harder than either of us have ever fought in our lives."

Finn nodded, thinking back to his final confrontation with Bloodletter at his trial, and how that had led to Owen's death and him beating Corbin Radcliffe senseless with his bare hands. That memory had never left him. The squelch of his fists against pulpy flesh. The crunch of bone. The roar of blood in his ears. It haunted him and he'd hoped to never have to repeat such acts of violence again. It seemed that this was not to be his fate.

"I'll do whatever it takes," Finn said, ensuring there was no doubt in his voice, even though there was doubt in his heart.

"Then get ready," Elara said, raising her crossbow.

Before he could ask what he was getting ready for, Elara sprinted from cover and ran directly toward the new prosecutors. Finn was left reeling, unable to fathom what his former mentor was planning, then a shotgun blast rocked the sky and a dragon's breath round scorched the snow clear, the flames licking at Elara's heels. Walter loosed a javelin, sending the spear hurtling toward his mentor like a Nimbus rocket launching, but she dove at the last moment and the weapon pierced only air. Elara recovered, found cover, then aimed and fired in one fluid movement. Finn expected her target to be Walter or Zach, the two greatest threats, but instead the dart thudded into the shoulder of "Inferno". Tonya yanked out the bolt and for a moment she didn't appear to be badly hurt. Then the poison set to work and she collapsed in the snow, shotgun crashing to the ground.

"No!" Ivan roared, throwing down his pistol and glaive and rushing to Tonya's side. Elara tried to get another shot but Sabrina and Walter had her zeroed in and she dared not peek her head out of cover. Then Ivan dragged Tonya back to the where Voss and the other prosecutors were watching, out of range of Elara's bolts.

"What are you doing, Herald, get back out there!" Voss demanded. "You are a Prosecutor of Zavetgrad and your duty comes before all else!"

"Fuck duty!" Ivan yelled, shoving Voss off him. "I order you to save her life. Fly us to the medical center, now!"

Voss recoiled from his former student, face flushing with rage.

"You don't give me orders, boy!" Voss snarled, grabbing Ivan's arm and yanking him up. "I am the Chief Prosecutor. You will do as I command!"

Ivan shook Voss off him then drew his rapier and pressed the tip of the blade beneath the man's chin.

"I am the Regent Successor of Spacehaven," Ivan hissed, as blood trickled from Voss's chin and down the blade of the rapier. "Your rank and title mean nothing to me. You will do as I command or you will be put to death!"

Voss clenched his hands into fists and the other prosecutors stood by, hands ready on their weapons should Apex give the order to subdue Ivan, but Finn knew that the man would not. Ivan was royalty, descended from the founders of Zavetgrad. He was the Authority and Voss was nothing but a gold.

"Very well," Voss spat, pushing the blade away from his face. "But on your head be it."

Ivan threw down the sword then carried Tonya into the skycar. Voss spoke to Frost and though Finn couldn't hear the words, he surmised that Apex had passed the mantle of command to the next highest-ranking member amongst them. Voss then entered the skycar and the rotors accelerated, lifting the vehicle off the ground and removing the bulk of the prosecutor's cover.

Finn saw his chance and stole closer, loosing a burst of fire from his sub-machine gun. The weapon crackled and bullets smashed into concrete and armor, chipping away at their defenses and forcing Frost and the others behind the crash barrier that stood in front of the fence. No-one was killed or even badly hurt, but that had not been Finn's intention. He wanted them to know that despite outnumbering them three-to-one the outcome of the fight was far from certain.

"New prosecutors, get back out there!" bellowed Frost. "And watch for Redeemer. He's swapped his laser for a lowly prefect's weapon. He's afraid to face you. Use his fear and remember that you are superior. You are all gold and they will always be beneath you!"

This time the cry of "Frost!" reverberated through the air. Where Apex was pompous and theatrical, Frost was like a sergeant major, rallying his troops and instilling within them the courage to fight. Finn pulled his eyes from the iron sight of the submachine gun and saw Frost hand out expandable riot shields to Walter, Sabrina and Zach. The barriers were effective against incoming fire and would allow the prosecutors to get close enough to use their deadly weapons and skills.

"Keep them occupied," Elara called over to him. "And stay alive..."

Elara activated her chameleonic armor and became a shimmering blur, moving toward their enemies like a heat haze dancing across the horizon. Finn advanced too, firing aimed bursts at the prosecutors to distract them from his mentor's stealthy assault. The bullets pinged off their riot shields and kept them subdued long enough for Elara to strike. Walter and Zach were her targets, but Sabrina continued directly for him, shield covering her slender body. Finn cursed and continued to fire, trying to skip shots off the concrete and into Sabrina's feet or shins, so that he wouldn't have to fight her, but still she came and then the weapon clicked empty.

Finn threw down the submachine gun and drew his baseball bat, and at the same time Sabrina discarded the shield and came at him with both Sai. He considered trying to reason with her but Sabrina's face was twisted with rage, furious at him for abandoning not only her, but her brothers and sisters in arms too. She slashed and stabbed the weapons and Finn was forced onto the back foot, parrying as best he could with his crude bat. Blades pierced his armor and scratched his face, and his survival instinct took over. He didn't want to fight Sabrina but he didn't want to die either. Using her rage and momentum against her, he dodged her next attack and crashed the bat into the small of Sabrina's back with all his might. She cried out and dropped to her knees, Sai slipping from her fingers as they curled like wizened branches from the shooting agony wracking her body.

Finn spun around, ready to smash the heavy bat into Sabrina's face and end the fight, but he couldn't do it, and in that split-second of hesitation, she pulled a snare from her armor and threw it at his feet. The trap activated and Finn's legs were entangled, like a boa constrictor wrapping itself around him. He tried to fight it but his struggle only tightened the snare's hold and he fell. Then Sabrina was on top of him, Sai in hand, pressed to his throat. Her eyes were wild but wet with tears and he could feel her body trembling against his.

"I'm sorry," Finn said. If he was going to die, he wanted her to know that. "I didn't want to leave you."

"Then why did you?" Sabrina cried, fighting back tears. The tip of the Sai had pierced his skin but Finn felt nothing other than sadness and regret. "I trusted you. We were a team!"

"Sabrina, I can't stay in this place, you know that," Finn said.

It felt oddly cathartic being honest with her for the first time in nine weeks. He nodded toward the other prosecutors and the movement of his head forced Sabrina to cut him more deeply.

"I'm not like them, and I don't want to be," Finn added, meeting her eyes. Tears fell onto his face and into his mouth, salty and hot. "I don't think you do either."

Sabrina gritted and bared her teeth, torn between fulfilling her orders and becoming "Ruin", the stone-cold killer the Authority had trained her to be, or remaining Sabrina Brook.

"Fuck, I don't want to kill you!" Sabrina snarled.

"Then don't," Finn said.

"I don't have a choice," Sabrina said, words falling from trembling lips.

"We all have a choice," Finn said. "And I choose to say fuck Voss and fuck all of them, because this is wrong Sabrina. What we are. What we do. This is wrong. You must see it?"

The Sai bit deep and Finn closed his eyes, anticipating the feel of sharp metal sliding into his neck, severing arteries and cutting his throat, but instead the blade was pulled away. Then the snare trap was released and his legs were freed. Sabrina sat back, still straddled over him like a cage fighter about to unload a beatdown, but her fists were unfurled.

"I knew I'd regret liking you, chromeboy," Sabrina said, smiling. "So, what now?"

Before he could answer, Sabrina was speared through the back by a golden javelin. The tip of the weapon punched through her heart and sternum, covering Finn with blood so thick he choked on it. Sabrina's eyes were still fixed onto his, for a brief moment alive with shock and fear. Then the light left them and she toppled off his body, dead.

27

JUST A GAME

Finn pulled the spear from Sabrina's back and lay her down in the snow, blood from the wound painting a frame of red around her broken body. Her eyes were still open, fixed in shock from the moment when Walter Foster had taken her life. He gently ran his fingers across her eyelids to close them then arranged her hands onto her stomach. She looked oddly peaceful, at ease in a way that he'd never seen her before. The he looked up and saw Walter smiling back at him, hammer in one hand and another of his five golden javelins in the other. The man was fifty meters away, close to Frost and the other prosecutors. They each had crossbow bolts dug into their armor, but none had penetrated deep enough for Elara's poison to take effect.

"Enough games!" Frost yelled.

Finn shook his head. *Games... Death is just a game to these people...*

"Now let's you see how you traitors fair against real Prosecutors of Zavetgrad."

Walter and Zach regrouped behind Frost, Garrote and

Blitz, then together the five remaining prosecutors advanced. Elara deactivated her armor and appeared beside him, though he'd felt her presence even before the chameleonic shield had fallen, like the subtle pull of a planet's gravity tugging on a passing comet at the outskirts of its influence. He picked up Walter's spear, wet with Sabrina's blood, and stood by his mentor's side.

"Do you think we can take them?" Finn asked.

After a short pause, Elara replied simply, "No."

Finn drew in a lungful of ice-cold air but as the sound of his own breath eased into the sky, it was replaced by the drum of rotors. He scanned the horizon, spotting a dozen prefect skycars headed their way from the central Authority sector, a few minutes out, at most. On-board was a small army of officers, no doubt tasked with capturing them alive, if possible, but Finn had no intention of becoming the Authority's prisoner.

"I always thought I'd die in a trial one day," Finn said. "I guess today is as good as any."

Elara nodded. "I should have died so many times already. At least this way, I get to kill people who actually deserve to die."

The two prosecutors, both chromes from Metalhaven, strode out toward their enemies with a confidence that belied their slim chance of success. Five on two might have been possible had they been fighting drunken workers in a bar brawl, but to believe they could defeat five fully-trained and heavily-armed Prosecutors of Zavetgrad was a flight of fancy. Owen would have asked him why and Finn would have given the answer he always did. *Because fuck them, that's why.*

Switching his grip on the bloodied spear, Finn prepared

to thrust it at Walter's throat, determined that he at least kill that bastard, if no-one else, when suddenly two offenders appeared from behind the concrete crash barriers in front of the fence. Finn and Elara stopped, as did the five prosecutors, then two more offenders appeared, then another three, until finally a group of ten workers stood between them. Finn recognized only one of the men and women, the chrome he'd met in the Seedhaven mini-sector who called himself Trip.

Frost extended an arm across the chest of Walter and pushed him back, anxiously watching the offenders, who were alternating their gazes between Finn and Elara and the five other prosecutors.

"What the hell is going on?" Trip asked. The others had gathered between him, as if the man from Metalhaven had become their leader. "Aren't you supposed to be killing us, instead of each other?"

"This is an Authority matter and not your concern, offender," Frost growled. "Stay out of it or you'll be next."

Trip laughed and shook his head. "We'll be next no matter what," the man from Metalhaven said, pointing out the critical flaw in Frost's logic. "Why the hell should we stay out of it, when you're just going to kill us anyway?"

Frost thought for a moment. Finn had never considered him the smartest of the prosecutor mentors, but if André Regan had a talent beyond killing, it was staying alive.

"You want an incentive, then listen up," Frost said, stepping two-paces forward.

Finn wondered if this was perhaps to show that Frost wasn't afraid of the offenders, but he'd be a fool to discount their threat, and Frost was no fool.

"Offenders, I offer you a chance to earn your freedom!"

Frost bellowed, drawing a little from Apex's theatrical style. He then pointed to Finn and Elara. "These two are traitors of Zavetgrad. Help us to capture these terrorists and in return you will all walk free, your crimes forgiven!"

The prosecutor paused to let that sink in and there were chatters of nervous excitement amongst the ten workers, though Trip remained impassive.

"This is your one and only chance at life," Frost continued, drawing his speech to a rousing conclusion. "Take it!"

The offenders continued to chatter, most directing their questions and suggestions to Trip, who didn't take his eyes off Frost for a second. Finn glanced at Elara, but her expression also gave nothing away, so Finn was left to speculate by himself.

What will they do? He wondered. *What would I do in their boots?...*

Then the truth of the situation became clear to him, like an epiphany, and he wasn't worried anymore. The offenders might have hailed from different sectors and be wearing different colors, but they were all workers under the boot of the Authority and Finn knew that they wouldn't trust the prosecutors' lies any more than he would. Stood where Trip was now, Finn would tell Frost to shove his offer up his ass.

Trip then held up his hands and the chatter diminished. The man also stepped forward, like two generals meeting one another in the center of the field to parlay before the battle started.

"Don't believe any of his bullshit," Trip said to the others, and Finn allowed himself to crack a smile. "So long as the

Authority exists, people like us will never be free... I say we fight!"

Frost stepped back and the other prosecutors shuffled their feet and anxiously adjusted their holds on their weapons. There was disharmony amongst the workers and one man, a red from Volthaven, voiced his concern.

"But we're just workers," the red said. "We don't know how to fight."

"I do..."

Elara Cage advanced toward the group of offenders, stripping the gold trim and edging from her armor as she did so, and casting it into the snow.

"I was once a worker like you, and I will stand with you now against the Authority." She raised her roundel dagger high. "Metal and Blood!"

The cry was electric and Trip punched a fist into the sky.

"Metal and Blood!" the man roared, and the reply from the other nine workers was immediate, a rallying cry almost loud enough to shatter the barrier fence.

"So be it," Frost grunted. "Then you all die today."

Frost held his hand outstretched and Walter pressed the grip of the prosecutor's blood-stained warhammer into the man's palm. Frost twirled the weapon, which was as natural in his grasp as a chisel in the hands of a sculptor, then limbered up his shoulders, ready to give the order to fight, but Finn had a condition and was quick to make his demand.

"Not him," Finn said. He pointed his spear at Walter, who grinned. "He fights me, and only me."

Frost scowled then looked at Walter and nodded his assent. Walter split away from the group and Finn moved out to face him, one-on-one, as they had done so many times in the octagon in the training hall. After nine weeks of contests the score was even. This would be their deciding battle.

"Metal and Blood!" Elara cried, aiming her dagger at Frost.

Her cry was returned in force and the offenders charged with The Shadow fighting amongst them, as one of them for all to see, but Finn wasn't watching. He had eyes only for Walter "Vigor" Foster.

"We all knew that you were rotten," Walter said, spinning the spear to display his skill with the weapon. He smiled. "Well, apart from Sabrina, anyway. She liked you and see where that got her."

"It got her stabbed in the back by a cowardly piece of shit," Finn replied. "You never could win by fighting fair, could you? Some perfect gold you are."

Walter gritted his teeth and almost took the bait. Nine weeks of constant hostility and interrogations by robot evaluators had taught Finn patience, but Walter had never been a patient man, and his temper almost got the better of him.

"I'm going to deliver you to Ivan myself," Walter said, still circling him. "If you think that prosecutors and prefects can be brutal, wait till you find out what a Regent will do to those who cross him."

"Ivan isn't a Regent, he's just a whiny little bitch, who gets everything he asks for, because his daddy is Mayor," Finn said. He'd been bottling up his vitriol for months and now it was overflowing. "And you're worse," he added, spitting the words at Walter. "You're just a gutless sycophant, clinging to Ivan's coattails. You think you're special, but whatever bottle they poured you out of was tainted like sour milk."

Walter bristled and Finn knew he only needed to push a little harder to make the man break.

"The truth is that I feel sorry for you, Walter," Finn said. He spat into the snow. "I feel sorry for you, because despite everything you've been gifted, you're just a small man failing to live up to expectations. You're not better than me, Walter. You're beneath me and you always were."

Walter finally snapped and lunged at Finn with his spear, striking so fast and hard that the tip of the weapon cracked the sound barrier. Finn was ready, dodging the initial thrust and parrying the follow up, which hit the shaft of his javelin with the force of an earthquake, shaking his bones and causing his teeth to grind together like millstones. He backed away, patient and wary, dodging and blocking Walter's increasingly frenzied attacks, waiting for the one opening he needed.

Then his chance came and he took it. Walter overreached and the momentum of his thrust carried his body forward and across the blade of Finn's spear, which sliced through the man's unarmored thigh close to the groin, cutting deep into the muscle. At first, Walter didn't seem to notice, but as he spun around, putting weight onto the injured leg, it collapsed under his mass. Crying out in pain, Walter dropped to one knee, clasping his hand to the wound, which was spurting blood like a punctured water main. Finn's prosecutor training had taught him the weak points of the human body, and Finn had been a diligent student. The femoral artery had been cut, and though he didn't know it yet, Walter Foster was a dead man.

"You bastard, I'll kill you!" Walter snarled.

The man tried to stand, but it was impossible and the

more he struggled, the more rapidly blood leaked from his body. Vigor thrust at Finn with his spear but he was safely out of range. It was like a man fighting in the dark, lashing out at every smear of light, blind to where the real threat was. Finn watched his former classmate and shook his head.

"The perfect gold…" Finn sneered. "Engineered from the best genetic stock in Zavetgrad and conditioned from childhood to be a Prefect of Nimbus." He laughed in Walter's face, which cut the man more deeply than his spear had. "Look at you now."

Walter roared and dragged himself toward Finn, but for each agonized lurch forward, he only needed to take a step back.

"You can't do this!" Walter roared, exhaustion and blood loss finally compelling him to stop. "I'm a Prosecutor of Zavetgrad. A pure gold! I order you to help me!"

Finn shook his head. The words he'd spoken earlier had been designed to incense Walter and make him become impulsive, but now he realized they were true. For all his gifts, he found Walter Foster to be a pitiable man.

"Everything you have was given to you," Finn said. He adjusted the grip on his spear, ready to throw it. "But everything I have was earned with blood."

Finn launched the spear at Walter's heart and buried it deep into the man's flesh. Walter grasped the shaft of the weapon and tried to pull it out, but Vigor's vast strength had finally left him, and with one last muted gasp, he collapsed into the snow and died at Finn's feet.

28

NOT ALL OF US

FINN TURNED his attention to the other fight that had been raging at the same time as his battle with Walter Foster, but he saw that it was already over. To his relief, Elara was still standing. Together with the ten workers from Metalhaven, they had overwhelmed the prosecutors – a mob tearing down the Authority – but victory had not come without sacrifice. Nine of the of the ten workers had fallen too, leaving only Trip alive, wounded but not critically. The cost of revolution was high, Finn realized, but it was a price worth paying.

He walked up to Elara and they exchanged subtle nods to indicate that they were both okay. Then he cast his eyes over the bodies of Frost, Garrote and Blitz, which were little more than battered meat and blood-stained armor. He felt nothing when he looked at them, but seeing Zack, broken like a puppet with its strings cut, somehow hit differently. He'd never gotten to know the man and what he'd learned he didn't like, but they had shared the ordeal of prosecutor training, and despite his flaws, Zach had been a comrade of sorts. Yet he would not mourn his death, just as he would not mourn the passing of Walter Foster or any of the other prosecutors, even Sabrina. In the end, they were all part of a system that kept hundreds of thousands of men and women enslaved against their will. And if you were with the Authority then you were against Finn Brasa.

"Finn-Finn!" Scraps yelled, zooming into view. "Skycar ready. Finn and Elara come soon?"

"We'll be right there, pal," Finn said, smiling at the robot.

"Hurry-hurry!" Scraps said, anxiously. The robot pointed in the direction of the Authority sector and Finn saw that the prefect skycars were dangerously close, yet still not within weapons range.

"Get her started up, pal, and we'll be there before you know it," Finn said.

Scraps nodded and zoomed away, then Finn turned to Trip. His courage, and the sacrifice of those who had fought with him, was why he and Elara were still alive. They couldn't leave without him.

"Wait till I tell the lads back home about this," Trip said, tightening the knot on a makeshift tourniquet wrapped around his arm. "The Iron Bitch and The Hero of Metalhaven both here together with me!"

"You can't go home," Finn said, though he was amused by the notion that Trip's first thought was how he'd brag about his experiences over a pint or three. "Prefects are coming in force. You have to come with us. It's the only way."

Trip shook his head then pointed to the inky outline of the special prefect skycar, which was powering up as they spoke.

"You and I both know that piddly little thing will barely get the two of you across the Davis Strait to Haven," the man said. "With my fat ass on board too, all that will happen is we ditch enroute and drown in freezing cold water." Trip shivered at the prospect of what he'd just described then shook his head again. "I'd rather take my chances here than end up like that," he said. Then he grabbed Finn's hand with both of his own and shook it warmly. "Just don't forget us, okay?"

"We won't," Finn said. He knew better than anyone that when a chrome had made up his mind there was no changing it. "And we will be back. I don't know how or when, but I promise we'll find a way. Let everyone know that, okay? Let them know that Finn Brasa and Elara Cage won't forget them. Ever."

"I'll do that," Trip said. He nodded to the approaching fleet of skycars. "Now go, before they get into range and start filling us with holes."

Trip released his hand then bowed his head to Elara before backing away to reinforce the fact they were separating.

"Metal and Blood," Elara said, bowing to the worker in return. "Teach them our cry so that when the time comes, you'll all be ready."

"Metal and Blood," Trip replied, bestowing the words with the reverence they deserved. "Good luck."

Trip ran in the opposite direction to the approaching skycars, while Finn and Elara sprinted for the special prefect vehicle that he hoped would carry them over the fence and eventually to Haven. Neither of them spoke, but even if Elara had said something, the rush of air flowing past his ears had rendered him deaf. With their skycar in sight, Finn allowed himself to feel a measure of hope then in an instant it was ripped away. Elara fell and hit the snow-covered concrete hard. At first, Finn thought that she'd only stumbled on something hidden beneath the white powder, but when she didn't get up again he slid to a stop and clambered to her side, heart in his mouth.

"What's wrong?" Finn said, desperate. Elara was on the concrete, slumped over to one side, arm wrapped around her body. "Come on, I'll help you."

Finn tried to get her up, but she was a dead weight, and she waved him away.

"It's over, Finn," Elara said.

Finn shook his head, then he saw blood leaking into the snow and he lifted Elara's arm to see that she'd been shot.

"Sniper..." Elara said, nodding toward the skycars. "A lucky shot." She snorted a laugh. "Not so lucky for me." Already her face was drawn and her words were becoming slurred.

"Go, Finn," she said, trying to push him away. "Go, before they get you too."

"No, fuck them!" Finn snarled. Even as he cursed at the prefects, bullets were skipping off the concrete around them but he didn't care. "I'll carry you to the skycar. You'll be okay!"

"Finn, no..."

He ignored her and tried to pick her up, but with the mass of her armor and his own wounded and exhausted body, he didn't have the strength, and merely managed to stumble a few meters before they both collapsed into the virgin snow, tangled together like the roots of a tree.

"Finn, for once in your life, stop fighting," Elara said, dragging herself away from him. "You can't save me, but I'm begging you to save yourself. Save yourself or this will all have been for nothing."

"I can't leave you here to die!" Finn said, raking tears from his eyes. "Too many have died for me already. I can't lose you too..."

Elara sighed. "This isn't about you, Finn, it never was. It's about what you represent. It's about the change you can bring. Whether you like it or not, you're the spark that will light the fuse that will bring down the Authority and even Nimbus itself. I know you don't want it. You probably don't even deserve it. But it's on you, Finn. And if you can't do it for yourself or for me then do it for Owen."

Her words hit him like a warhammer to the chest and he reeled back from Elara, stunned. Bullets continued to skip off the concrete all around him, and a round even ricocheted off his shoulder, but still he couldn't move.

"I warned you about Juniper," Elara continued. It was another gut punch even harder than the first. "I warned you and still you told her about us. So this is on you, Finn. That's twice now you've fucked up and someone else has paid the price. Make it the last time."

Elara turned her head away from him. "Now go..."

The prefect skycars were making their descent and Finn could hear commands being barked at him over PA systems, but still he sat in the snow, too stunned to move or even think.

"Finn, go!" Elara roared, kicking him in the chest and knocking him to the flat of his back. "If you care anything for me then go!"

Finn didn't remember getting to his feet. He didn't remember running to the special prefect skycar or strapping himself into the seat. And he had no idea how the vehicle became airborne and who was flying. All he knew was that he'd left Elara Cage to die and that even if he managed to escape, he'd never forgive himself for as long as he lived.

29

MAKE THE CALL

The skycar's rotors screamed as they labored hard to drag the flying vehicle into a steep climb, like a Nimbus rocket reaching for the orbital citadel. Bullets were pinging off the skycar's armor as the prefects gave chase but the vehicle was as defiant as its passenger and continued to climb.

"Hold-hold!" Scraps said. "Close-close!"

Scraps, loyal and courageous beyond measure, was doing the flying. The little robot was connected to the skycar's controls, using the head of the evaluator as an interface, while employing all of his own electronic guile to push the vehicle to its absolute limit. The nose of the craft was aimed at the top of the fence but their rate of ascent was slowing and alarms were blaring inside the cabin, warning them of an imminent engines stall.

"More powa!" Scraps yelled, bashing his hands onto the evaluator robot's head, like trying to whip a horse to go faster. "Climb-climb!"

"We're not going to make it," Finn cried, gripping the

arms of his chair so tightly his fingers ripped the faux-leather covering. "We're too heavy!"

The special prefect skycar comprised only the pilot's cabin and a small passenger compartment in the rear. Finn twisted his neck to look into the rear section and saw the seats loaded with equipment and weapons.

"Scraps, open the passenger doors!" he yelled to the robot. "Shake out whatever we can!"

"Roger-roger!" Scraps said, tapping his hand to his head in a sort of salute.

The rear doors sprang open and the skycar rocked from side-to-side so violently that Finn thought he might be thrown outside too. Weapons and boxes were cast out, spiraling beneath them like bombs and striking the cockpits of the pursuing prefect skycars. Then the doors swooshed shut and the nose of the craft tipped up by a couple of degrees so that it was now pointed above the summit of the electrified fence. It wasn't much but it was enough. *It has to be...* Finn told himself.

"Hold-Hold!" Scraps yelled.

The robot was covering his eyes with his hands, peering through his little metal fingers. There was nothing more he could do. They either made it or they didn't.

Alarms screaming, the skycar shot over the top of the fence, scraping its belly over a pylon and causing sparks of metal and electricity to explode around them. The cockpit was filled with brilliant light and Finn was blinded. Then the nose of the craft dipped sharply and for a horrifying few moments they were falling, until the craft leveled and the engines eased from a labored scream to a measured thrum.

"Did we me make it?"

Finn's question was met with the flash of a detonation and the punch of a shockwave as one of the pursuing skycars crashed into the fence and exploded. He craned his neck to see a fireball spreading across the fence, ten meters below the summit. Then another skycar hit and exploded with the same violence, followed by another and another until the sky was turned orange and black with fire and smoke.

"We okay!" Scraps said. The robot had immediately returned to his cheerful norm. "Thems, not so much," he added, hooking a little metal thumb toward the incinerated prefect vehicles.

Burning ordnance and exploding fuel tanks sent debris rocketing into the sky like missiles, while the fence crackled and sparked for hundreds of meters along its length, causing the lights in the city to flicker and dim from Seedhaven to Metalhaven and everywhere in-between. It was a lightshow a thousand times brighter and more spectacular than any fireworks display that had been put on for a trial.

"Workers in every district in Zavetgrad will have seen that," Finn said, forced to squint his eyes to continue watching. "It's just a shame they won't know why it's happening. If only there was a way we could let them know."

"Finn can!" Scraps said.

"How, pal?" Finn asked, turning away from the explosions.

Scraps tapped the C.O.N.F.I.R.M.E. computer on Finn's wrist then drummed his fingers onto the head of the evaluator robot.

"Use fancy 'puter," Scraps said. "Bad Juniper has access, so Scraps has access!"

Finn frowned at the device on his wrist but even if Scraps

was right that it had access to the Authority central computer system, he didn't know how that helped him. Then he saw the time on the display, which read 21:46 hours. More than half of Zavetgrad's worker population would be piled into smokey recovery centers, downing pints of strong ale, laughing, joking and probably fighting with one another.

"Can you get me access to TV screens?" Finn asked. The kernel of an idea was germinating in his mind. "If we can hack the network, we can reach hundreds of thousands of workers and let them know what happened!"

"Already done-done," Scraps said, looking justifiably pleased with himself. "Scraps clever. Finn made him so!"

"No, you did that all by yourself," Finn replied, laughing. "In fact, I think you're the smartest person in all of Zavetgrad."

Scraps giggled and waved his arms in the air like a kid who'd just been told he was going to the zoo. Then his little metals fingers flashed across the screen of the C.O.N.F.I.R.M.E. computer and a light shone from the dashboard of the skycar directly into Finn's face.

"Finn connected," Scraps said, sitting back. "Talk-talk!"

"What, now?" Finn said.

Scraps nodded and smiled. "Camera live. Speak-speak!"

Finn looked into the camera lens and his mind went blank. *What the hell am I supposed to say?* he asked himself. Then he remembered everything that Elara had told him about the failed revolution and about Haven, and he realized that all he needed to say was the truth that had been hidden from the people for over a century. He knew it was a risk to expose hundreds of thousands of workers to information considered so dangerous that the Authority killed to keep it secret, but they couldn't kill everyone. Zavetgrad would fall apart without the work sectors and the Nimbus project would collapse with it. In the end, he had no idea what consequences would follow but he'd already made up his mind. The people deserved the truth and he was going to give it to them.

"I don't know if you can hear me, but if you can, then put down your pints and listen, because we don't have much time," Finn began. "My name is Finn Brasa, though you may know me as the Hero of Metalhaven." He laughed weakly. "But I'm no hero and I'm sure as hell not a leader. I'm just a chrome from Metalhaven, or at least I was until the Authority tried to make me a gold. But I'm not a gold. I'm a Metal and I'm going to tell you something that the Authority has kept from you for over a century."

Finn leaned in closer and peered into the lens even though the light stung his eyes and made his head thump. He imagined thousands of men and women, weary from a day's toil and a little drunk, all sat in silence watching and waiting on his every word, which meant he needed to make every word count.

"A hundred and twenty-seven years ago, workers like us rebelled against the Authority and almost brought them down," Finn continued. "The survivors of that failed revolution, all of them chromes like me, founded Haven. They were the first Metals but they were not the last. Despite what you may have heard, Haven is real and it's a place for all colors. All workers. It's out there, waiting for you, just as it's waiting for me. I'm headed there now, as we speak."

He wet his lips and thought of his cockroach-infested hovel of an apartment, and the reclamation yards where he worked tirelessly every day without reprieve, and of the wellness centers where people were forced into sexual slavery, and of the gene banks that stole his very life essence. He thought about how every aspect of his life had been controlled by the Authority and bile rose up into his throat.

"Why am I telling you this?" Finn said, leaning in closer still so that his face, bruised and blooded, filled the entire lens. "I'm telling you because one day you'll all be free too. It won't be today and it won't be the next day, but it will happen. I promise you that. In the meantime, do nothing. Work your jobs, drink your pints, smoke your cigarettes, and survive. When the time comes to fight, you'll know. But make no mistake, the price of freedom must be paid in blood. Metal and Blood, Stone and Blood, Seed and Blood…"

He pictured Owen, smiling and joking with him in yard seven, and Melody and Khloe who had also died in the trial along with so many others over decades. The losses were too numerous to count, the suffering too great, but in that moment, all of it paled compared to the crushing guilt and regret he felt for leaving Elara behind. He felt her absence like a hole in his chest. Finn drew in a deep breath and let it out slowly. Scraps was looking at him, anxiously tapping his wrist to tell him that time was short. He nodded to the robot and stared back into the camera lens, and into the hearts and souls of his people.

"I am Finn Brasa, a chrome from Metalhaven. I am your brother. And one day, if you remain strong, I will be your redeemer."

The light shining into his face vanished and Finn blinked away the wetness in his eyes.

"Signal jammed," Scraps said, throwing his arms out wide.

"Did the message go out?" Finn asked, flopping back into his chair. He felt utterly broken, as if he'd just worked a sixteen-hour shift.

Scraps shrugged, though the robot didn't look unduly flustered, which he took to be a good sign. Scraps then bounced off the evaluator robot's head and launched himself onto the cockpit dashboard. "Look-look!" he said, pointing through the glass.

Finn sat up and saw that they were over water. He looked behind and Zavetgrad was already in the distance, its towering, electrified walls looking suddenly tiny as the distance between them rapidly increased. Sentry guns placed around the Seahaven coastline tracked them but the weapons were not programmed to fire on one of their special skycars.

"Davis Strait!" Scraps said, still pointing to the water. "We made it!"

Finn smiled and gently patted the top of his robot's head.

"Yes, pal, we made it," he said, softly. "But not all of us."

30
HAVEN

The skycar jolted as it passed through a rough patch of air and it shook Finn awake. He hadn't planned on sleeping but the comfortable seats and heated interior of the skycar, coupled with the mesmerizing drone of the rotor engines acted like a sedative and put him out like a light. Finn sat up, still feeling stiff and tired, and rubbed his eyes. Then he rubbed them again because what he saw outside the cockpit glass confused the hell out of him.

"Did we turn around?" Finn said, frowning at the mass of land they were approaching.

"Nope-nope!" Scraps said. "That Disko Island!"

"The island where Haven is?" Finn asked, sitting up straighter. The robot's answer had kicked his drowsy mind into gear.

"Yep-Yep!" Scraps said, brightly.

Finn rubbed his eyes again then peered out across the barren, rocky terrain that was rapidly enveloping them, but he couldn't see anything that resembled a city or a town or even a small hamlet.

"Then where's Haven?" Finn asked.

Scraps shrugged. "Beats me!"

He scowled at the robot. Scraps was often unreasonably cheerful, but Finn didn't consider venturing deep into a barren wilderness with no supplies of any kind to sustain them to be a matter worthy of cheer.

"I'm going to need you to do better than that, pal," Finn said.

He was trying to express his earnest intentions without sounding cross with Scraps. After all, he'd saved his life. Suddenly, an alarm sounded and an orange indicator on the cockpit dashboard began flashing.

"What's that?" Finn asked, feeling in his bones that it was bad news.

"Low fuel," Scraps answered. "Maybe twenty min-mins."

"Twenty minutes until we're out of fuel?"

Scraps nodded and the hope and optimism Finn had felt after learning they'd reached Disko Island vanished like their depleting duel supply.

"Are you saying that if we don't find Haven in the next twenty minutes that'll we have to ditch the Skycar?" Finn asked.

"Yep-yep!" Scraps replied.

"Honestly, pal, I don't know why you're so cheerful," Finn said, his frustration starting to show. "We're not exactly kitted out for wild camping and we shook out all the supplies in order to get over the electrified fence."

"Scraps knows," the robot said, still remarkably unconcerned. "But no problem."

"And why is that?" Finn said.

Scraps pointed out of the window. "Because Haven finds us!"

Finn scowled at the robot then scowled through the glass. At first he saw nothing but endless emptiness, then his eyes were drawn to two objects just above the horizon line. He thought they might be birds, as rare as they were, but they were too big and too fast. Then he realized they were skycars and that they were headed straight for them.

"Are they prefect skycars?" Finn asked, staring at the console but none of the displays revealed anything useful.

"Nope-Nope," Scraps said.

"Then whose are they?"

One of the skycars flew past so close that its wake buffeted their smaller vehicle. Then tracer rounds flashed over their heads and the second skycar buzzed them, even closer than the first.

"What the hell?" Finn said, ducking instinctively. "Are they crazy?

"Unidentified skycar, squawk your ID or we will destroy you," a voice said, crackling over the internal comm system.

Scraps pointed to a headset hung up beside Finn and he pulled it on, heart racing.

"Hostile skycars, don't shoot, we're not from Zavetgrad," Finn bellowed, then cursed because that wasn't exactly what he'd meant to say. "I mean, we are from Zavetgrad, but we're not from the Authority."

There was dead air for a few seconds and Finn noticed that the pair of armed skycars had formed up behind them, guns pointed at their engines.

"Unidentified skycar, squawk your ID," the same voice said. "I will not ask you again."

"Damn it, we don't have an ID," Finn said, punching the arm of his chair. "I'm Finn Brasa. I stole this skycar and made it out of the city." He thought for a second then added, "Metal and Blood..." hoping that the phrase might be the key to his survival.

"Skycar, did you say your name is Finn Brasa?"

"That's right!" Finn replied, breathless.

"Switch to visual comms at once."

Finn was about to say that he didn't know how when Scraps operated his console and the bright light that had shone into his face when addressing the workers of Metalhaven lit up again. He looked into the lens and waved, feeling immediately foolish for doing so. The face of the pursuing skycar's pilot appeared on one of the screens. It was the face of a serious man considering the sobering prospect of shooting them down.

"Unidentified skycar, we have designated you Skycar FB-one, please release all controls to my authority," the pilot said. "Fail to comply and I will shoot you down."

Finn looked to Scraps but his robot was already on the case. Then the consoles all switched to different but equally indecipherable displays, apart from one screen, which read, *Remote Piloting Activated*. The two combat skycars then formed up on his wings, so close that Finn could see the face of the pilot he'd spoken to clearly without needing to look at the monitors.

"We will guide you in, skycar FB-one," the pilot said. "Do not touch the controls."

"I haven't touched the control since we left," Finn said, pushing himself back into his seat.

He saw the pilot frown and realized his answer made no

sense but the man didn't question him and returned to navigating his own craft. Seconds later, they all banked right and adopted a new heading, though to Finn it still seemed that they were venturing into endless nothingness.

"Skycar FB-one, we are approaching Haven," the pilot's voice said, after ten minutes of aching silence. "Landing will be on automatic. Do not touch the controls."

"You got it," Finn replied, pressing his hands between his thighs to make certain they weren't near any of the buttons or levers. "What's your name, anyway?"

"Keep this channel clear, FB-one," the pilot replied, gruffly. "Starting final approach now."

Finn looked out of the window and was about to ask where or what they were approaching when he saw something. There was a flat section of ground with a circular area that was completely clear of rocks and other natural features. Then lights lit up around the circumference and an obelisk-shaped tower punched through the snow. It took Finn a moment to realize that it was a gun tower, not unlike the weapons platforms that surrounded Zavetgrad.

Another alarm squealed in the cabin and this time Finn didn't need to ask the cause, because one of the displays was flashing the words, *WARNING: TARGET LOCK*, in bright red letters. Finn gasped and looked at the pilot escorting them, but the man appeared unconcerned, as did Scraps, so he bit his tongue and let it play out.

The skycars dove suddenly, still in perfect formation, then as Finn's car approached the center of the circular plateau, the escorting vehicles peeled away. Seconds later they touched down with a hard thump and were immediately swallowed by whatever they had landed on. Black walls raced past the windows and a heavy shutter closed above them, like the iris of a camera lens. The cabin was pitched into darkness, save the glow from the console screens, then the elevator came to an abrupt stop. Moments later the skycar was shunted from behind and picked up by an enormous robotic arm that swung them out into a chamber and dumped them unceremoniously on the ground in a dark corner of the mysterious space. Floodlights switched on outside, dazzling after so much darkness, then the doors of the skycar were forced open.

"Hands in the air!" a voice yelled. The man sounded like a prefect and Finn complied out of habit. "Step out, keep your hands where I can see them!"

Finn followed the instruction, and Scraps jumped onto his shoulder as he pulled himself out of the vehicle. Then the lights were dipped and Finn finally saw the man who had given the order. The skin on his square face was craggy and his hair was streaked with grey, suggesting a degree of experience that few workers in Zavetgrad ever lived long enough to achieve. A nametag on the breast pocket of the man's uniform read, *RILEY* in capital letters.

A door opened in the otherwise empty chamber and a woman walked in. From the silver in her hair, she also appeared to be in her early fifties, like the hard-nosed man aiming a rifle at him, but unlike that grim-faced solider, she didn't look it. She wore a grey suit, well made and cut, like the suits golds in the Authority sector wore, but she didn't walk like a gold, who strutted and swaggered, so full of themselves. Instead, this woman approached like she was walking to a podium to give an important speech, effortless, elegant and self-assured.

"Thank you, General, you can stand-down your men," the woman ordered.

"Ma'am are you sure?" the craggy-faced soldier replied. "We still haven't confirmed this man's identity."

"I'm sure, Will," the woman said, gripping General Riley's wrist and pulling the aim of his rifle down. "I'd know that face anywhere, since it was just on every TV screen in Zavetgrad." The woman smiled and flashed her eyes at Finn. "And beyond Zavetgrad too." She 'tsked' then sighed, elaborately. "You were barely out of Zavetgrad for a few seconds before inciting rebellion. What are we going to do with you, eh?"

"Who are you?" Finn asked. He had a million questions rattling around his aching head but at that moment the woman's identity was the one he most wanted an answer to.

"My name is Penelope Everhart," the woman said. She sighed and shrugged. "I know, it sounds pretentious but I didn't get a choice in it. Most people just call me Pen."

The woman then smiled and patted General Riley on the shoulder.

"Apart from the ones who call me, 'ma'am', even though I tell them every single day not to."

"Ma'am is the correct honorific for the Principal of Haven," General Riley grunted.

"Yes, but it's so..." Pen searched for the right word, waving her hand in a circular motion as if trying to hurry up her thought processes, before adding, "... it's so authoritarian-sounding, don't you think?" Finn simply stood with his mouth open. "And I think you've had enough of authority for the time being, isn't that right, Mr. Brasa?" Pen added.

"Or can I call you Finn? Or Hero? Or Redeemer? I'm really not sure which."

"Finn is fine," Finn replied, his voice little more than a timid squeak.

Pen smiled then looked past him and into the skycar behind. Its engines were slowly cooling, the metal pinging like a hot kettle. "Is it just you?" she asked.

Finn felt his stomach knot. "Yes... Elara didn't..." The words stuck in his throat. "She didn't make it..."

Pen nodded and her head tilted down by the slightest fraction. "I understand," she said, softly.

She sighed heavily then lifted her chin and smiled, switching from somber to sunny as easily as Scraps could do, like flipping a switch. She turned and began walking toward the door that had remained open. She got about five or six meters before stopping and looking back.

"Well, are you coming?"

"Coming where?" Finn asked, still in a daze.

"To Haven, of course," Pen said, frowning at him. "You're here for a reason, Finn, and we should get started right away."

"Now?" Finn said. He looked at his prosecutor uniform, chrome and gold and stained with blood, some of which was Elara's. "But I don't know what to do. I'm don't know why I'm here."

"All in good time," Pen said, smiling.

The words jangled around his mind. He knew he'd heard them before. *But where, when and who?...* Then it hit him. They were the same words Elara used whenever Finn got ahead of himself. He looked at Pen and staggered closer until he could see the emerald green in her eyes.

"You're Elara's mother?" Finn said, though it sounded unbelievable.

"Yes," Pen said. "In a biological sense, at least."

She turned again to leave but Finn couldn't move. His legs had simply stopped working. Pen then appeared by his side. In his dazed state, he hadn't even seen her approach, like she'd been wearing Elara's chameleonic armor.

"I'm so sorry," Finn said, unable to hold back tears. "I tried... It's my fault..."

Pen hooked her arm through his and Finn used her as a crutch.

"Elara knew what she was doing," Pen said, speaking softly again and without judgement. "She thought you were worth the risk."

"But I'm not," Finn said, shaking his head and casting tears onto Pen's grey suit, creating darker spots where the liquid soaked into the material. "I fuck up everything. I'm a curse. You're better off without me."

Pen smiled and shook her head.

"I just saw you address more than four hundred thousand workers, none of whom believed their lives would ever get better, until they saw your face," Pen said. "You gave them hope, Finn, but you also gave them something else. Something we've been trying to find for decades. A symbol. Someone to believe in. Someone who will fight for them and whom they will follow when the time comes."

"But I'm not a leader," Finn said.

"No, you're not," Pen said and this admission shocked him. "Not yet, anyway. But you will be." She cocked her head to one side. "Assuming you still want to take down the Authority, of course?"

"I do," Finn said. That, at least, he was certain of. "I want to tear that place down brick by brick then launch a rocket at Nimbus that will shatter it to a billion pieces."

"Good," Pen said, smiling again. She released Finn's arm then set off toward the open door.

"Then come with me, Prosecutor of Metalhaven," Pen said. "We have a rebellion to plan."

The end (to be continued).

CONTINUE THE STORY

Read about Finn's adventures in Haven and beyond in book #3 of the Metal and Blood series, Liberator of Metalhaven. Available from Amazon in Kindle, paperback and audiobook formats, and in Kindle Unlimited.

ALSO BY G J OGDEN

Sa'Nerra Universe

Omega Taskforce

Descendants of War

Scavenger Universe

Star Scavengers

Star Guardians

Standalone series

The Aternien Wars

The Contingency War

Darkspace Renegade

The Planetsider Trilogy

G J Ogden's newsletter: Click here to sign-up

ABOUT THE AUTHOR

At school, I was asked to write down the jobs I wanted to do as a "grown up". Number one was astronaut and number two was a PC games journalist. I only managed to achieve one of those goals (I'll let you guess which), but these two very different career options still neatly sum up my lifelong interests in science, space, and the unknown.

School also steered me in the direction of a science-focused education over literature and writing, which influenced my decision to study physics at Manchester University. What this degree taught me is that I didn't like studying physics and instead enjoyed writing, which is why you're reading this book! The lesson? School can't tell you who you are.

When not writing, I enjoy spending time with my family, playing Warhammer 40K, and indulging in as much Sci-Fi as possible.

Printed in Great Britain
by Amazon